MY STORY
ONE
BRANDAO'S
DASH THROUGH
LIFE

Copyright © 2024 Leo Arthur Brandao

All Rights Reserved

DEDICATION

This book is dedicated to all those who have made me who I am today. My family, my friends, my mentors, my coworkers, my neighbors. Anyone who has had an impact on my life, which is virtually anyone I have had contact with, as we all affect one another in some way. In his book, "*Some of My Best Friends Are Black: The Strange Story of Integration in America*," Tanner Colby says, "You are the sum total of the people you meet and interact with within the world. Whether it's your family, peers, or coworkers, the opportunities you have and the things that you learn all come through doors that other people open for you." As you pass through those doors, may your journey be as enjoyable as mine was and is. Thank those who have opened doors for you, and be mindful of the doors you open for others.

ACKNOWLEDGMENT

I would like to thank all those who helped by contributing to the content of this book, either just by being a part of my life or by actually contributing content. I spent many hours having conversations with my brothers and sisters, recording stories of their lives while I was away to help me fill in the gaps, as my memory wasn't always the best. Some of the stories they shared were not included in this book, not because they weren't interesting but because they were just too complicated to sort out and may have reflected events that I would rather not include for various reasons. I thank those who contributed photos of their families as well. I would also like to thank those who encouraged me to have this book published, as it was initially intended only for the purpose of passing a legacy down to my children, grandchildren, nieces, and nephews. And I thank those who helped me to put it into its final format so that it is readable and enjoyable. And most importantly, I thank God for guiding me through all the days of my life.

CONTENTS

DEDICATION iii
ACKNOWLEDGMENT iv
ABOUT THE AUTHOR vi
FOREWORD viii
THE BRANDAO ADVENTURE 1
CHAPTER ONE: THE BEGINNING 2
CHAPTER TWO: THE SIBLINGS 30
CHAPTER THREE: DO I REALLY WANT TO BE A PRIEST 56
CHAPTER FOUR: BEGINNING MY MILITARY CAREER 67
CHAPTER FIVE: RETURN TO THE LAND OF THE BIG BX 77
(or Awful Air Force Base, Oh My God, Nebraska) 77
CHAPTER SIX: PEASE AFB NEW HAMPSHIRE 88
CHAPTER SEVEN: BACK TO OMAHA 93
CHAPTER EIGHT: OFF TO GERMANY AND HAHN AB 100
CHAPTER NINE: RETURN TO THE STATES (BOLLING AND ANDREWS) 112
CHAPTER TEN: RETIREMENT BECKONS, A NEW CAREER BEGINS 126
CHAPTER ELEVEN: RETIRED AGAIN – WHAT DO I DO NOW 145
APPENDICES 152

ABOUT THE AUTHOR

Leo Arthur Brandao was born September 22, 1948, to Lillian and Arthur Brandao. He lived in Cape Cod, Mass, until he left for college in 1966, then joined the Air Force in 1970. After serving 26 years, he retired in Maryland just outside of Washington, DC. He worked another 20 years as a defense contractor for Northrup Grumman. He continues to live in Maryland. He and his wife, Barbara, have been married for over 50 years and have two grown sons, Christopher and Adam, a granddaughter named Caitlyn, and a grandson named Trevor. His most important accomplishment was accepting Jesus Christ as his Lord and Savior, as nothing is more important than that. He is proud to be a "conservative" and values the principles that made America a great and godly nation. Principles grounded in the Bible. And prays that the American people will someday return to those values and principles.

FOREWORD

Hi there. There is a song that was published in 1919 by an anonymous author which says, *"This world is not my home. I'm just a-passing through."* Most likely based on Hebrews 13:14, *"For here we have no continuing city, but we seek one to come." (KJV)* The Living Bible translation actually uses the words, *"For this world is not my home..."* One day, I was born, and one day I will die. That is the fate of the physical body. But what about the spiritual body? That lives on forever. It came from God and was implanted into the physical body. And when the physical body is no more, the spiritual body will go to the place where it will spend eternity, to one day be reunited with a glorified body. Psalm 90:10 says, *"The days of our years are threescore years and ten; and if by reason of strength they be fourscore years, yet is their strength labour and sorrow; for it is soon cut off, and we fly away."* Folks, that's 70, maybe 80 years. Some may even live to be 100 or 110. In 2 Peter 3:8, it says, *"But, beloved, be not ignorant of this one thing, that one day is with the Lord as a thousand years and a thousand years as one day."* Genesis 5:27 says Methuselah lived to be 969 years old. That's still less than a day to the Lord. Do the math, and you'll see our time here is a drop in the bucket. So, what do we do within that time? Well, the following is an account of how I spent that time, that little dash that appears between our birth year and our death year. Isn't it interesting that we place a little dash between our birth year and our death year? I looked up the definition of a dash in Webster. Some of the definitions were "to go in a great hurry," "a rush, sudden movement like a sprint," and "verve." These are some things that can apply to our life. Of course, in the following pages, I have not included everything that has happened in my life. That would be too overwhelming. I mean, over 27 thousand days is a lot to remember, especially when you don't keep a journal (one of my regrets). The big question is, did I use my time wisely, or did I waste it? Will God say to me, *"Well done, good and faithful servant"* (Matthew 25:21), or will He refer to me as *"Thou wicked and slothful servant."* (Matthew 25:26)? Only God knows, and I guess I'll find out when I see Him in Heaven. I thought I'd share some of the highlights of those years, some adventures or, more often, misadventures. This is not meant to be a tell-all or to confess all my sins, so if that's what you expect, you'll be disappointed. It's just a brief history, a few anecdotes, and some trivial facts. So here goes. Please enjoy.

"He hath shewed thee, O man, what is good; and what doth the Lord require of thee, but to do justly and to love mercy, and to walk humbly with my God?"

- *Micah 6:8*

THE BRANDAO ADVENTURE

CHAPTER ONE: THE BEGINNING

"Now, the Lord had said unto Abraham, Get thee out of thy country and from thy kindred, and from thy father's house. Unto a land that I will show thee." Gen 12:1

Ever since I can remember, my father worked for the Daniel Brothers Contracting Company on Cape Cod. His primary responsibility was tending to the estate of the Parlett sisters on Eel River Road in Wianno. This was a beautiful estate along the West Bay with a boathouse, a well-manicured yard, and the pride of the estate, the rose garden. At least, this is what my memory holds.

It was while working here that he suffered his heart attack when I was fifteen while loading a lawn mower onto his pickup. He drove himself to our family doctor, Dr. Jacques. After examining him, the doctor sent him home and told him to get some rest. He had another attack that night and was rushed to Cape Cod Hospital. He spent about a week in intensive care but was removed from the ICU as the doctors felt he was recovering fine. We were told that he would be home on Monday following Mother's Day. But then, that Saturday night or rather Sunday morning, about 2 a.m., May 10, 1964, the telephone rang, and our lives were changed forever.

But I'm starting in the middle of the story, and maybe I should go back to the beginning. But where is the beginning? When I was born? When a young 14-year-old named Arthur landed in America from a volcanic island somewhere off the coast of Africa called Fogo, Cape Verde? I understand he was brought to America by Arcenio Lopes, who eventually became my Godfather.

I guess I could call this chapter "From the Cape to the Cape." I don't know a whole lot about this time period. After all, I wasn't even a figment of Arthur's imagination. I suppose he came to America, like many others to seek his fame and fortune. At the age of 17, he joined the United States Army, where he served as a cook. He was stationed at Otis Air Force Base in Falmouth but did spend some time overseas during World War II. He returned to the United States aboard the U.S. Hospital Ship "Dogwood". Returning to civilian life following WWII, he ended up working for the Daniel Brothers of Osterville as a Landscape Gardener, attending to the Parlett Estate, and living in

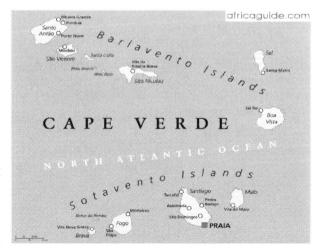

the town of Osterville. Osterville was founded in 1648 as "Cotacheset". It was primarily a seafaring village, the home of sea captains, shipbuilders, salt workers, cranberry growers, and oystermen. The name of Osterville did not come into use until 1815 as a result of a misprint. The name had been changed to Oysterville since it had become a center for the harvesting of wild oysters (oystering).

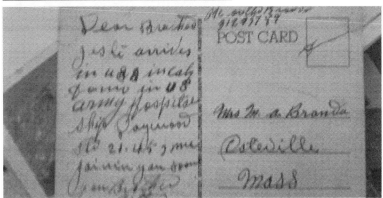

Meanwhile, a young woman by the name of Lillian Jean Abraham was living in the city of Worcester, Massachusetts, with her mother, Mary, and father, John, along with sister Anna and brothers George, Allen, and Michael. Actually, I was told that her birth name was Leah Jean, but somewhere along the line, it was changed to Lillian. Her birth certificate, however, reads Lilly G. Abraham. One of her brothers introduced her to a friend of his named David Anderson, who offered to teach this young lady how to drive. During this time, a relationship developed, and even though Anderson was married, he ended up fathering a child with Lillian, a boy whom she named Dennis Daniel. (A little side note: Dennis was born February 12, Abraham Lincoln's birthday; his mother's maiden name was Abraham, and the doctor who delivered him was Dr. Lincoln.) The relationship continued until Lillian became pregnant the second time a few years later. Realizing that the relationship was wrong and that she would never wed this man, she decided to leave the city. Encouraged by her dear friend, Sally Salazar, who shared her Lebanese background, she decided to move to Cape Cod. She somehow managed to find a little shack on Old Mill Road, where she took up residence.

As it turned out, this small shack was just down the street from where Arthur was living. Each day, when he passed by her "house," he would see her hauling water from the well. He realized how hard she was struggling, being pregnant and caring for a small son. He would often reach out to her with food and other necessities. The struggle became so intense that she was considering sending Dennis back to Worcester to live with his biological father and putting her unborn child up for adoption. Arthur told her that if she married him, he would adopt her children as his own, and so, on November 22, 1946, Arthur's birthday, the two of them became husband and wife. And on one stormy night, January 20, 1947, when the weather was so bad, they could not get to the hospital, her daughter, Leonna, was born. And Arthur, true to his word, formerly adopted both as his own. Dennis said the happiest day of his life was when Arthur asked him if he would like to be adopted and have him as his father. Dennis told me it made him feel really special. Then, in 1948, some very significant events occurred, among them the recognition of Israel as an Independent Jewish State, the assassination of Mahatma Gandhi, the opening of the largest airport in the world, Idlewild in New York (JFK International today) (Trivia for you trivia buffs: What 60s show's theme song are these lines from, *"There's a scout troop short a child, Khruschev's due at Idlewild, ...where are you?"*), the founding of NASCAR, the U.S. Supreme Court ruling that

religious instruction in public schools violates the Constitution (McCollum vs. Board of Ed.), Hells Angels was founded, Truman signed the Marshall Plan, Civil Air Patrol became part of the USAF as did the Woman's Air Force (WAF), the Berlin Blockade Began and the Berlin Airlift takes place, Executive Order 9981 is signed by President Truman (ending racial segregation in the military), USAFOSI is founded, the UN adopts the Universal Declaration of Human Rights, just to name a few. There were also some significant births that year, including Al Gore (former VP), Jerry Mathers (the Beaver), Clarence Thomas (Supreme Court Justice), Christa McAuliffe (American teacher killed in the Challenger disaster of 1986), and too many actors, actresses and musicians to mention. And, also that year, September 22, to be precise, I came along.

I was told I was in such a hurry that I couldn't even wait to get into the hospital room, but I arrived in the hallway of Cape Cod Hospital in the village of Hyannis, in the Town of Barnstable, in the land known as Cape Cod in the Commonwealth of Massachusetts, aka, The Bay State, named for the Massachusett, one of the many tribes which once inhabited the area. I believe the name means something like "near the great hill." Hyannis itself was named after a sachem (chief) of the Cummaquid tribe whose name was Iyannough. They have a statue of him on Main Street in Hyannis. But all that is fodder for another book and another time. Back to me. I was christened Leo Arthur (Leo after a cousin whom my mother loved and who was killed in a bicycle accident…incidentally, the same individual after whom my

older sister was named…and Arthur after my father, of course. These names were chosen because my mother thought I would be her last child. But then came Mary Jean, Arthur James, Jr, Anna May, Peter John, Theresa Louise, and finally, Marcia Marie. There was one miscarriage after she had Anna, and the doctor told her she should not/could not have any more children after that. And then three more came along. More about the siblings later.

Coming home from the hospital brought us to 366 Old Mill Road, a house shared with my Uncle Nina (Manual), my father's brother, and his wife, Aunt Lilly. (Actually, her real name was

Lillian Francis.) How about that - two brothers having wives with the same name? I believe we stayed here until I was about four when my father built the house at 437 Old Mill Road, just down the street. I can actually recall when it was being built. I have vague memories of walking through the framework.

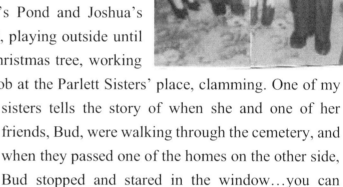

Eventually, I was old enough to join my brother and sister at school, so I started at Osterville Bay Elementary School, 93 West Bay Road (Opened in 1915, closed in 2008). My first-grade teacher was Mrs. Childs. My second-grade teacher was Mrs. Adams.

Some highlights growing up. Playing at Micah's Pond and Joshua's Pond, walking to the A&P through the graveyard, playing outside until dusk, exploring the woods, getting our annual Christmas tree, working the cranberry bogs, accompanying Daddy to his job at the Parlett Sisters' place, clamming. One of my sisters tells the story of when she and one of her friends, Bud, were walking through the cemetery, and when they passed one of the homes on the other side, Bud stopped and stared in the window…you can imagine the reaction of the residents.

In 1960, I was promoted to what was then called Junior High and attended Barnstable Junior High School, located at the end of High School Road in Hyannis. Today, it is a Catholic School, St. John Paul II High School, but at that time, it housed the seventh and eighth graders. Graduating from there, I went to Barnstable High School located on West Main Street. There were three different enrollment classes that we could sign up for. General, Business, and College Classes. Additionally, there was the Vocational School where you could learn a trade such as auto mechanics, carpentry, plumbing, or other "blue collar" type work. I initially signed up for the General Courses, which, besides the normal academic classes, allowed me to take some vocational courses, so I signed up for agricultural-type classes, including Future Farmers of America. Since I grew up doing landscaping, I felt this was appropriate. But then the

guidance counselors stepped in "doing their job" and convinced me that I belonged in the College Classes. So many of my classes were switched, and I was no longer able to take the agricultural classes. There was nothing really fantastic that I remember about my high school days. I remember a few of the teachers and some "really insignificant stuff." For example, I remember playing a game in one of my tenth-grade classes where we had to have our "partner" guess the name of a song using charades. I remember I had the song by Barbara Lewis, "*Make Me Your Baby*." Another time, I believe it was in Paul Germani's class, we had a little party, complete with records. The song "*Monday, Monday*" was playing, and when it got near the end, there was a slight break in the song, and it seemed like it was over. At that point, Mr. Germani went to remove the record, and it came back on, and he jumped back. Now, how insignificant is that to remember it. Weird. My yearbook only had a few signatures in it. My Sister Leonna, my old girlfriend, Sharon, my friend Laverne (more about them later), and one teacher, interestingly enough, Paul Germani.

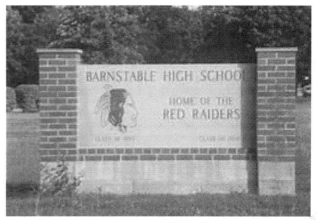
The caption under my picture reads, "He that is slow to anger is better than the mighty." So, I guess I must have had a reputation for being mild-mannered. In the back of our yearbook, we had the "Class Will." I left "wreckless driving" to Bob Stewart. My pet peeve was supposed to be "the Idiot Box," i.e., the television, but instead, it reads, "the idiot ox." Go figure. And under "Remembers," I wrote "the night in the swamp." Maybe I'll explain that a little later when I talk about my brother, Junior. I didn't go to the proms as I wasn't much of a dancer, but they were nice. Junior Prom theme was "Atlantis," and the Senior Prom theme was "Winter Wonderland." Later, I wrote a poem about these years entitled "BHS 66". You can read it in the appendix if you'd like.

Eventually, I graduated high school and went on to college. Somewhere along the line, as an altar boy, I had mentioned to Father Tosti that I was interested in becoming a priest. He took it upon himself to get me accepted into a College Seminary called St. Mary's, located near the small town of St. Mary (previously known as Hardin's Creek) in Marion County, Kentucky. So, that September, I was leaving home for the first time. St. Mary's was beautiful. The town itself was

just a crossroads with one general store and a post office. Situated on a working farm, the school was founded in 1821 and consisted of a number of buildings: Byrne Hall (named after one of the founders, William Byrne), Columbia Hall, and "The Abbey." At one time, it was the oldest extant college in Kentucky and was the third oldest Catholic College originally founded for boys in the United States. The original settlers of Hardin's Creek were immigrant Catholics from Maryland. The school was initially going to

be built by Father Charles Nerinckx, who was a local pastor. He had to abandon his plans due to a disastrous fire that destroyed the buildings that had been erected. When the Reverend Byrne replaced him as pastor, he realized the need for a boys' school and founded the college. The school not only held a college but also a high school. The school was temporarily closed following the Civil War due to financial problems, and when it was reopened in 1871, it was taken over by the Fathers of the Congregation of the Resurrection.

Postcard view of the St. Mary's campus. Byrne Hall is the central building with the tower.

Because the initials after their name was "CR," we referred to them as "Clerical Rejects," as almost all of them had some quirk that we either found amusing or frightening. Out of respect for them, I won't mention the names, but one used to never let anyone look inside his room. He used to open his door a crack, look up and down the halls, and then slip in. Another used to walk around the campus with a sharp pencil in front of him, and if you didn't get out of his way, you'd get jabbed. Maybe I'll share some more stories about them later. One interesting story was that of "Zeus." "Zeus" was a bull that had been purchased by the school to service the numerous cows that provided income for the school. A barbed wire fence had been erected to keep him away from the cows until it was time for him to perform his responsibilities. One day, Zeus decided to try and jump the fence to get to the cows. This resulted in $2,000 worth of worthless bull. I remember the annual bonfire that we held in the fall; the trips on Wednesdays to the "Cedars of Lebanon Rest Home (a Senior Citizen Home) located in Lebanon, KY, where we talked and sang with the residents; and our annual hikes out to St. Joe, to a small one-room schoolhouse. On these occasions, the headmaster of the school would declare a holiday for the students, and we spent the remainder of the day entertaining them. I had my first introduction to the arts here, as I worked backstage as a prop manager for numerous plays, such as "Oliver Twist" and "Guests of the Nation." I enjoyed working backstage and

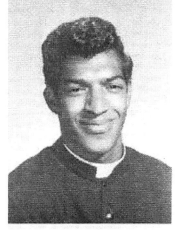

didn't care much for the limelight of the stage. I also had my first taste of the "no-nos" while here. One day, we had a field trip to Louisville, for us a major metropolis. While walking around, several of us passed a "strip club" and decided to go in. One of our company felt this was wrong and did not want to accompany us so we agreed to meet later. When we met up, he was stoned drunk, and we had to try really hard to sober him up before we met with the priests for our return to the school. By the way, this was my first and only visit to a strip club. And it happened while in seminary. Naughty, Naughty. Some of the noted alumni from St. Mary's include Joseph Cardinal Bernardin, Archbishop of Chicago (1982-1996), Martin Spalding, Bishop of Louisville (1850-1864 and Archbishop of Baltimore (1864-1872), and Augustus Hill Garland, 11th Governor of Arkansas and Attorney General of the United States, just to name a few. (Added note: the school closed in 1976 and was converted into a low-security prison. We had the opportunity to visit it while visiting my grandson in Kentucky but weren't allowed onto the grounds) Eventually, the diocese transferred me out of St. Mary's (which had nothing to do with the visit to the strip club) and enrolled

BROTHER JOHN ABRAHAM
Holy Redeemer Mission House,
Methuen, Mass.

me in St. John's College in Brighton, MA, a suburb of Boston. Things changed here. I got involved in other activities (good ones, like helping at one of the local churches), but as a result, my studies suffered. I was losing interest in remaining in the seminary. Some of it may have been the reality of the priesthood. My interest in the priesthood had been fostered by my admiration of Father Tosti and my idolization of Father O'Malley (Bing Crosby) from the movies *"Going My Way"* and *"Bells of St. Mary's."* My exposure to some of the priests at St. Mary's and St. John's kind of shattered the image I had.

Not that they were bad, but it just wasn't what I had imagined. So, the bottom line was that the following August (1969), I decided I wasn't going back. I knew that if I didn't go back to school, I would be hot for the draft (Vietnam was still going on strong), so I enlisted in the United States Air Force. My mother was shocked to say the least, as she was especially proud of me for wanting to become a priest. One of her favorite nephews (Cousin John) had done so, and she had much respect for the priesthood. But she loved me and supported me. I went in on the delayed enlistment program, so even though I signed up in August 1969, I wasn't called up until the following May. In the meantime, I had to get a job.

Speaking of jobs, I sure have skipped a lot of stuff. Let's save the military stuff for later and talk about some of the jobs I've had over the years prior to going into the military. My longest job was working with the A&P in Osterville. I worked in the produce department every Summer after turning sixteen. Even when I came home from college. I really enjoyed working there and met a lot of great people, especially college girls who were on the Cape for the summer and needed a part-time job. One of these girls was Marilyn. She and I shared the same birthday, and we hit it off fairly well as friends. I always wanted to go out with her but never had the courage to ask her as I felt we came from opposite sides of the track, as it were, and I didn't know how it would be accepted by her family. I did walk her home a few times and met her parents. Nice folks, I thought. I found out many years later that she would have gladly said yes had I asked her out. Had I not enlisted in the Air Force, I would have had the opportunity to become a produce manager at one of the Island stores (Nantucket or Martha's

Vineyard). Since the A&P was only a summer job, I had to find employment during the fall, winter, and spring periods. Besides a paper route, I also worked as an usher at the movie theater in Hyannis, in the

distribution department of the Cape Cod Standard Times, and in a candy/chocolate-making store on the main street in Hyannis (I forget the name). Additionally, I mowed lawns and worked on the cranberry bogs with my father. Hard work was instilled in me early in life and has served me well. Well, so much for an overview. What say we go back and look at some of the stories I remember for those first 18 years from birth to graduation and college? And while we're at it, we can talk about my brothers and sisters. But where do we start?

Well, I already mentioned where and when I was born and where our first house was. As a matter of fact, my sister Anna and her husband live in that house today (as of 2023). And my youngest brother had a trailer right behind the house where he stayed in the summer. The wintertime found him either in Florida or back at Cape Verde, living among some long-lost relatives. More on that later. Much later. What do I remember about that time of life? Well, there was a grapevine in the backyard. Loved eating the grapes. And my uncle

made wine. I think he also had a pear tree and apple tree back then as well. There was an outhouse, too. A two-seater, if I recall correctly. Let's see, there was Mom, Dad, Dennis, Leonna, me, Uncle Nina, Aunt Lilly, and I believe at some time, Junior Vierra and Patricia (Patsy) Roderick lived with us as well. They were two foster children being raised by my aunt and uncle, who had no children of their own. And the family grew. A year or so later,

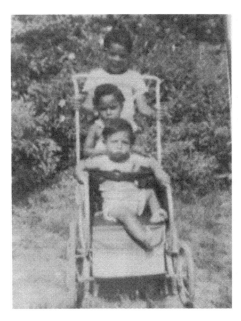 

my sister Mary was born. Mary Jean, to be exact. Following her came Arthur Jr. Actually, he was Arthur James, and since my father had no middle name, Junior wasn't 100% accurate, but who cared? A pattern was being formed – boy, girl, boy, girl, boy, so I guess the next was to be a girl. Somewhere during this time, my father built the house at 437 Old Mill Road, just a quarter mile up the road. Actually, he owned a lot of land on Old Mill Road. Other places in Osterville as well, but, somehow, he lost all the rest, bought by his bosses, but kept the land on Old Mill Road. I kind of think he was taken advantage of. Perhaps he needed money. At any rate, many years later, while checking county land records, I found the sales agreements. But that's water under the bridge. So now we're in the new house. Two stories with a full basement. Two big bedrooms upstairs, one for the girls and one for the boys. A little "tunnel" connected the two rooms, accessed by

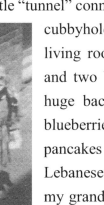

cubbyholes in the wall. A big kitchen, living room, dining room, one bathroom, and two bedrooms downstairs. We had a huge backyard, plenty of woods, lots of areas to play. Wild blueberries allowed Mom to make us some delicious blueberry pancakes and other goodies. Did I mention my mom had a Lebanese background? My grandfather came from Lebanon, and my grandmother from Syria. Anyway, she sure could cook some of them Lebanese dishes. My Auntie Anna and her family would sometimes visit from Worcester. Her family consisted of Uncle Charlie and cousins Danny (Scuffy), William (Sonny), Sister (real name Lillian), Leona (Lonnie), Dorothy (Dotty), George, Joe Reeks (Sister's husband) and sometimes Uncle Allen. Lots of food would flow then. Sometimes, we would take a trip to Worcester to visit them. Of course, in those early days, we didn't have the superhighways, so a trip to Worcester took a few hours, so it became quite an event and a rare one at that. We never went hungry. We had a big garden out back, and we raised all kinds of animals. Most memorable was "The Pig." Every year, we would get a pig, and when it was big enough, it was butchered and provided plenty of meat. There are a lot of stories surrounding the pigs. Occasionally, they would escape from the pen and go wandering down the street. The neighbors would call, and we'd have to go round it up. Sometimes,

we'd ride the pig like it was a horse. I remember my older brother coming home on leave from the Marines with some of his buddies and challenging them to ride the pig. Inevitably, one would fall off and end up in the muck. One such guy was Russell. He fell off, and the pig chased him around the mud. Had to be embarrassing for a U.S. Marine. Dad could never be around when it was killed. I guess he couldn't bear the sight of watching it die. A friend of his, Joe Perry, took care of that. My dad had good relationships with the people in town. I guess because he worked for a lot of important people, and they respected him for his hard work, his honesty and his integrity. He told me once that your name was the most important thing you had, and you should never do anything to tarnish it. He would always get the leftover produce from the A&P so we could feed the pig with it (after we removed any "good stuff" for ourselves. After all, there were a lot of mouths to feed. One of the people he worked for was Victor Adams. I believe he was a town selectman. Mrs. Adams was one of my teachers. He also worked for Albert Hinckly, the Chief of Police, as well as the Fraziers, the Goodspeeds, and the Greicos. I'll tell you a story about them later when I share some of the tales of my brother Junior and me. I will mention one thing here regarding the people he worked for and the respect they had for him. He had been left an estate in Wianno by a man named Alex Monroe, whom he had worked for. Because he did not want to fight the family over the inheritance, he gave it up.

Back to the house. Did I mention about the basement? For some strange reason, there was a small mirror embedded in the concrete floor. Many years later, after my father's passing, I found out what it was for. I think it was my uncle that educated me on this. They used to hold dances in the basement. And, of course, the ladies wore dresses. Well, you can figure out the rest. I never said my dad was perfect. He was a hard worker and a good provider. Unfortunately, he did drink quite a bit. But then, I guess, most of the men did. Some of the women, too, I reckon. I never recall either my mother or my aunt drinking. From what I understand, my dad had a hard life growing up. His father, Peter, was extremely strict. Owned lots of land in Cabo Verde on Fogo, and dad and his brothers had to work hard. I remember one time my dad brought me into the bathroom, dropped his pants and showed me all the scars on his legs caused by his father. His admonition to me was to NEVER do anything that would cause him to beat me like that. That lesson stuck really good, and I never gave him cause. Except maybe one time. Remember when I mentioned the Greicos earlier? Well, that story almost got me that beating. But you'll have to wait to read about it.

Back to the house and the land. Up the road, just to the north of us, lived a couple (Yaya and Tony). I remember well that

Dad would spend lots of time there drinking. We'd just cut through the woods to their house, or Dad would drive his truck over, and they'd be sitting out back of the little shack they called home, drinking and playing music. For some reason, I recall the summer of 1967, they would play the song, *Whiter Shade of Pale* by Procul Harem over and over, and we could hear it through the woods. Another one of those weird and insignificant things one recalls. Music has a way of bringing things to memory. As long as we're speaking of neighbors, to our left was the Cabrals and west of us, again, through the woods, lived the Barbozas. A little west of them lived the Hurtts, John and Bea and their kids, John, Bruce, Laverne (Debra), Terry, Bud, Jay and Marva. Growing up, I always thought that Bea was a beautiful woman, though I never mentioned that to anyone. Something about her smile, I think. We remained friends until she passed. I would visit her every time I came home, and I think she really appreciated it. All of us kids would play together until it was time to come in. Mom had a bell outside the breezeway door, and she could ring it when it was time for us to come in. With no computers, no video games, and no television programs (except some Saturday morning cartoons and prime-time family shows), we spent as much time outside as we could doing all kinds of things. Building forts in the woods, picking berries, and going to the pond (either Micah's or Joshua's).

Someone said it best on Facebook, and so I'll repeat it here with some minor editing. It applied to anyone who grew up around that era. "I grew up in the small town of Osterville, MA. It is on Cape Cod, some 40-odd years ago (in my case, 75+). This was during a time when everyone treated each other like family. Our parents talked to the neighbors, and we all knew everyone. We ate pork chops, meatloaf, steak and potatoes, hot dogs, hamburgers and homemade biscuits and gravy. We also ate whatever Mom made for dinner, with NO exceptions. We went outside to play. We left our houses as soon as we could in the morning or after school and stayed out until time to come in. We rode our bikes everywhere. There were no smartphones or tablets to keep us occupied. We swam, fished, camped out, played hide and seek, kickball, tag, dodge ball, kill the guy with the ball. We had water balloon fights, dirt clog fights, football, stickball, basketball, and soccer. We built forts, lit our own sparklers, and caught lightning bugs. Sometimes, we even made up our own games. Did I mention that we rode our bikes everywhere? We jumped ramps, and if you fell down, you would just get back up and keep on going even though the palms of your hands were scratched up or your knees were bleeding. We weren't afraid of fake guns or walking after dark. We respected our parents, our teachers, and the American Flag and were scared of the school principal. We said the Pledge of Allegiance EVERY morning at school. We watched our mouths around our elders because we knew if we disrespected any adult there would be a price to pay. We were spanked when we needed it and learned our lesson from that spanking. I would not trade anything for the childhood we had. We had enough, and we had love, and all of that made us the adults we are today."

We had our share of fights, too. I remember one time, getting hit in the head with a rock, with blood gushing down my face. This happened up by my aunt's house, and we had to run home with the blood coming down my face. I don't think I had to go to the hospital, though. Those injuries were all a part of growing up. We had other friends who didn't live so close but would visit them on occasion when my father took us there to visit with their parents or conduct business. There were the Perrys, the Pinas, the Pells, and the Lopes. My Godfather was, in fact, Arcenio Lopes. I remember him having a beautiful daughter, actually three, but only one that I was particularly interested in.

Sometimes, my dad would take us with him when he went to visit his cousin Joe. Joe was an old, single guy who lived by himself on Route 28 in Centerville, about 4 or 5 miles from us. It was always a boring visit. We'd sit there and couldn't do anything. Joe might offer us a soda. Anytime you said thanks, he'd respond in his gruffy voice, "Thanks don't pay no bills." One thing he did do was to collect clothes and stuff every year and send them to his relatives in Cape Verde. I remember him having barrels around in which he would stuff anything that he was going to send. I'm sure there are a lot of stories around this time, but memories fade. Wait a minute. We're still missing some siblings. We ended with a boy, Arthur Jr., so the next had to be a girl. And it was…Anna May. But Mom and Dad didn't stop there. She had a miscarriage following Anna, and the doctor told her she shouldn't or couldn't have any more children. He was wrong. This time a boy's turn, and Peter John (Named after both grandfathers) came on the scene. Followed by, of course, another girl, Therese Louise (who, with her husband, Peter, lived in "the house that dad built" following mom's passing). Then came the spoiler, Marcia Marie. My mother, of course, was expecting a boy and had bought all boy's things. And for some reason, since she broke the boy-girl chain, we all knew she was the last. And she'll always be the baby of the family. Well, let's move on…or backward as the case may be, as we start filling in the holes.

I mentioned that I spent a lot of time working with my father. When I was old enough, I started going with him after school. He would get off of his Parlett job, his "7 to 4" if you will, and would pick the boys up, and then we'd go to one of the other homes that he would take care of. It might have been the Goodspeeds, the Fraziers, the Adams, the Greicos, the Aylmers, or…wait a second. The Aylmers. I remember Karen. You might say she was my "first love." I was, well, young enough to be playing in the leaves while my dad raked them. That's what I remember – playing in the leaves with Karen. And that's all I remember. I think she had a brother named Thomas. At least, I think that was his name.

My father drove a Kaiser – don't remember the year or the color, but he also had a 1946 Chevy pickup truck that he used for work. Don't remember a whole lot about that, either. Somewhere along the line, he picked up an Edsel and a Rambler with a rear-facing third seat. And I'm sure he had to replace the '46 pickup with a later model. My brother Junior and I used to work a lot together. (See my speech, "Dad and I at Work," in the Appendix, which I gave in 1994 for Toastmasters-more on Toastmasters Later.) One day, my father dropped us off at the Greicos, who had an estate on Sea View Lane along the water. A beautiful place. They only used it during the summer and weren't there at the time. A lot of the folks were like that. Anyway, Dad left us there and went to another job. We finished up and began exploring and found the wine cellar. Remember when I said I almost got the beaten dad had threatened me with? When he returned for us, we were both drunk. I think we found a bottle of rum. What I really enjoyed doing was going with him to the Parlett estate. There we could go clamming, fish, walk along the water or swim. One winter day, we tried to walk across the partially frozen ice. Bad idea.

Fortunately, nothing bad happened, but we were cautioned never to do that again. I mentioned the Fraziers and the Adams. Well, they owned cranberry bogs on the Cape, and in addition to working at their homes, we also worked on the bogs come harvest time. At first, we would just carry boxes down to the men, picking the berries with the scoops. In later years, we could also pick the berries that were along the ditches while the men used the machines to harvest the rest of the bogs.

Of course, it wasn't all work and no play. There was plenty of time for fun. One of the annual events that we all looked forward to was the San Antonio Festival. It was held just up the street from us in this field. In the middle of the field was this tall telephone pole, and the men would fashion a "tree" on it that could be raised and lowered. It was in the shape of a two-dimensional Christmas tree, and it would be covered with all kinds of fruit (pineapples, oranges, apples, bananas, and a bunch of other stuff. After all the singing, dancing and eating was over, all the kids would be released to attack the tree and grab as much stuff as they could as the tree was being lowered. At the very tip of the tree was tied a bottle of liquor, and once everything was stripped from the tree, it would be raised back up. Then, at a given signal, all the adult young men would dash to the tree to see who could get to the top first and retrieve the bottle. My older brother, Dennis, was the victor one year. Also, all the men would take all the change they had and throw it up in the air, and the kids would scramble to get all they could. The festival was initially held at my Uncle Nina's house right out in the front yard. But then, as it grew in number, my dad decided to donate some land for it, and it was moved close to the end of Old Mill Road, midway between Swift Avenue and Starboard Lane. Speaking of Starboard Lane, that was one of my favorite roads to travel, especially when I had a young lady with me. The road was deliberately constructed to reduce speeding because there were a lot of wealthy homes on it. It consisted of numerous dips and turns and made for an exciting ride for us daredevils.

Growing up, we all had our own stories to tell. Stories of bad mishaps, doing things we shouldn't have been doing, exciting stories, scary stories, and just plain fun stories. Just to share a few, I'll try to include some from each of the siblings.

One day, when my sister Terry was about 9, she was riding her bike down Autumn Drive, a fairly steep road. When she put on her brakes, she made the mistake of applying the front brakes instead of the rear brakes, and went head over heels over the handlebars. As she had been moving at a fair pace, her whole face was scraped really badly. She rushed home, and since my mother didn't drive and my father was at work, mom proceeded as best she could by washing her face and, applying all kinds of creams on it and bandaging it up. Terry had to stay in the house for weeks because, as I said, her face made her look like a "monster." Eventually, it did heal, and she turned into a beautiful young lady. It wasn't until many years later, when she went to the doctor for an examination, that she found out that her nose had been broken.

I mentioned that mom didn't drive, and dad was always working, so if we wanted to go anywhere, it was usually by foot, bike, and sometimes hitchhiking. Sometimes, we could get an older sibling to take us places. This was the case with Terry and five others when they wanted to go to the County Fair Grounds, which were about 12 miles away. My sister, Leonna, drove them there and told them that if they wanted a ride home, they were to be at the gate at 10:00 p.m. sharp. Well, they arrived at the gate about 10:02, and there was no Leonna. They waited a while, but with no cell phones back then and no way to contact her, they started walking. About 2:00 a.m., they arrived home. Leonna, who had been having a heated discussion with my mother for not going back to pick them up, told them, "When I tell you to be somewhere at a particular time, I don't mean a minute later." Older siblings often have a way of doing the discipline. I remember once when I sassed my mother; it was my older brother who chased me, and when he caught me, he taught me a lesson about never disrespecting mommy.

Junior and Johnny had their share of stories as well. One time, they took a ride to visit the Lopes girls  who lived in Falmouth. Junior didn't have a license, but he did have an old Ford. They got some plates from somewhere, put them on the car and drove to Falmouth. As they were driving home, Junior noticed the dreaded flashing blue lights behind him and eventually pulled over. When the officer approached the car and asked for Junior's license, he handed him my father's expired license. After all, they had the same name. After looking at the license (remember my father was born in 1909, Junior was born in 1951), the officer started laughing so hard and proceeded to tell

Junior to park the car on the side of the road. Junior says, "I'll park it in my driveway," and takes off for home. By the time he pulled into the driveway, the cop was right there (after all, the address was on the license). Needless to say, they didn't drive anywhere for some time after that.

When Johnny was old enough to drive, he decided one day to take my neighbor's car to go pick up his girlfriend, Robin. The neighbors were away at the time and had asked my older brother Dennis to keep an eye on the car and the house for them. Well, when Dennis noticed the car missing, he, of course, called the police. I believe Johnny ended up crashing the car. Since Johnny was very young when Dad died, he really didn't have a father figure around while he was growing up, which may help to explain some of his wilder antics.

One time, he was mowing the lawn when the neighbor's kid, Mark Barros, asked him about the little chute on the side of the lawnmower. You know, the one where the grass is supposed to come out and be caught by the grass catcher if it's attached. Well, Johnny, being wise, told him to stick his foot in there and find out. Then he made the mistake of leaving the lawn mower running while he went into the house to get something. And Mark went ahead and stuck his foot into the chute. Another trip to the hospital.

Johnny once broke into the House and Garden Shop on Main Street in Osterville and came home with a BB Gun, some camping equipment, and a cash register. When Mom asked him where he got the stuff, he said someone gave them to him. Right, a cash register? Of course, Mom called the police.

Then there was the time Johnny decided to be an entrepreneur. He and his friend Dukey had to pass through the office at school for some reason and saw the rolls of tickets for lunches and milk. They stole a roll of each and were selling them to the kids for half price. Johnny made a little money, the kids got a deal with their lunches, and the lunch teachers were wondering how the kids had tickets when they didn't sell them to them.

Johnny wasn't the only one to get in trouble with the law.

Dennis had learned to drive Dad's 1946 Chevy pickup when he was only eight. Back in those days, you could get away with it because there wasn't too much traffic on the road. Usually, he would drive Daddy home when he got drunk. But one time, when he was eight years old, he got stopped on Old Mill Road. He was raking leaves with Daddy when Daddy told him to finish up while he went three houses down to check on something. Dennis loaded the leaves in the truck and then started driving the truck down the road to where my father was, and he stalled the truck. It just so happened that a cop was nearby. The cop came over to the stalled truck and, seeing Dennis in the driver seat, asked him what he was doing, and Dennis replied, "I'm driving my father's truck. As the cop asked him where his father was, my father came walking up the street. He cussed Dennis out, in Portuguese, all the way home.

Junior and I did a lot of things together, especially after I got my license. One time, we tried to go into the landscaping business together since we were both familiar with it. One guy had just recently bought a house, and as we were passing by, we noticed that the yard had not been prepared, and we offered our services to prepare and plant his lawn. He hired us, and we did the job. When the lawn did come up, it was the worst job you ever saw. You have to start somewhere.

One Christmas, we needed a Christmas tree. When we were young, and Dad was still alive, the family would all go out together into the woods and find the perfect tree. But this one year, I believe it was the Christmas of '68, we had been driving around and noticed these beautiful "Christmas" trees. Only problem was…they were in somebody's front yard. Did we let that stop us? Of course not. We came back later that night. I told Junior to drop me off with the saw and come back in about five minutes or so. I cut the tree down, brought it to the side of the road and waited…and waited…and waited. A dog was barking in the background, time was going by, and I was getting a bit nervous and antsy. Finally, about a half hour later, Junior shows up. He had gone to the package store about a mile down the road and had lost the keys to the car. It took him all that time to find them.

Another time, we had been driving around listening to music with our older cousin, Danny, or Scuffy as we used to call him. We wanted to hear the song *"They're Coming to Take Me Away,"* by Napoleon XIV, a big hit that particular year (1966). We stopped on Main Street in Osterville so we could use the phone booth outside of Peggy's Newsstand. By the way, this was also our local soda shop. Anyways, Junior tried to call the radio station and lost the money in the phone booth. For some reason, the call didn't go through, so he starts pounding on the phone booth. A cop was patrolling the street and came over to see what was going on. Junior explained to him what happened, and the cop told him that the only way he could get the money back was to notify the phone company. And my cousin starts whistling and saying you can get it out with a screwdriver. Did I mention Scuffy had a relationship with the police? I think they all knew him from some of his antics. He was always doing something crazy. We'd be sitting in a restaurant, and he'd be pretending he was picking blueberries or flies out of the air and eating them. Sometimes, when we were in the car, he would stick his foot out and scrape the road, or tell us he was going to lean out and lick the road. I remember one time my brother Junior tied a rope around the door jamb to keep Scuffy from opening it so he couldn't do one of those crazy things.

Another time, the three of us were going to the carnival. Scuffy worked a lot with the carnivals and could always get us passes. At the time, I had my Black Studebaker, but I had problems with the tires. Junior had gotten an old Ford from somewhere that had good tires, so we had taken two of the tires off the Ford and put them on the Studebaker. As we were driving to the carnival, Scuffy asked if anyone wanted some "uppers" so we could stay out late. Junior said sure, but I said absolutely not. No one was going to be taking any pills while in my car. So, Junior and I had an argument, and I told him if he wanted to take them, he could get out of the car, and I stopped the car. He said if he was getting out, he was taking his tires with him. Anyway, we got into a little scuffle in someone's front yard, and they proceeded to call the police. When the police finally arrived, we told them it was just a family disagreement and it was over. Then he noticed Scuffy and said, "Don't I know You?" Forgot all about me and Junior. Since no one was pressing any charges, he let us go, and we continued on to the carnival with a story to tell later on.

One time, Junior came home after drinking. He thought he heard a prowler out in the yard, and so he took a rifle down from the gun rack. It belonged to my older brother, who had built a house across the street, but for some reason, he left the gun rack at Mom's. Anyway, Junior got the rifle down and loaded it, and it went off and shot through the floor of the kitchen. At the time, my sister Terry was sleeping on the other side of the wall in the living room (don't know why), but she woke up startled. Junior started shaking really badly after he realized what might have happened had the bullet gone through the wall instead of the floor. Needless to say, the gun rack was removed the first thing next day.

One time, when my Sister Mary was in Junior High School, she had to stay after school. The late bus did not drop us off in front of the house but rather at the end of Old Mill Road, about a mile away from home. Walking home from there was usually not a problem, but this particular day, there was a terrible blizzard. The teacher should never have kept her after school. She started walking home in the blinding snowstorm with freezing temperatures. After walking about a quarter mile, she was so cold and tired she was ready to give up and started to lay down at the bottom of the cemetery. It was at that time that my brother Junior showed up. She could not even see his face until he was right next to her because of the snow coming down so hard. Mom had sent him to find her. Anyway, he helped her up and got her safely to my Uncle's house. Uncle Nina helped warm her up by giving her some wine and a blanket. Junior went home to let Mom know she was OK. Uncle Nina then brought her home. My Mom was really mad at him because she had asked him to go pick her up, and he wouldn't.

The late bus would drop us off at the end of the road, but the regular bus picked us up in front of the house. During inclement weather, all the neighbor kids would wait in our house until the bus arrived. One day, one of the mom's, Dolly Barboza, complained because she didn't feel it was right that the bus stopped in front of our house and not at the end of Oakville Ave, which happened to be her street. It was only about 300 feet from our house, but the bus driver agreed to do it. So, during inclement weather, those who were waiting in the house had to watch for the bus and then run down to the corner to catch it. At least they got some exercise.

Another story about Mary was when she was playing baseball. Not very athletic. She didn't too often get a hit. One time, she hit the ball really good and started running. She fell down and hurt her knee really badly with blood flowing down, but she was so excited about hitting the ball that she got up and kept running, oblivious to the fact that she had blood oozing down her leg.

Can't forget some stories about Little Marcia. She had her stories growing up as well. One time, she and Michael Barros decided they would paint Mom's little white dog green. Neighbors had to take a second look when they saw this green dog running down the street. Another time, Marcia and Michael were playing and evidently got into a little fight, and she began biting his finger, nearly biting it off.

Well, I'll get back to some more stories later, but I seem to be losing my place with these side stories. Many of these stories were passed on to me as I had already left to go to college and wasn't around when they happened.

While growing up, I became involved with the Church. Church was a big part of growing up. Both Mom and Dad were Catholics (which explains the large family). Dad would go to Church every morning before going to work. He would also cut flowers and bring them to the Church. Besides going to Church every Sunday, we also attended Catechism classes on Wednesday. The Church was Our Lady of the Assumption Church, located at 76 Wianno Ave. (It was originally founded as an outreach mission  of St. Francis Xavier Church in Hyannis, the home church of the Kennedy's. It was dedicated in August 1905 and formerly established as a parish in 1928. The pastors who served during my time were the Rev William J. Buckley (1943-1960) and Rev John T. Higgins (1960-1966). The Curates, or assistants, were Rev John Driscoll (1947-1950) and Rev Ronald A. Tosti (1962). I was baptized here on August 28, 1949, by the Rev Driscoll. My Godparents were my Dad's good friend, Arcenio Lopes and my Aunt, Anna Scobie. I received my First Communion here by Rev Buckley on May 13, 1956. The Altar Boys affectionately referred to Father Tosti as Ronnie the Rat, as his initials were R.A.T. I served as an Altar Boy for a number of years and then as a lector. My brother Dennis said one time he heard me praying the "Our Father" in my sleep, so I guess I was destined to follow the Lord one way or the other. I enjoyed serving as an Altar Boy. I didn't get too involved in any school activities, so this gave me something to do. I remember when Fr Tosti took us Altar Boys to the wake for our Assistant School Principal and

 member of our Church. After the wake, he treated us all to ice cream at "The Four Seas Ice Cream" in Centerville, a Cape Cod fixture since 1934 and our favorite place to go for ice cream. When he dropped me off, I said, "Thanks for the good time, Father." Before realizing we had just come from a wake, so using the phrase "good time" was probably not appropriate. *Mea culpa, mea culpa.* I still remember some of the Latin that we had to learn. In today's lingo, I guess you could roughly translate that as "My bad." As I mentioned, instead of Sunday School, we received our Catechism classes on Wednesday at the "Cenacle." The Cenacle was staffed by the Sisters of the Missionary Servants of the Most Blessed Trinity. The sisters served in the Parish through the late 1960s. In addition to Our Lady of the Assumption Church, the Parish was also responsible for two outreach chapels, one in Cotuit and one in Santuit. Eventually, Father Tosti

went on to build the largest Church on the Cape, Christ the King Parish in Falmouth, replacing the two little chapels. One year, I broke my foot while working at the A&P. We had this huge steel plate that we used to keep the garbage room door closed so the critters wouldn't get in there. I forgot that it was leaning against the door when I opened the door to put the trash in. The plate fell on my foot and broke it, and I was in a cast and on crutches for a while. What does this have to do with the

Church or Fr. Tosti? Well, this was during the summer while I was attending Seminary. As my foot was getting better, I decided to walk downtown one day and was escorted by three young ladies from North

Carolina who were visiting our neighbors (Chubby, Debbie and Patricia W.). When I bumped into Fr. Tosti on Main Street, I had one arm around one young lady and the other arm around the other (for support). Fr. Tosti took one look at us, shook his head, and said, "Well, I guess there's safety in numbers." Another time, he chewed me out for wearing a Mason ring that I found. I had no idea what it represented, but he told me to get rid of it. Besides serving as Altar Boy and Lector, I also served as a part-time janitor and did clean-up work around the Church. An interesting side note. My future wife also attended Our Lady of the Assumption Church. Only the one she attended was in New Bedford, MA.

I can honestly say that I enjoyed my childhood years. I was never into sports, so aside from recess activities, I never got involved in sports. Very seldom went to any games. My excuse was I had to work.

When I wasn't working, we were playing. Like I mentioned earlier, we built forts and had lots of neighborhood kids to play with.

Once I was old enough to get my own job, I started working at the A&P in Osterville, as I mentioned earlier. The manager, Bob McCarthy, was a parishioner at our Church, as was the head cashier, Evelyn Whitely. So, getting the job was not a problem. But I had to prove I was a good employee, and so I worked hard. I loved working in the produce department.

A group of young lectors.

Occasionally, I had to help with bagging or stocking, but that wasn't my primary job. I eventually got really good at what I was doing. I would package the produce with this machine we used that had rolls of plastic wrap and a thin wire for cutting the wrap, and I got really fast at doing it. One day, while shucking corn to prepare it for wrapping like six in a package, I asked one of the butchers if he could sharpen a paring knife that I used for shucking the corn. The knife was so sharp, allowing me to shuck the corn even faster. As this was a summer job, and Cape Cod was a resort area, we had a lot of summer visitors (as well as employees) of the female persuasion. College girls were there to have a good time. Oftentimes, they would come into the store wearing bathing suits. The room where I worked had a swinging door with a window that looked out onto the floor. Shucking corn with a sharp knife and looking at girls walking in the store in bathing suits proved to be a not-so-good combination. I still have a nice scar on my thumb from that experience.

Today, everything is computer-run, so if the computers go out, the stores have to shut down. Many of the cashiers today cannot even make change unless the computer tells them what the change is. Not so in those days. I remember once when the power went out. Did we shut down because the cash registers couldn't run? Not on your life. Believe it or not, they pulled out cranks for the cash registers, and all the guys would team up with one of the cashiers, and when she hit the keys, we turned the crank. Never see that happen today.

I met a lot of friends while working at the A&P. Mostly girls but a few guys. Of course, I can't remember all the names. I already mentioned Marilyn. We had a couple of sisters from Braintree, Karen and Andrea. I also met a guy named Amos Diaz and made the mistake of introducing him to my sister. If I got my story right, he was initially interested in one of my younger sisters who wasn't interested and convinced my older sister to help her out. So Leonna did, and she and Amos eventually got married. It proved to be a not-so-good marriage because he was more interested in his bike and his freedom than he was in the married life. But they did produce one beautiful son whom they named John Anthony. I believe the name

John was chosen after my younger brother. We called him Tony. I'll talk more about Leonna and Tony a little later, as they played a significant role in my future.

I already mentioned the other jobs I did besides the A&P. One of them being the candy "factory" on Main Street in Hyannis. That was an enjoyable job. I didn't actually make the candy, as we had the chocolatiers who did that. My job was pouring the chocolate into the various molds and, of course cleaning up the molds and utensils. But it was fun watching them work as they made these creations. Plus, I got to taste a lot of the chocolate. Another time, as I mentioned, I worked for the movie theater on Main Street. Back in the 60s, we didn't have these mega-theaters that we have today. Each town had one theater and would show one movie or perhaps, on occasion, a double feature. When it opened in 1911, it was called the Idle Hour Theater but was renamed in the 1930s to Center Theater. It was destroyed by a couple of fires in 1971 and 1972. My job consisted of ushering people to their seats, making and selling popcorn, and changing the marquee sign whenever the movie changed. We had to go outside with a stepladder, climb up, and remove the old plastic lettering and replace it with the name of the new movie, one letter at a time. Of course, I also got to wear a nice uniform and fancy hat. A couple of movies I remember playing were Alfred Hitchcock's "Psycho" and "Mary Poppins". I remember with Psycho, we had the exact time of the shower scene posted, and no one was admitted into

the theater after that time. One of the things that I remember with "Mary Poppins" was the fact that grown men would come out of the theater with tears in their eyes. I really didn't understand why until many years later. Of course, one of the good benefits of working at the theater was that you could watch any movie you wanted for free and eat the popcorn. I usually went home with leftover popcorn and nothing tastes as good as that movie-theater popcorn. I read recently that popcorn is a theater's biggest income producer as it is marked up 1200-1400%, and the aroma permeates the theater, enticing people to buy it. And, of course, you need to follow up with a drink. The movie theater wasn't the only place where we could watch movies. We also had the drive-in theaters, which came to be known as "Passion Pits." Patented in 1933 by Richard M. Hollingshead, Jr of Camden, NJ. Drive-in theaters reached their peak in popularity in the late 50s and early 60s. It proved to be the ideal place to take your date, especially if you weren't really interested in watching the movie. It was also a great place for a family outing because it was cheaper than taking the whole family to the movie, the kids could play on the playground, and you could bring your own food with you, so you wouldn't have to spend money at the concession. We could also sneak some of the kids in by covering them with blankets or hiding them in the trunk just before we pulled into the theater. We would go to the one located on Route 132 in Hyannis (it's now a shopping center) or the one on Route 28 in W. Yarmouth, which closed around 1980. Most drive-ins are closed now, but you can still find a few. Maybe they'll make a comeback.

Back to jobs. The third job I had in Hyannis was in 1969-1970. After I dropped out of college and enlisted in the delayed enlistment program, I wasn't sure when I would be called to report. I was told it would be months. Therefore, I got a job working in the distribution department of the Cape Cod Standard-Times. It's  still in the same location today (319 Main Street) but was renamed Cape Cod Times in 1970. When they changed their name, they ran a front-page editorial that said, "We adopted the new name because we want it clearly known that we are an independent Cape Cod newspaper, printed and published on the Cape, by Cape Codders, for Cape Codders." My daily job was to work on "The Fly." This machine was an extension of the press. As the paper came off the press, it was collated and folded and would travel along this conveyer belt to the point where I would stand. I would grab 25 papers at a time and wrap them using the tying machine with twine, and then stack the papers on the floor where someone would pick them up and load them into the waiting trucks. This had to be done very fast so that the papers did not stack up on the conveyer belt and I got to be pretty good at it. In addition, we would insert the sale circulars twice a week. I believe it was in the Wednesday edition and the weekend edition. My future wife Barbara also worked on inserting the inserts. Shucks, I gave away her name and haven't even got to the point where she entered into the picture, which was in 1969. I'll talk more about how we met later, but first, I have to get through the college years. Let me just say that she was living next door to my sister Leonna and nephew Tony, and that's where we met, but the details will have to wait until later.

I entered high school in 1962. Barnstable High School was and is still located on West Main Street in Hyannis. It's changed a lot since then. Much has been added on, and the vocational school is no longer co-located with it. Had the chance to tour it during my 50th class reunion in 2016. In 1963, I became a sophomore, doing fairly decent in school. But tragedy struck that year for the nation. My sister, Leonna, had planned on throwing a surprise anniversary party for Mom and Dad on their anniversary, November 22. And everyone knows what happened Nov 22, 1963. President Kennedy was assassinated. Jack Kennedy was much loved in Massachusetts, especially Hyannis, since it was there where he maintained residence, Hyannisport, actually. The Kennedy Compound. I got to go there once when the president was away, of course. The father of one of my classmates was the elder Joe Kennedy's chauffeur, and Bruce invited me and a few other guys over one day to play some touch football. Well, anyway, with the assassination, my sister had to postpone the party until the following year. But she never got the chance. Dad died the following May. I already mentioned how he died, but things happened that week that were unusual at best.

First off, let me say that I was amazed that my father was able to get himself to the doctor after suffering the first attack. Secondly, I believe the doctor made a mistake in sending my father home instead of to the hospital right off. Premonitions abounded that week. My mother had a dream, and I'm not sure of all the details, but it included my sister Mary taking off, my father being missing, as well as some other details. In addition, a day or two before he died, Mary had decided that she was going to go to the hospital to see him. When we found her missing, we all assumed she had run away. She had gotten about a mile from the house when she stopped to rest. Meanwhile, the police had been called, and a search had begun to try and locate her. The hospital was informed to remove any radios from my father's room to ensure he did not hear any newscasts regarding her disappearance. A neighbor, Norma Perry, and her date were returning from their prom and found her over by the cranberry bogs on the corner of Old Mill Road and Five Corners Road and brought her home.

I am a bit fuzzy on all the details following his death. I remember the funeral procession came by the house for those who were not able to participate. I remember my Uncle Nina crying. The first time I ever saw a man crying. I do not think I cried, and if memory serves, I think my sister Leonna scolded me for "not caring." It was a devastating blow to all of us, especially the younger children. The youngest, Marcia, was too young to really understand what had happened, and she kept asking Mommy, "When's Daddy coming home?". But we all survived. I was out of school for a few days, and when I went back to school, I ended up getting detention because I didn't have a note. I never told them why I was out because I guess I thought they would know. When my mom found out, she chewed them out, and they apologized. Mom was strong, and she kept us all together. The two sisters that my Father worked for, the Parlett Sisters, gave my Mother what I believe was almost a year's worth of my Father's salary to help us through. He was buried at Mosswood Cemetery in Cotuit. Doane, Beale and Ames was the funeral parlor that handled the funeral. Dad had some insurance and veteran benefits, but Mom still had to do some work to help make ends meet. She cleaned homes for a while. And, of course, the older kids pitched in what they could. And life went on.

I turned 16 in September of 1964 and was able to get my license. The first time I drove was with my Uncle Nina. He had this big old Lincoln Continental. I think it was a 1959, built like a tank. We were riding down the mid-Cape highway, Route 6. I do not recall where we were going, but all of a sudden, he pulled over to the side of the road and got out. He walks over to the passenger side, opens the door, and tells me to slide over behind the wheel. Then proceeded to let me drive as he told me what to do. Well, I got my license, but of course, I didn't have a car and didn't have enough money to get a car. After my father died, I was able to take over many of the jobs that he had, mowing lawns and the like and was able to earn some money. And the following spring, I started working at the A&P. In the fall of 1963, my father bought a brand new 1964 Chevy pick. I remember Mom not wanting him to do it because she was afraid that if anything happened, she would be stuck with payments. Well, of course, her premonition came true. I am not sure how the truck was paid for after Dad died, but it was probably through the insurance. When he died, all of us kids got a trust fund, but we wouldn't get it until we turned 18. For some reason, Dennis was the only one who didn't get any because he was already over 18. So, Mom decided to give him the truck. But I could drive it if I needed to go someplace. I remember when he was going to sell it. My brother Junior and I were talking, and we realized that he was planning on selling the truck the next day, so we decided to take it for one last ride. For some strange reason, we decided to drive down the dirt roads that went along where the power lines were. I guess we were just being adventurous. I was probably driving faster than I should have when the road ended abruptly, and there were some tree logs blocking the way. I couldn't stop in time. The truck ended up stuck on the logs, and we tried as we could but were unable to free it. We ended up walking to where we could find a phone and called my uncle who ended up coming to get us and helping us get the truck out. Mom and Dennis weren't too pleased with us. Remember back when I was talking about my yearbook, and I said, "I remembered the night in the swamp." This is the incident I was referring to. In 1966. I got my very first car, a 1960 black Studebaker Lark. One day, I was walking down Main Street in Osterville and spotted this beautiful light blue Studebaker Hawk parked at the gas station with a "For Sale" sign. I fell in love with it, but unfortunately, it cost more money than I could afford at the time. I would look at it every chance I could, and then, one day, it was gone. I had my heart set on a Studebaker and finally found the Lark. It was not as beautiful as the Hawk, but it was affordable. It cost $200. That would be the equivalent of about $3,500 - $3,600 today. I had saved $100, and my dear sister Leonna gave me the rest as a graduation present. The remainder of 1966 was marked by adventure after adventure (or, should I say, misadventure) in that car. I mentioned stories with my cousin Scuffy, my brother Junior and myself. Well, most of them happened in this car. One night, we were coming past Our Lady of Victory Church in Centerville, South Main Street. There were these two girls walking down the street, and just as we drove past, my cousin reached out the door as if he was going to grab them, and they went running up the hill towards the Church. He must have scared the daylights out of them. Not very nice. I already mentioned the tires, the carnival, and the phone booth incident. We used to love to cruise Main Street in Hyannis because, well, that's what you did in those days during the summer. Just cruise up and down the streets. I remember one time we were coming back from Yarmouth after getting some fried clams late at night from the A&W. We were stopped at the light on Main Street by the movie theater, and my sister or brother let out the biggest sneeze anyone would have ever heard. And before you know it, the cops were standing next to the car. Another time, Leonna and I were sitting in the parking lot at Zayres waiting for someone, and a cop came up to us and accused us of making out, "parking" is what we called it then. Leonna let him have it. "I'm with my brother, and I'm going to be making out?" She was never afraid to speak her mind. I think that car was a magnet for the police. Another time on Main Street down by where the "Egg and I" is located now, I remember Officer Freddy Rivers pounding the top of the car with his flashlight because I failed to stop when he signaled me. I honestly didn't see him until the last second. Fortunately, when you're only creeping at less than five miles an hour, you don't really pose a danger, but he pounded on the roof of the car and said, "When I say stop, you stop." Another time, I went to visit the Lombas who lived on Betty's Pond Road across from the Melody Tent. The Melody Tent is probably one of the most famous entertainment venues on the Cape, always hosting some of the biggest names in show biz. One of only two continuously operated tent theaters in the round in the United States, it was originally known as the Cape Cod Music Circus. It was owned by David M. Holtzmann, a theatrical attorney, who changed the name in 1951. In 1990, it was purchased by the South Shore Playhouse Associates, a not-for-profit organization. It's still in use today, but it only operates May through September. Every show is always crowded, and they, of course, have the police directing traffic. But back to the story. When I was pulling out of Betty's Pond Road after my visit, the cop who was directing traffic pulled me over to the side of the road and accused me of making the turn into Betty's

Pond Road on two wheels. Can you imagine that two wheels, indeed? I liked visiting the Lombas (John, George, Charlie, Betty and of course Loretta). Many years later, when I started writing poetry, I wrote one about her. Don't know if I ever shared it with her. John one time threw a rock through the windshield of my Studebaker. I was getting ready to leave, and he said if I left, he would throw the rock, and he did. Oh well. I had some crazy friends. Their house was on a slight hill, and one day, I noticed some liquid was leaking from the car. I backed the car down the hill and lit a match to see if it was gasoline that was leaking. Yep, it was. Fortunately, I had backed the car far enough away that it didn't cause a problem. I was giving their mom a ride somewhere once, and being the perfect gentleman that I was, I opened the car door for her. When I shut the door, the side window came crashing down. She was afraid that was an omen of what lay in store. A few years later, I bought a 62 Ford Galaxy, and when the salesman put the inspection sticker in the window and shut the door, the window came crashing down, and the first thought I had was this incident with the Studebaker. One of the things we liked to do was to write all over the car with white shoe polish. We would write clever sayings or names of songs, etc. It would all wash off, so that was no problem. One time, when we were doing this, one of my sisters found a broken 45 record and gave it to my brother Junior and asked him to write the name of the song on the car. After he wrote down the song, which happened to be "*Red Rubber Ball*" by Bryan Highland, he threw the record like a frisbee, expecting it to go flying into the woods. Unfortunately, his aim was off, and the record hit me in the head. With blood oozing out, I had to go to the hospital, where I received about four stitches. This happened shortly before I was to leave to go to college, so I ended up taking the stitches out myself while at school.

One of my favorite tricks was to pull into a vacant parking lot, put the car in reverse, turn the wheel, and get out and watch the car go around in circles by itself. I was giving a girl a ride one day and did this. Was she ever mad? And I already mentioned I loved giving girls rides down Starboard Lane, our private little roller coaster.

Speaking of girls, I probably should take a few paragraphs to talk about some of the girls I have known and "loved." There have been a few. Yvonne and Barbara were sisters, and their ages corresponded to my brother and me. Nothing serious ever developed from that, though. I already mentioned Marilyn and Loretta. Both were silent recipients of my poetic talents. Another was Cynthia. There was something special about her that I really liked, but I never told her. And then it was too late. I don't really remember when I started dating Sharon. But she was the only girl that I ever went steady with. We dated for a couple of years. Influenced by shows like "Man from Uncle" and the James Bond movies of the sixties, I once rigged a tape recorder inside my briefcase so I could press a button on the handle, and it would start recording. I taped Sharon without her knowing it, and when she found out, she wouldn't speak to me for two weeks. But we survived that. Another time, I was over at her sister Dean's house. That's where Sharon was staying at the time, and I was going out with her that night. While I was sitting in the living room waiting for Sharon to get ready, I called Dean's dog over. She owned a little beagle named Queenie. Only problem was, when I called the dog, I called, "Here, Dean". I rank that up there with my most embarrassing moments. I don't think Dean cared for me very much after that. She probably didn't care much for me before that. I continued to date Sharon even after my first year in College, but during my second year, we decided we needed to break it off. There was no future in it since I was destined to become a priest, or so we thought. She went her way, and I went mine. We'll come back to my love life later.

Let's change the subject a little bit as we move on to the next chapter.

CHAPTER TWO: THE SIBLINGS

"As arrows are in the hand of a mighty man, so are children of the youth. Happy is the man that hath his quiver full of them: they shall not be ashamed, but they shall speak with the enemies in the gate."

Psalm 127:4-5

Before I continue with my story, I'd like to take a moment to encapsulate the lives of my siblings. I've already talked a bit about them, but they each have their own story to tell. I make no attempt to capture their entire journey in these next few words, for that is up to them to do in their own unique way. Here, I would just like to summarize what I know of their lives journey and leave the blanks for them to fill in.

We start first of course with Dennis, the oldest and elder of the family. I've already talked about his beginning, being born February 12, 1943, his mother's surname being Abraham, and the delivery doctor being Dr. Lincoln. But another connection with Lincoln is that Abe had a cousin ten years older than him named Dennis, Dennis Hanks, to be precise, the son of Nancy Hanks, who was an aunt of Abe's mother. Dennis and Abe became close friends and even shared a room in the cabin for a while. Well, back to my brother. At the age of fifteen, he lied about his age and joined the United States Marines. I make no claims as to his sanity. I know little of his tour of duty except that he spent part of it cruising the Mediterranean. I suppose if you want to take a cruise to that part of the world and can't afford it, the Marines is one way to do it. I already mentioned that he used to bring some of his  fellow Marines home with him on furlough and let them ride the pig. After the Marines, he did a number of different things. I know he drove the big rigs for a while, working for Baxter Transport Trucking Company. I had the opportunity to ride with him one time as he drove to Rhode Island, and I remember him driving through a line of trucks with inches to spare on either side. Then he asked me if I wanted to back out. Joking, of course. I was quite impressed with the way he handled the rig. He eventually became the night foreman at Baxter's for over 20 years. Another talent he had was dating some very nice-looking young ladies. I seem to recall Almeida and Ramona, whom I believed he dated, but I can't say for certain. He eventually married Candias (Candie) Pena and had a beautiful daughter, Denise, who gave him two handsome and talented grandsons, Devon and Jaden. I remember when he built the house across the street from where we all grew up and even helped him do some things in the house. One thing that sticks in my memory is something the stonemason who was building his fireplace said to me. He said, "The only difference between an amateur and a professional was that the professional knew how to cover his mistakes." In 1972, Dennis opened his own tuxedo business called Dennis-John Formals and was in business for over 35 years. He started it as a mobile business working out of a van but then got some space by sharing a building with Butchie Perry, who ran a barbershop. He eventually moved to a new location and ultimately opened multiple stores across the Cape. He asked me if I wanted to go in partnership with him, but unfortunately, he asked me right after I reenlisted in the Air Force, and so he went into partnership with his brother-in-law, John, hence the name Dennis-John Formals. (Dennis-Leo wouldn't have worked anyways). When his brother-in-law wanted out of the business, Dennis once again called me to see if I was interested, but this followed my second reenlistment. The timing was just not right so I guess it was not meant to be. My younger brother, Peter John, eventually went to work for him, and since the

business name was Dennis-John and everyone called him by his middle name, the assumption was that the two were partners. Somewhere along the line, Dennis started working at night for the Community Action Committee at Safe Harbor, a Domestic Violence shelter. He worked there for over 20 years as a Security Supervisor. Initially, he worked here at night while working the business during the day. It seemed he was always working. He eventually sold the business but continued working at the Center. In his later years he started driving for Uber and Lyft as well. He made a good impression on his passengers and even picked up some terrific regular fares, as he tells it. He also loved his Goldwing motorcycle and would ride whenever he could, along with our brother Johnny and Junior Viera. One time, the three of them rode up to Canada together. I would have loved to have made that trip with them. A few times when I would visit him, we played golf together, with him

mercilessly putting me to shame. He enjoyed golfing, but that was not my forte. He enjoyed playing poker as well with his brothers-in-law, friends, and nephews. I remember times when he would be playing with Harry and Henry (one African-American and one caucasian) and would make some strategic comments that would get them going at each other while he sat back and enjoyed their arguing. Dennis had the opportunity, along with some other family members and friends, to visit Cape Verde Islands, the home of our father, and to meet more of our distant relatives. A trip he thoroughly enjoyed. I'm sure Dennis has many tales to tell, but we may never get to hear them. Dennis was a victim of the COVID-19 pandemic and went home to be with the Lord on January 26, 2021. The mark he made on the Cape is reflected in the following article from the Amplify POC Cape Cod by Tara Vargas Wallace. (Used with permission)

What's good about Cape Cod? Tara here, and I have a different kind of entrepreneur story to share with you today.

Like many of our stories, this is a story of a hardworking businessman and devoted father and grandfather named Dennis Brandao. This is also a love story about the strong, unbreakable bond between a father and a daughter – a bond that transcends time and even death. This is a story about a woman who is transforming her pain and turning it into something beautiful in her plight to honor her father's memory – and that of the other nearly 450 victims who succumbed to this terrible virus this past year on Cape Cod.

Dennis, who owned Dennis-John Formals for 38 years, recently passed away from COVID-19. The local Cape Verdean-owned business had several locations across the Cape.

When my good friend Denise shared with me what she is doing to honor her father – and the other nearly 450 COVID victims on Cape Cod – I was moved to tears and knew I had to do whatever was in my power to help amplify her efforts.

I came to know this wonderful family almost 20 years ago. My friendship with Denise Brandao Harris and her father began when I worked with them both at Safe Harbor, a local domestic violence shelter. And although Denise and I were more like ships passing in the night – relieving each other from our alternating shifts – Dennis and I worked side by side together, on and off for years. As the head of the shelter's security, Dennis had a natural protective nature about him. Something that put me and everyone else at ease, as the threat of a client's abuser showing up at any given moment was always a possibility (and did, in fact, happen on my shift once).

Dennis worked at the shelter mainly for health insurance benefits, while he also ran his own businesses and was an active member in the NAACP, Kiwanis Club, and St. Anthony's Cape Verdean Club. He would spend hours telling me stories about Denise and his two grandsons, Devon and Jaden. He was a loving and super supportive father and grandfather. As a woman who grew up without a father of my own, I remember being a little envious of Denise and thinking I wish I had a dad like Dennis.

As my friendship with Denise and my coworker's relationship with Dennis grew over the years, Dennis took me in almost like a daughter - making sure to invite me to his family BBQ because he knew I did not have any family here and he knew I needed to be in his words, "around my culture and my own people." He also had Puerto Rican relatives (my people), and when I decided to get married at the tender age of 20, with very little support and resources, Dennis offered to suit up all the men in my wedding in the latest tuxedos, free of charge.

He was a solid guy – always there to help a friend, and he would even go to the local high schools to measure kids and drop off tuxedos for prom out of the kindness of his heart. Denise, like her dad, always worked a couple of jobs as a single mother of two growing boys and still found a way to be an incredible

mom. Always getting to their games and karate events and baking homemade treats from scratch for their class and team events. I would always comment about how she put the rest of us moms to shame as we all worked two to three jobs as well, but when our kids needed baked goods, you better believe the rest of us were making pit stops at the bakery section in our local grocery stores and picking up some premade brownies and cupcakes – because ain't nobody got time for all that!

Whenever I would comment about Denise putting us mothers to shame, she would comment with a compliment as sweet as her homemade treats

and say something like, "Tara, what I do for my family, you do for our community. We're both superwomen, just with different superpowers."

Always a supportive friend, showing up at community events I'd helped organize over the years – with her sleeves rolled up, ready to put some work in – that is the kind of person Denise is. As solid as her father.

And as you can imagine, as his only child and daughter, Denise has been beside herself with grief since her father's death. Unable to find a local one-to-one grief support resource to help her through her anguish, she knew she had to do something to honor her father's death. And so, this is where the real story comes in and hopefully where you can all help – Tara Vargas Wallace.

Hello,

My name is Denise Harris, and I am starting up a Cape Cod Covid Victim Memorial for all the residents we lost on the Cape. My father, Dennis Brandao, was one of the Covid victims who passed away in January.

Since his death, I have been trying to find a way to honor him and the other victims and their families. While I watched other towns memorialize their victims, I noticed there was nothing done on the Cape. So, I reached out to the Town of Barnstable, the BPD, State Rep Kip Diggs and Mass DOT.

Everyone so far has jumped on board and is willing to back me in whatever way is needed. We all seem to think it would be great for our town and the community.

I am in the process of purchasing 500 flags and hopefully having the victims' names, towns and dates of their passing printed on them and placing them on the Hyannis Airport Rotary for the month of May.

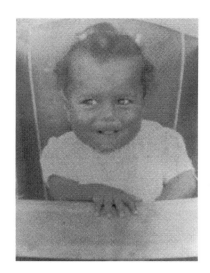
Next in line is big Sis, Leonna. I've mentioned her birth to you as well, January 20, 1947. Being named Leonna, after our cousin Leo, just like I was, may have provided us with some kind of bond. She was always there to lend a helping hand. She was with me when I was hit in the head with a rock. She helped me buy my first car, and being close in age, we were able to share some moments together, some of which I have already shared with you in the first chapter. When I was talking to her one day preparing to write this book, I asked her to share some of her early memories. One story she told me was how she and the Cabrals, some of our neighbors, used to let the air out of people's tires while they were at Joe's Twin Villa. I'll tell you about Joe's when I talk about brother Johnny. Leonna was a great big help to everyone after our father died. She drove us places, she made sure we pulled our weight around the home and she was like a second mother to the younger siblings. Of course, she could be a bit bossy and pushy at times, but we love her. She is one of the ones who kept pushing me to publish this book.

She married Amos Diaz and had a wonderful son whom they named John Anthony. I believe he was named after my younger brother as a result of some bet, but I'm not positive. Eventually, she and Amos divorced, and she was left to raise her son on her own. She did a wonderful job, not only putting him through college but herself as well. As I mentioned earlier, she and Tony lived across the hall from my future wife, Barbara, and she was the one responsible for introducing us. She built her first home directly behind the home we were raised in. Having the Barnstable High Vocational School build the home made it  very economical for her. But life threw her a curve ball, which is all part of her story, which I won't get into here. Suffice it to say that as a result of a series of events, her son ended up in prison. Circumstances led her down a path of travel, missionary work, and serving others in a most meaningful way. She spent fourteen years working for the State of Massachusetts as a social worker. She has traveled to places I could only dream of. Places such as the mountains of Quetzeltenango, Guatemala, Guyana, Panama, Honduras, Costa Rica, Nicaragua, and Ghana, West Africa. She attended the Mayan Indian School, Centro Mayo De Idiomas, and studied the language and culture of the Mayan Indians. She has devoted much of her life to helping those in prison as a result of Tony's

incarceration and has authored a number of books, some of which reflect part of her story. Some of her titles include *"Touching Lives: Heartfelt Stories of Lives, Losses and a Failing System," "World of Healing and Hope," "Our Lord Forgave You: Letters and Deeds of the Incarcerated," "No Freedom – No Existence," "No Voice, No Hope," "How Can I Make It Through," and "Inspired by the Holy Spirit, An Inspirational Book of Poetry."* She is the founder of New Vision Organization, which, as their website states, is "helping to restore the lost and forgotten men, women, and youth." Through this ministry, she has brought countless numbers of people together throughout the country, working as volunteers to help those in need and to reexamine and improve our prison systems. Through her Blog Talk Radio program, she has been able to interview those who are advocates for the abused as well as those who have suffered abuse. Her life has served as an inspiration for many.

Next in line, we come to Mary Jean, born on January 25, 1950. Mary married Vincent Lai, an immigrant from China. I believe she met him at a Chinese Restaurant, the Dragon Light, in Hyannis. He was a cook there, and Mary was a waitress. He had asked sister Anna out, but she said no, and so he asked Mary, and she said yes. It seems Mary always had a passion for the Orientals. I recollect a birthday party to which a number of individuals were invited, one of them being a Chinese friend of mine, Dennis Chang. I believe the whole party was planned so that she could get Dennis to come. Throughout most of the party, Dennis sat in a corner of the living room, surrounded by girls. Mary hardly got the chance to talk to him. Mary ended up with four beautiful children: Chin Wah (Mary), Tri Wah (Jennifer), Chuck Wah (Chucky), and Sung Wah

(Vincent or Kenny as we called him). When her oldest daughter, Chin Wah, was born, they decided to send her to China to live with her grandparents so she could learn the language and culture. When Mary wanted to bring her back, Vinny refused, so Mary had temporary custody papers drawn up for me so that I could go to China and bring her back. Fortunately, Vinny relented and had her brought home before I had a chance to go get her. Mary's life was filled with ups and downs, as I have shared a small part of her story with you. She has suffered from epilepsy for as long as I can remember but has always persevered. She and Vinny either owned or worked in a few Chinese restaurants over the years.

Two that I remember were one in New Hampshire and one in Boston. I remember helping out one week in the Boston restaurant when they were having some difficulties with help. I am certain that she has many stories to share, and perhaps she or one of her children will commit those stories to a book of her own. I've already shared her near-death experience during the blizzard. Later, I'll share her trip to Omaha with you as well. One day, while visiting Terry's, there was a phone call, and I answered it. The person on the other end asked if Mary was there, and I told them no, she wasn't, but I was her brother. Could I take a message? The individual said something to the effect that he was not calling to threaten her but was calling as a friend. He told me to tell Mary she didn't know who she was dealing with and that she needed to back off. It turned out that Mary was planning on divorcing Vincent and was seeking for half the assets, which included the restaurant. Unfortunately, the Chinese mafia was involved in some way, and this person on the phone was calling to warn Mary about their influence and what they could do. Somehow, the situation got worked out, and the divorce was called off. There were a lot of good times, too, for the Lai family. Vinny was a very hard worker, working six days a week with most shifts from 10 a.m. to 9 p.m. Trips to Chinatown for the family were not unusual and often Vinny would wake the family at 11 p.m. so they could have a late-night family dinner. In 2019, Vinny moved into a nursing home, where he remained for a few years. His health started deteriorating, and in January 2021, he moved in with his son, Chucky, and soon thereafter went home to be with the Lord.

Next on the list (and right smack dab in the middle) is Arthur Junior. Born January 18, 1951, he was probably the most generous of the family, always willing to lend a hand to someone in need. Junior was always willing to help folks who were in trouble. One day, when the family was having a big cookout celebrating something, maybe the Fourth of July, Junior stumbled upon a family that was having car trouble. Having checked out their car, he found out they needed a new starter, I think. Don't really remember what it was. But he brought the family over to the house, told them to stay there and enjoy themselves, and he would take care of the car. He went and got the part they needed, installed it, and got the car running. That was the type of guy he was.

He followed in the footsteps of our older brother, Dennis, by studying auto mechanics in school, dropping out in the tenth grade and joining the United States Marine Corps just like Dennis. Junior and I did a lot of things together, as I have already mentioned. With only about three years between us, we were able to hang out a lot together. Although I can't remember too much of our childhood years, I'm certain we played a lot and got into trouble together. I mentioned our working with my father and some of the trouble we got into in that arena. I guess 1966 was our closest year since I had my license and a car and, well, you know, teenagers. A couple of times, we dated sisters. But I went off to college, and Junior, as I said, joined the Marines. He wasn't as fortunate as Dennis and didn't get to do the Mediterranean Cruise, but he ended up doing a tour at DaNang, Republic of Vietnam. With the good Lord on his side, a result I'm sure of my mother's constant prayers, he came home safely. He married twice, once to Vicky and once to Sandra, fathering four sons, Troy S., Arthur James Jr., Christian L., and William J. Unfortunately, at the age of 27, he was at a party, and that was when he collapsed. Though he was rushed to the hospital, he did not survive. He became a member of the infamous 27 Club. This is an unofficial club whose members include various musicians, actors, artists, and athletes who have died at the age of 27. The

list includes such names as Jimi Hendrix, Kurt Cobain, Janis Joplin, Jim Morrison, Amy Winehouse, and about 75 others. My mother always blamed "Agent Orange," but it was never proven. For those not familiar with it, "Agent Orange" was a very controversial chemical defoliant used by the U.S. Military in Vietnam. It was used to deprive the North Vietnamese guerillas of concealment in the trees as well as destroying part of their food supply. Its effect on the people exposed to it led to many lawsuits and claims for compensation with the Department of Veterans Affairs, with only a small percentage being granted.

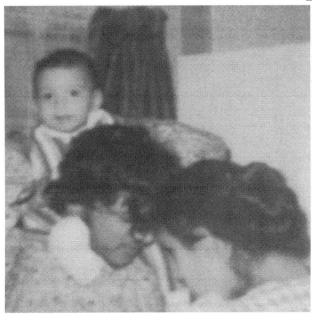

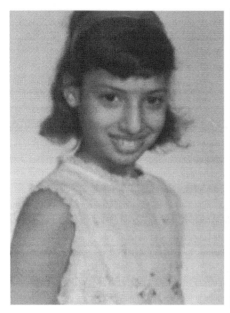  

Next, we come to sister Anna May. When I left home to go to college in 1966, Anna was only 13 or 14, having been born on August 22, 1952. Since I wasn't around during her teen years, I can't tell you how much trouble she got in. She'll have to do that herself. When she was 16, she met a marine friend of Junior and became engaged to him. She went to New York with him to meet his parents, and because he wanted to get married immediately and she didn't, she ended up catching a bus and going home. About ten years later, through a series of circumstances, she met Harry Hunt, and on 15 August 1981, they got married, and together they raised five wonderful kids: Eric, Harry Jr, Robert, Arthur and Jennifer. She graduated from Barnstable High School and went on to work in a variety of areas, mainly in running a daycare for kids with special needs in Boston. She moved into the house that I first called home, the one where I spent my first four years on this earth. You can see her love for children by looking into her backyard: swimming pool, slides, merry-go-round, shuffleboard, horseshoes, and all kinds of toys for the kids to play with. Me too, whenever I get a chance to visit. After all, I'm just a kid in disguise. Anna has been a mainstay in the family and a prime force in the annual family reunion, which I will talk about further down the road. One of the stories that Anna recently related to me was when we were at Hathaway's Pond one summer. When it was time to go home, one of my friends, Charlie Kaminsky, said he would take her home. As they neared the house, Charlie asked Anna if she really wanted to go home, and she said no. So, the two of them went down to Dowses' Beach in Osterville, where they stayed and talked until 4:00 O'clock in the morning.

Following Anna, we come to Peter John, named after both grandfathers, Peter Brandao and John Abraham. Johnny, as we called him, was born on August 16, 1956, and went to be with the Lord on October 15, 2017. Since I left home in 1966, Johnny was only nine years old. Even though I was home during the next three summers, we did not hang out much together since he was so much younger. And then, I joined the military and only saw him every four years after that. It wasn't until I moved to New Hampshire in '76, and after brother Junior died, that we began spending time together. And even then, the times were short since I left for Omaha and then Germany. Johnny lived a very full life and had a quality about him that was very magnetic. Everyone who knew him loved him. He fathered many children by various women, and yet all of them were very close. His children include Rachel, John James, Sharae, Peter Jr, Amber, another Peter, and Marcia. We recently met another of his children whom we didn't even know existed as a result of her and Peter doing DNA testing. Their results were so close that they connected, and now Melissa has brothers and sisters she never knew before. I never sensed any animosity amongst any of his children or their mothers. Johnny had a carefree spirit and loved being on the go. He enjoyed his motorcycle, and I will never forget the time he came to D.C. to visit me on Memorial Day 1993. We took a ride into the city, not realizing that Rolling Thunder was in town. If you're not familiar with Rolling Thunder, here is a brief history from their website:

Rolling Thunder Washington, DC, Inc., and its mission began as a demonstration following the era of the Vietnam War, which was a difficult time in our history. Many of America's military were killed or missing in action (MIA), and their remains were not being returned home or respectfully buried. There were also reports of live prisoners of war (POW) who were left behind when the war ended. In 1987, Vietnam veteran Ray Manzo (CPL, USMC), bothered by these accounts, came to DC with his idea and met and enlisted the help of fellow veterans to organize a motorcycle demonstration to bring attention to the POW/MIA situation. Choosing Memorial Day weekend for the event, they envisioned the arrival of the motorcycles coming across the Memorial Bridge and thought it would sound like "**Rolling Thunder**." The first Run in 1988 had roughly 2,500 motorcycles and riders demanding that the U.S. government account for all POW/MIA. It continues to grow every year, becoming the world's largest single-day motorcycle event. Now, with over a million riders and spectators combined, Rolling Thunder has evolved into an emotional display of patriotism and respect for all who defend our

country. Later on, I actually went to a couple of their meetings, but I never joined the organization. So, this was the fifth year of Rolling Thunder, and there were literally thousands of bikes there. Johnny felt in his glory. After parking his Honda, we got off and walked around, with my video camera rolling and Johnny interviewing people as we walked. Acting just like a reporter, he got people, perfect strangers, to talk to him. One of his remarks was, "Dennis, eat your heart out," sending a message to our older brother.

One time, I happened to be home on his birthday, and we were hanging out together doing different stuff. As we were heading home, he wanted to go to Joe's Twin Villa to have a few drinks. I had stopped drinking by this time and didn't want to go to a club, and I explained that to him. He said, no problem, just drop him off. I said OK and asked him how he would get home. He said don't worry about it. I had not been back over at Terry's for 10 minutes when he came rolling in with some lady. He worked fast. A little side note concerning Joe's Twin Villa. "Sloppy Joe's," as it was lovingly called by the locals, was begun as a speakeasy during the prohibition era by the Diggs family. At first glance, it looked like a small shack set on the edge of the woods with a large parking lot out front and two red doors.

During the 1950s and 1960s, it was a highly popular club, having the distinction of being an integrated club. No matter who came in, everyone was treated the same, and if you had to wait outside to get in, so did everyone else, regardless of your social status. Whether it was one of the Kennedys, a major sports star (the Patriots brought all their new members there), or a Hollywood celebrity (such as Arnold Schwarzenegger), you were treated no different than one of the locals like my father. Once inside, the unspoken rule was that you would not ask for autographs. Everyone was there just to relax, have a good time, and enjoy some good food, drink, and music. Weekends would find a DJ and a live band performing. Because of the standing rule that everyone was treated equally, there was a time when Johnny almost got in a fight with one of the Kennedy clan. He had placed his quarter on the pool table, and the rule was that whoever placed their money on the table would get to play the next game, in order of when the money was laid

down. It happened that the Kennedys were playing on the table and were not going to allow Johnny to play. They were informed of the policy, and fortunately, the situation was diffused before it got out of hand. Unfortunately, Joe's closed in 2008 and fell into disarray, and as of this writing, it has been overtaken by shrubs and other greenery. A fence now surrounds the small building and parking lot. Who knows, maybe someday it will be designated as a historic landmark. However, it is my understanding that the property upon which the Villa was located actually belonged to the elder Joseph Kennedy, who happened to be friends with the family and leased the property to them for 100 years. That time period is nearing its end, and I believe once the lease expires, the Villa will be torn down, and some type of housing will be built. Time will tell. Back to Johnny. Johnny loved to golf and play pool and would always relish the chance to beat me any time he could. And that was just about every time we played. I've already told you about some of his antics growing up, and I often wondered if I had been home if he would have gotten into less trouble or if he would have enticed me into joining in his capers.

Like two of his brothers before him, Johnny quit school and joined the Marines. However, since Johnny didn't like following orders, he and the Marines soon parted company.

In his later years, Johnny decided he didn't like the cold weather. So, during the summer, he would stay in his trailer behind Anna and Harry's house, but in the Winter, he would head south to Florida to spend time with Marcia and then, later on, to Cape Verde. Some of the family members had been invited to take a trip to Cape Verde to visit my father's place of birth and meet some distant relatives. Johnny fell in love with the place and even had a small business there, as well as a girlfriend. The winter before he died, he was there and suffered a small heart attack.

Here, Johnny is pictured with Mary Gomes, originally from Falmouth, on a sea cruise. She loved Johnny because he used to prepare food and put on a big spread in the Community Room of the Douglas

House for the residents, elderly and disabled. The Property Manager planned a Cruise for the Residents, and Johnny was invited to join them.

The last time I saw Johnny alive, we visited the gravesite where Dad, Mom, and Junior were buried. Johnny, with his usual carefree attitude, laid down on the ground and said something to the effect that that was his spot. Three months later, his prediction came true, and on October 2, 2017, he joined his parents and his brother.

Next, we go to Theresa Louise. If you didn't know that she was the second youngest, you'd think she was the matriarch of the family. Terry was born on July 27, 1958. She is probably more like Mom than any of my sisters. Always working either in the house or in the garden, I always wondered how she does it. Like Johnny and later Marcia, I missed her growing up years being away at college and the military. I'm sure there were many wonderful antics that I would love to have seen. Terry's life was filled with its ups and downs, as was everyone else's, but she always managed to stay good-spirited. On 17 July 1976, she married Peter Rivera, and they split their time between the house on Old Mill Road and their house in Puerto Rico. She raised four terrific kids: Peter, Matthew, Josh and, of course, Teresa. When she took over the house after Mom died, she kept it pretty much the same with some improvements. Raising different kinds of animals and having a terrific vegetable garden, she could supplement her food supply without having to rely on grocery stores. Her biggest claim to fame, in my opinion, is the beginning of the Family Reunion, along with help from Anna. She started it as a means for the family to get together once a year. Soon, it included not only the local family but relatives from as far away as Boston, New York and even Cape Verde. Through these reunions, we met relatives we never knew existed. The reunions were held each year during the last weekend of July. This time period coincided with Terry's birthday and the anniversary of Mom's death.

I came across these comments on Facebook once, and I thought I'd share them here.

From Teresa Knight: Such a great weekend (referring to the mini-reunion on Aug 25). Pig roast Saturday, clam bake Sunday, pond, park, family game night, storytelling, reminiscing over old pictures, "Mom's Club" and Camp Mendes in between. Yesterday, we took time to go to the cemetery with four generations where my grandparents and uncle are buried to pray. My mother and her siblings are so inspirational to me. My Aunt Anna was like a second Mom. Mary was one who always had new ideas or dreams. Marcia made sure we had fun and always experienced life. Uncle Dennis was always a hard worker with a big heart. Uncle Leo was always full of faith in God and full of jokes. Peter John was always the one that we teased and had fun with, but if we had car troubles was there to help us out. My Mother, Theresa, is always the one that keeps

the family together. Growing up, I had a very limited time with my grandmothers and only ever met one great aunt that I remember. I am so lucky that my daughter has not only the BEST grandmother but wonderful Great Aunts and Uncles to learn from. I only wish that we could do this more often.

FROM Chin Wah: No one could say it any better, Teresa. Before your mom, Sitto held this family together. She always had something delicious on the stove, and we always sang or whistled a tune as we cleaned. I remember spending weekends with her, and we'd get dressed up to go to church in front of her TV in the living room. She had Easter egg hunts and grandchildren's day because she couldn't make it to everyone's birthday. Most of all, she made all of us feel like her favorite.

Gail Whelden: Yes, Ma did. When me and all your aunts and uncles were growing up, Ma kept going and always had an ear for any problem you had. END OF FB COMMENTS

You can see from these comments why I believe she is more like mom than any of the other sisters.

We looked forward to making these annual treks back to the Cape until 2020 when they were canceled for two reasons. One was the breakout of COVID-19, and the second was that Terry was diagnosed with cancer. In February of 2023, Terry lost her battle with the Big C, but her spirit remains with all of us. Her daughter and nieces revived the Family Reunion and continue to make it a reality.

 And finally, we come to Marcia Marie, born July 2, 1961. As I mentioned earlier, Marcia should have been a boy to keep the pattern up, but when she turned out to be a girl, we knew the pattern was broken, and she would be the last. Though she wasn't a boy physically, she was a tomboy, always playing rough. One thing about Marcia, she was always full of life. She liked to party and enjoy life to the fullest. She  once told me of a time she and some others stole some tomatoes and were throwing them at passing cars until one guy stopped and pulled out a gun. Good thing they could run. Another time, she and her friend Michael fell into a hole full of red ants. Have her tell you that story.

Marcia decided not to graduate from Barnstable High School but rather followed her brothers' pattern, quitting school and joining the Army. I'm surprised she didn't join the Marines. She went in as a Communications Specialist and  considered going airborne, but that didn't pan out. Once the Army found out she didn't have her high school diploma, they told her she had to leave and could come back once she got her GED. She did eventually get her GED but, by that time, decided not to go back into the Army. Instead, she moved to Boston to stay with her sister Anna and became an exotic dancer. Here, she met and married Alan Hopkins and had two sons, Danny and Corey. After five years, she divorced Alan and later met and married Pablo Ortega. She moved to Florida, studied at Southwest Florida College, and worked at Shell Point Retirement Community in Fort Myers for about 15 years. Unfortunately, her marriage to Pablo didn't work out, and they ended up getting divorced as well. She must have had a passion for the name Paul (Pablo) because she

 met and dated three more with that name, the last one for 22 years plus. She currently (as of 2023) lives in Cape Coral, Florida, where she works taking care of the elderly, working very long hours, sometimes cooking, sometimes cleaning, sometimes  walking the dog, and sometimes just being a friend. Marcia, like Johnny, loved the party life.

CHAPTER THREE: DO I REALLY WANT TO BE A PRIEST

"If any man serve me, let him follow me; and where I am, there shall also my servant be: if any man serve me, him will my Father honor." John 12:26

Back to my story. The time had finally come for me to go off to college. I had no idea what was in store, but I boarded the bus and headed off to Kentucky.

I arrived at St. Mary's, and to be honest, I can't even remember the moment I arrived. I mentioned earlier that the college was converted to a minimum-security prison called the Marion Adjustment Center. This center is part of the CCA Corrections Management Program. Their website lists the following as their vision and mission: Vision: To be the best full-service adult corrections system. Mission: Advancing corrections through innovative results that benefit and protect all we serve. And Values: Having PRIDE in all we do; Professionalism, Respect, Integrity, Duty, and Excellence. They have facilities in 20 states as of this writing, from New York to California and Texas to Montana. Hopefully, their vision can be expanded to even more prisons. If the grounds of St. Mary's are any indication of their facilities across the country, it's a positive note. The grounds of St. Mary's were beautiful. It was a working farm and had plenty of wide-open spaces. At least while I went to school there. We had the opportunity to visit there a while ago but were not allowed on the grounds and had to view it from a distance.

We were assigned rooms in either the Columbia or the Abbey with one roommate. The first year I was in the Abbey. The second year, I had a room in the Columbia with a fellow named Ken. We'll get back to Ken later. My first roommate, Ray, introduced me to musicals. Prior to this time, I didn't really care about musicals at all. Probably because I never watched them. The first one I recall watching was *Mary Poppins,* and I already told you about that. Ray had a record player and a whole stack of musical soundtracks, and he would play them all the time. I was introduced to such show tunes as *Oklahoma*,

South Pacific, Auntie Mame, Meet Me in St Louis, and a whole bunch more. At first, I was annoyed and complained, but you know what? I grew to like them. Now I really enjoy them, at least the ones I think are good. My own opinion, of course. Listening to the soundtracks encouraged me to watch some of the movies when I could. There are still many that I haven't seen and probably never will, but I will enjoy the music. A prime example is "*Hair*". I like most of the music from that, but I have never actually seen the movie or the show. Maybe someday, I will, but for now, I'll just enjoy the music.

I really enjoyed St. Mary's. I loved the fact that it was in the middle of nowhere. The town itself was, as I mentioned earlier, just a crossroads in Marion County. Most of the employees were residents of the town, and many were related. I remember the three Porter sisters who worked in the cafeteria: Susan, Elli, and Stella. For some reason, I liked Stella more than the others and even wrote a poem about her. Speaking of writing poems, it was here at St. Mary's that I first began to write. I'll share more about that later. All the workers there were very friendly and helpful. I don't think there was anyone that I didn't like. I mentioned some of the activities earlier. The bonfire was one of the biggest events held in the fall. We would gather anything that would burn: fallen trees, broken furniture, old fence posts, whatever we could find. There was an old stone quarry where the fire was held. It was shaped like an amphitheater, and we could sit around it telling stories, singing songs like Kumbaya, and just having a jolly good time. We also held a Spring and Fall Festival, complete with games, food, and other fun activities. One year, we even raffled off a car to make money for the school. And, of course, we invited the local town folk. Another annual event was our hike to St Joe's. This was another very small town about seven miles away, and we would hike out to it. This was strictly voluntary, and not everyone participated, but those who did had a great time. We would arrive at this one-room schoolhouse, and the headmaster would declare a holiday for the students and suspend classes. We'd spend the rest of the day with them playing games, encouraging them, singing, and just talking with them, answering questions and just generally having a good time. Then, we'd have to hike the seven miles back to St. Mary's. Tiring but rewarding. Another rewarding experience was our weekly trip to the Cedars of Lebanon Rest Home located on South Harrison St, Lebanon, KY. According to the Village of Lebanon website, the home itself "has a rich history and is listed on the historical register. It is located in the Rosenwald School, which served the African-American community of Marion County as a high school from 1931 to 1962, at which time the school system was integrated. After sitting vacant for some time, it was converted into a nursing home" and is still in use today (as of this writing). Every Wednesday afternoon, we would visit with them, share a meal, sing some songs, and just talk with them. For some of these senior citizens, we were the only visitors they received. They loved to sing the old hymns, especially the women.

Students Preparing to Hike to St. Joe's

The Cedars of Lebanon

Other school activities included sports of all sorts. Well, maybe not all sorts, but we did have a varsity basketball team and a football team, both the college and the high school. And we had a fall field day where we played all kinds of different activities. Things like relay races, track meets, 3-legged and sack races, and piggyback races. Well, you get the idea. It's not one of your bowl-contender colleges.

Leo, Gip, & Bill Hanging Out

We also had plays, variety shows and movie night. I always worked backstage and enjoyed doing props and changing scenery. That was really cool because we did not have curtains, so we had to change the scenery while the audience watched. We did this by wearing all black and cutting the lights out, so we had to change the scenes in the dark. Every Saturday, we had a movie night and would get to watch one of the latest movies that was out. One week, the movie was *"Georgie Girl"*. We had a review committee made up of senior students and staff who had to review all movies shown to determine if it was appropriate for the audience, which included both high school and college students. Well, this committee decided that this particular movie was not appropriate and would not show it. Of course, we protested, but to no avail. The following Sunday morning at church service, the organist decided to play the theme song from the movie. Don't recall if he was punished for it or not. But the students enjoyed it.

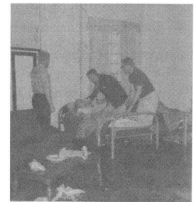
One of the Many Plays

Of course, it wasn't all fun and games. We did have to attend classes. After all, that is why we were there. The first two years were called First and Second College, and the last two were First and Second Philosophy. Since I was only there for the first two years, I never got into the philosophical classes. Most of our classes were your basic college courses, but we did have a focus on Latin. After all, Latin was the language of the church even though the Second Vatican Council (1962-1965) authorized the widespread use of the vernacular languages in the Mass instead of Latin. However, we still had to learn it. Our Latin professor was Father Joseph Scharfenberger, who was also the Director of Apostolic Work. His classroom was in a converted chapel. His desk sat on a raised dais, and I was fortunate to have a front-row seat right at the foot of his desk. One day, he was sitting at his desk, as he would often do, and he was droning on and on. I kind of had my head down, resting in the palm of my hands. I was paying attention, but I guess I gave the impression that I wasn't. He started tapping my desk with his foot, and I ignored it. Then he leans over and slaps my face. Well, actually, it wasn't really a slap, more of a love tap, as we say. Anyway, he hits me and says, "Wake up, Brand-dah-o." That's how he pronounced my name, with the emphasis on the middle syllable. I told him I wasn't sleeping and that I was paying attention. At the end of class, he told me he shouldn't have slapped me and, as an apology, I could skip class the next day. Later that afternoon, I passed him on campus and asked him if he meant what he said about me skipping class. And he said, "Of course, but you gotta pay the consequences." Unfortunately, the written word does not convey the manner in which he said it because he had a unique way of expressing himself. That evening, I conferred with one of my classmates in order to get his opinion on whether I should go to class or not. He told me what I already knew. I could skip class and possibly get marked absent, or I could attend class and have Father Joe tell me I had no guts. He had a way of saying, "You got no guts," with his hands, palms up, going back and forth. Anyway, I did not go to class, and he didn't mark me absent. He made up for it another time, though. The dismissal bell had just rung, indicating the end of class, and, as usual, when the bell rang, we all stood up to leave. Father Joe holds his hands up to stop us and says he decided to take attendance. Then he added, "If any of you don't think I should take attendance after the dismissal bell, you're free to leave the room." Since I sat at the front of the room and the door was right near me, I got up, walked over to it and waited for him to call my name. After all, I was second or third on the list alphabetically. Well, he skipped my name and continued on, so I walked out. When he got to the end of the list, he called my name. Since I was no longer there, he said, "Oh, Brand-dah-o isn't here," and marked me absent. Another one of his quirks was the four "sacred tiles." The floor of the dais was covered by one-foot square linoleum tiles, and he had four of them marked as "sacred tiles." What this meant was that if you stood within those four tiles, you were free to say anything you wanted to, and you would not have to face any consequences. I think it was honestly meant to be a place where you could feel free to speak your mind, kind of like the confessional. I really don't recall anyone ever taking advantage of those tiles. At least, not in our class.

Fr. Bernie & Fr. Sheridan

We did have a lot of colorful professors who taught us. Who could forget the Reverend Patrick Sheridan and his rival, Father Bernard Baldwin? Father Sheridan was the College's Spiritual Director. He was an elderly type, very polished and sophisticated, with a British accent (or maybe Canadian). He had a purebred dog named Queenie that he would walk with across campus, sometimes with Father Bernie. Father Bernie, on the other hand, had a mutt. He was the Dean of Students, was a much younger priest, let us address him as Fr Bernie and was pretty laid back. The two of them were always taking shots at one another, playfully, of course. Father Sheridan especially had fun comparing the two dogs.

Broadcasting a B-Ball Game

As you may have gathered from my antics with Father Joe, I liked to have fun at the college. I didn't participate in sports, but I did get involved in other activities. I was secretary of the Camera Club, and I tried my hand in the darkroom for a while, developing my own pictures. I already mentioned my theater involvement. I was also a part of the Chi-Rho Club. The Chi Rho (also known as Chrismon or sigla) is one of the earliest forms of Christogram, formed by superimposing the first two capital letters, chi (X) and rho (P), of the Greek word ΧΡΙΣΤΟΣ (Christos), in such a way that the vertical stroke of the P intersects the center of the X. You have seen it on the vestments worn by priests. The Chi Rho Club was actually a gardening club, and we helped maintain the grounds around the campus. I enjoyed doing this since it was part of my background. We also had our own radio station, WSMC. My roommate, Ken, was one of the announcers, and he would cover sports at the school. He even let me sit in the booth one time with him. It's not a big deal. I just thought I'd mention it. Ken and I had a lot of fun being roommates. We loved to play practical jokes on one another. One time, Ken decided to pull a big one on me. He knew the approximate time at which I would be returning to the room, so he unscrewed the light bulbs so the light in the room wouldn't turn on when I hit the switch. But he also opened both locker doors so that they would form a sort of obstruction when I walked into the room in the dark. He also placed the trash cans in the middle of the

floor, and then he hid under his desk. And waited. Soon, there was a knock on the door, and then the door opened. The light switch was flicked, and then someone walked in and hit the locker doors and said, "What the…" Then he opened the door wider so he could get some light in the room, walked over to the desk, turned the desk light on and saw Ken under the desk. It was Father Bernie. I don't really know what went through his mind, but Ken looked up from under the desk and said, "Hi, Father." And Fr. Bernie just shakes his head and walks out. I arrived soon thereafter and met the same fate. Ken was highly creative. Although not actively involved in sports, he enjoyed them, which is why he was the announcer on the radio station. He also invented a "football" game using football cards as players. He designed a football field on a felt cloth with all the yardage markings and goalposts and had elaborate rules for playing the game. Don't know if he ever marketed it or not, but he had fun playing it. He tried to teach me once, but it was too complicated for someone who wasn't sports-minded.

Well, I talked about some of the quirks of the professors, so it wouldn't be fair if I neglected the weirdness of the students, yours truly included. Several of us formed our own "underground society." It

Mock Sniper

included me, Ken, Bill, the Gipper, and maybe a couple of others. We would come up with these crazy stories and publish our "underground" newspaper, complete with pictures. Remember, I told you I tried my hand at photography and development. Well, some of the pictures we took were staged. As prop manager for the plays, I

Mock Execution

60

Staged Photo

Staged Photo

had access to the props, including dresses, guns, and other stuff. We developed our own symbol, which we called the "Retnun." Kind of like a Z with a line drawn through it. We staged executions, snipers, dead bodies, etc. We took the pictures in black and white, and I would develop them, and we would use them in the "paper." Our archenemies, our foes, were the "evil people" who occupied "The Bindery." The bindery was a place where they repaired books. It was run by the high school students, and they did a very good job of repairing textbooks, hymnals and any other tomes that needed repair. But we chose them as our nemesis. I even wrote a song about it to the tune of *"The Green Leaves of Summer."* The title was *"The Brown Leaves of Binding"*. It highlighted Tom, one of the High School Seniors and a few other folks. We used real events that took place on campus and converted them to our use, like when one student wrecked his car by hitting the front gate. That made it into the song. The song went like this:

A Time to be singing; A time to be gay
The brown leaves of binding have ended their days
It was pimps that once lived there; that once guarded the doors
Now, the bindery has fallen in the greatest of wars
With Evatt as their leader, a boy forty years old
Yes, the Bindery has fallen, so the story is told
It had started with Baker, who has now gone away
The symbol of pip-squeaks who no longer could pay
And then reckless young Dugan while he tried to escape
Had smashed his own Plymouth at the cow pasture's gate
Yes, the Bindery has fallen, and the world now is clean
And the brown leaves of binding will no longer be seen
Let us hope that this victory was not won in vain
That the evil that's wiped out was worth all the pain

Not the best writing in the world, but it was all in fun. Well, as I mentioned, we were in the boonies, and we didn't always have activities planned. And you can only study so much, so we had to keep our minds occupied. We didn't have computers or cell phones with all the computer games, so we had to design our own fun and games. Today, they do it all in the cyber world. Back then, the cyber world was whatever our minds could conjure up. I've mentioned my poetry several times so far. It was here at St. Mary's that I started writing. I'll include some of the stuff I wrote at the end. Those things that pertain to real life. But if you want to read any of the fantasy stuff, you'd have to get my book, "Leo's Collections," IF I ever get it published.

Ken in Front of Our Room -103 Baltic Ave

Because of my Lebanese background, I became known as the used camel salesman. Our room was 103 and was designated as 103 Baltic Avenue, and the door was adorned with signs that read Syrian Embassy and Used Camels for Sale.

Sometimes, I wonder how we survived those crazy years, but we did. Some of the comments in my yearbook were: "I really do not know what to say to you, Lao (sic), because you are so strange and crazy…I will pray for you."; "Mr. Brandao, in so much as I have sat next to you all year in chapel, and in so much as this has served to teach me mortification and tolerance for pain, let me thank you for this macabre chance to advance towards sanctity?"; "Leo, long live the revolution and the camel brigade."; "Leo, the last camel driver at SMC."; "Take care, Leo. May you never face a thousand camels, for this would not be true happiness." These should give you some idea of the craziness during those two years.

One night, there was a buzz around the campus. Many of us ran outside to see what was going on, and on top of the hill, we spotted what was a UFO, a strange light in the sky. It seemed to hover for a while and then disappeared. There was no sound coming from it, so we kind of ruled out a helicopter. We never found out what it was, so for us, it was an unidentified flying object.

I don't remember if it was the summer of '67 or '68, but one of those times when I was returning home, I stopped in Dayton, Ohio, to visit my cousin, Father John. I mentioned him in Chapter One. He was planning on driving to Massachusetts and had invited me to ride with him. I thought it a bit weird, but Cousin John had set us up with dates to go to dinner. One of the young ladies was riding back to Massachusetts with us. Cousin John eventually left the priesthood and married a nun. Don't know if it was the same woman or not.

As my second year drew to a close and we prepared to leave, I had expected to see everyone the next year, but during the summer, I received a notice from the Diocese of Fall River that I would not be returning to St. Mary but had been transferred to another school. No explanation was given, but since the Diocese was the one funding my education, I had no say in the matter. So, the following September, I reported to St. John's Seminary College in the Brighton neighborhood of Boston. The school was established in 1884, and the first class began on September 22, 1884, my birthday. Imagine that. At that time, it was called the Boston Ecclesiastical Seminary. It didn't become St. John's Seminary until 1941. St. John boasts a large number of highly successful alumni, including many Bishops and a number of Chief Chaplains. John P. McDonough and Henry J. Meade were both Chief of Chaplains for the Air Force, and Major General Paul K. Hurley was the 24th US Army Chief of Chaplains. The Rector when I attended was John A Broderick. Due to the continuing decline in enrollment since the 60s, especially in the wake of the sexual abuse scandal in the Archdiocese of Boston, much of the property was sold to Boston College, with the only campus left being St. John's Hall. I don't have a whole lot of memories of the time I spent at St. John's. A couple of memorable events not directly related to school were my participation in the Census for the Archdiocese and my assistance to one of the local high schools. During the census, we were required to wear our clerical collars and would go from house to house, knocking on doors and asking the usual census questions. It was interesting to watch people look out their windows to see who was knocking, and as soon as they saw the "collar," they would open their doors and be all pleasant. Of course, remember this was 1968-69. I doubt that today, they would be so eager to open their doors without seeing some kind of credentials beforehand. Nonetheless, back then, most would welcome me in, addressing me as Father, offering me tea and were willing to answer any questions. At least, the Catholics. If they weren't Catholic, they would politely tell me so, and I would move on. Part of our curriculum included helping the local parishes. I remember being a chaperone at one of the high school dances during the fall season. They were playing a game where you would have to pass an orange, which was held under your chin from one person to the next and the lines were made of girl-boy-girl-boy, etc. I was asked to participate, and not only was it very difficult to do wearing the "collar," but I also felt very uncomfortable doing it. Somehow, it just didn't seem appropriate. I never received any kind of yearbook for the year that I was there, and my memories of my classmates, teachers and classes are very dim. Academically, things were going downhill for me. I had trouble paying attention in my classes, and my grades were falling. I remember going to see the rector one day to get permission to get a part-time job. He informed me in no uncertain terms that with my current grades, that would not be feasible. At any rate, this was to be my final year in the seminary, although, at the time, I did not realize that. It wasn't until I had time to reflect on it the following summer that I made the decision not to return. There were probably other contributing factors to my decision. I think that if I had remained at St. Mary's, I would have stayed at least another year. I kind of missed the bucolic settings of the countryside. For whatever reason, I left school for the Summer with every intention of returning, but the Summer of 1969 turned things around. Bryan Adam's song, "Summer of '69," had special meaning for me. Of course, I would have to change a few words.

I still had my job at the A&P and continued working hard at it. I bought my second car that Summer. It was a 1960 Studebaker, just like my last one. The only difference was that this one was green. But before I bought my car, my sister Leonna was kind enough to loan me hers whenever I needed one. She drove a 1964 red Ford Galaxy. One day, something happened with the transmission as I pulled into a McDonald's parking lot. I wasn't sure what happened. All I know is that the car wouldn't run. I was so worried; I went and had a few drinks before calling her. That was a big mistake because now my sister thought I had been drinking, and that was what caused the problem. Don't remember if I ever convinced her otherwise, but she was a forgiving soul. She lived on Winter Street in Hyannis, and I would visit her often. Across the hall lived a young lady and her young son, Barbara and Billy. She was going through a difficult time as she was separated from her husband and preparing for a divorce. My sister suggested that if she needed to talk to someone, I would be a good choice because I was studying for the priesthood and was a good listener. Remember, this was before I made the decision not to go back. I had already broken up with my girlfriend of many years when I went away to the seminary,

Leonna's '64 Galaxie

and she had moved on. I wasn't involved in any relationships at this time. And I wasn't even thinking about dating. We talked a few times and became friends. Two things happened that should have been a clue to what lay in store. One day, while we were at my sister's house, there was a knock on the door. I happened to answer the door, and it was Barbara's husband standing there with another woman. He asked if Barbara was there. I told him yes and called Barbara to the door. When she came to the door, I put my arm around her while her husband asked her if he could pick Billy up that weekend. He never commented on the fact that I had my arm around her. Another time, we were in the hallway talking when Barbara's sister-in-law, who lived downstairs, came out the door. She saw us talking and asked Barbara what she was doing, and Barbara said, "I'm talking to my boyfriend." This was long before we even considered going out together.

Let me take a few moments here to fill in a little background on how Barbara got to be here in the first place. She has a very interesting family background that was grounded in the whaling industry in New Bedford. Her grandfather and granduncles served as whalers on a number of ships that sailed out of New Bedford, such as the schooner John R. Manta, which has the distinction of being the last New Bedford whaler. As a matter of fact, at the Whaling Museum in New Bedford, you can find some scrimshaw with the names of these men inscribed on it. If the reader is not familiar with scrimshaw, it is the whaler's art. Very intricate drawings were done on whalebone. Her father, James, did not pursue the whaling business but became a welder. He was also quite a talented artist. You can see some of his drawings in the appendix. James met Barbara's mother, Mildred Rose, in New Bedford, where they were married. Barbara was born in New Bedford on August 9, 1946. She lived at 153 Acushnet Ave. She was baptized at Our Lady of the Assumption Church on 6 April 1947. It was only a coincidence that the name of the church in which she was baptized was the same as the church in which I was baptized. Or was it? Her Godparents were

Scrimshaw at the NB Whaling Museum

Barbara with her Mom & Dad

Everett Rose and Elsie Fortes. She grew up in New Bedford, moving to Purchase Street and then 122 Potomska Street, attending Acushnet Avenue School (grades 1-6), Donaghy Roosevelt Jr High (grades 6-7), and New Bedford High. She has one sister, Jane, and a much younger brother named Mark. The age difference was such that when Barbara was walking down the street with Mark, many people thought he was her son. On 16 April 1966, she married William Carlos Rocheteau II, and on 7 September 1967, they had a son, William Carlos Rocheteau III. A short time after that, they separated, and Barbara moved to Cape Cod and filed for divorce, which was finally granted on 2 February 1971. And that is how she came to be living across the hall from my sister.

Well, the Summer of 69 wore on and eventually came to an end. While everyone was waiting for me to get ready to return to school, I had made the decision that I was not going back. But I also knew that not going back to school meant the draft. So, I went to New Bedford to the recruiter's office and signed up for the United States Air Force. Two of my brothers, Dennis and Junior, had already joined the Marines (my youngest brother, Johnny, would eventually follow suit). As honorable as that branch of the military was, it wasn't for me. Neither was the Army nor the Navy. Besides, the Air Force's birthday is 18 Sept 1947, only one year before I was born, so it was a perfect match. When I enlisted, I had signed up to be a Chaplain's Assistant. I figured this was still pursuing a career serving the Lord. As luck would have it, I was

Barbara, 2nd Row, Far Right

told I would have to wait a few months before I would be called to report. My job at the A&P was about over for the summer, and it wasn't until after I signed up that I found out that had they known I was not going back to school, they would have offered me a job as produce manager at one of the Island stores,

either Nantucket or Martha's Vineyard. But now I was going into the Air Force, so I had to pass it up. But I did have to get another job since I wasn't sure when I'd be leaving for boot camp, or as we called it, Basic Training. So, I got a job working for the Cape Cod Standard-Times. Meanwhile, what about my love life? Well, Barbara and I became good friends, but we still hadn't dated. Our first date was actually on Halloween when I asked her if she and Billy would like to go with me and Tony (Leonna's son) out Trick or Treating. We consider that our first date. During this time, Barbara moved a couple of times. Once back to New Bedford and then back to Hyannis. I remember hitchhiking all the way to New Bedford to visit her. Don't remember why I couldn't drive, but perhaps my car was not working, or it may have been later when I was home on leave.

When she moved back to Hyannis, she moved into a small house, which I thought of as a little doll house. We went out a lot after the Halloween date. She got a job at the newspaper, stuffing flyers into the papers, so we spent time doing that together. Saw several movies, mainly at the Drive-In (or Passion Pit), the first being *"Butch Cassidy and the Sundance Kid"* with Paul Newman and Robert Redford. We also saw a movie called *"Last House on the Left."* (Not recommended). Billy was in the back seat, and Barbara had to keep checking to make sure he wasn't watching it. It was a terrible movie. Besides going to the movies,  we would go out to eat at "Signor Pizza," one of the favorite hangouts in Hyannis located on the corner of Main Street and Sea Street. Of course, it has been gone a long time, but in the day, it was the place to go. One insignificant thing I remember was "S8." It was the number on the jukebox for the song "Sunny" by Bobby Hebb. For some reason, the waitresses loved this song and had written "Play S8" on a paper plate and put it on the jukebox, so it was played often. The "Dragon Light," which was across the street

from "Signor Pizza, was also a good place to hang out if you wanted some good Chinese food and drinks. It is still there to this day, and it holds many memories for many members of the family.

1969 turned into 1970, and as the months wore on, eventually, the time had come for me to leave. I took a bus to New Bedford, where I spent the night with a friend, and the next day, I would catch the bus to Texas, San Antonio to be precise, where I would begin my basic training at Lackland AFB.

CHAPTER FOUR: BEGINNING MY MILITARY CAREER

"Blessed be the Lord my strength which teacheth my hands to war, and my fingers to fight: My goodness, and my fortress, my high tower, and my deliverer; my shield, and he in whom I trust; who subdueth my people under me."

Psalm 144:1-2

As I stated earlier, I arrived at Lackland AFB in March 1970. Lackland AFB is the only entry processing station for the Air Force and is in San Antonio, Texas. On 1 October 2010, as part of the DoD restructuring, and under the advice of the 2005 Base Realignment and Closure Commission (BRAC), it became part of Joint Base San Antonio, aligning itself with the US Army Fort Sam Houston and Randolph AFB. But, in 1970, it stood alone, with its own rich history. Founded in June 1941, it was originally part of Kelly Field, but a year later, it became an independent organization called the San Antonio Aviation Cadet Center. In 1948, the same year I was born, it was renamed Lackland AFB after Brigadier General Frank Lackland.

There's not a whole lot to say about basic training. Most people know the routine. From the time you get there, they treat you like scum. Tear you down and then build you up into what they want you to be. Not as rough as the Marines or even the Army, but still six weeks of intensive training both physically and academically. At first, I must have been very nervous or apprehensive because it seemed like I was always goofing up something. My TI (Training Instructor) once told me that I could be a top airman if I would just get my head out of my …. Well, you figure it out. I worked hard at being the best I could. On our first weekend of liberty (a moment of freedom), a number of us were heading to the movies. As we were walking, this car came zipping around the corner, squealing tires. As he passed by, I tossed him a wave and the next thing I knew, he had slammed on his brakes, spun his car around, pulled up alongside us, threw the passenger door open, and ordered me to get in. Now, I don't remember what rank he was. Probably no more than a Staff or Technical Sergeant at most. But when you have no stripes, and this zebra orders you into the vehicle, you must obey. At least, that's what we were trained to do. So, I get into the vehicle, and he storms off. He asked me my name and squadron. I meekly asked him where we were going, and he replied, "To the brig, where smart asses like you belong." I had no idea what I had done wrong. Eventually, we pull up to my squadron, and he tells me to get out. We go into the building, and he asks who is in charge. No one was there because they were all out on liberty, except for one airman who was one of the squad leaders. This sergeant tells him that I was making fun of the military salute. I denied that and told him I was merely waving to say hello. He said, "You wave to everyone you see?" I replied that I was from Cape Cod, and yes, we did. Well, he wasn't too pleased with my answer and told Airman Black (the Squad Leader who was there) that I was to spend the rest of the afternoon scrubbing floors. And that was my first weekend of liberty.

Bertha

San Antonio Gardens

Eventually, I did get some time off and was able to visit San Antonio, the Alamo, to be precise. I remember studying about it in high school and was eager to see it. Although it was disappointingly small, when you consider what was accomplished there, it becomes that much more impressive. I remember meeting a girl while visiting San Antonio. She told me her name was Bertha Lozano and even gave me her address and phone number. For some reason, I remember that, but I also remember that both the name and number appeared to be false. There's not much more that I remember about basic training. Eventually, basic training was over, and our assignments came through. My first "assignment" was not going to take me out of Texas. In fact, it took me to Sheppard AFB, just north of Wichita Falls, Texas. It was here that I would receive my advanced training. This base was named in honor of Texas Senator John Morris Sheppard, who was a staunch supporter of military preparation prior to World War II. Although I had enlisted with the intention of becoming a Chaplain's Assistant (or 70130), my training was designated as a 60550, or Air Passenger Specialist. I was told that this was very similar to what I had requested, although I couldn't see how. Maybe it's because, in 1968, Eric Burdon and the Animals came out with a song called "*Sky Pilot*," a name given to chaplains. But I accepted it and learned "the trade." I do remember one thing prior to our classification. We were told to raise our hands in the air and wiggle our fingers. As we did that, the instructor said, "Good, you can all type." We eventually received the assignment that we would report to following the completion of our training. I was to go to McGuire AFB in New Jersey. One of my classmates, Wiley, received his assignment directly for Vietnam. We used to tease him about it, and anytime we would walk to the club or some other place, we would pretend to be the point man and let him know the coast was clear.

Well, I left Sheppard and headed for New Jersey after a short visit home. I arrived at the 438th Military Airlift Wing, McGuire AFB and began my first official assignment. McGuire is located about 16 miles southeast of Trenton, NJ, right next to Fort Dix. As a matter of fact, as part of the DoD restructuring, it is now known as Joint Base McGuire-Dix-Lakehurst (JB-MDL). It was initially established as

Fort Dix Airport in 1937, but in 1948 (again, my birth year), it was renamed in honor of Major Thomas Buchanan McGuire Jr., a World War II flying ace, who died on 7 Jan 1945 when his P-38 Lightning spun out of control and crashed on Negros Island in the Philippines during an aerial dogfight. Sometimes, my duties put me behind the counter processing

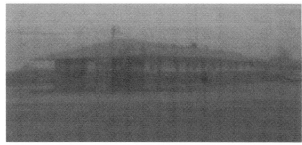
Royal Motel

passengers, but most of the time was spent loading the aircraft. I learned to drive three different types of tugs: a forklift, a step-truck for loading/unloading passengers, and the mobile conveyer belt used to move the baggage into the belly of the aircraft. I really enjoyed driving the tugs, especially when we were racing them. Most were automatic, but we had one that had a stick shift, and we would often practice popping wheelies with it. For a portion of my time there, I worked the night shift and slept during the day. Remember earlier when I said songs evoke memories and how we often remember insignificant things as a result? I remember one day, while I was asleep, I was working the night shift. I awoke to the sound of police sirens and the words, "This is the police. Give yourself up. You are surrounded." Needless to say, I jumped up, startled, only to realize that I was listening to a song on the radio by R. Dean Taylor called *"Indiana Wants Me."* The song had just come out, and so it took me by surprise. Now, whenever I hear that song played on the radio, I recall this incident. Barbara came out to visit me once while I was stationed there. We stayed at the Royal Motel just outside the base. We still communicated with each other with letters, but I don't recall if we ever talked about marriage. Her divorce had been filed, but it would take some time for it to be finalized. I made a few friends while stationed here, but none that really lasted over the years. The guys I worked with were basically good guys, but we all had our faults and did some things that we shouldn't have. When we worked the night shift, things were slow, so we passed the time playing cards. But we still got the job done. One day, one of my friends (Bruce and Mary) neighbors were moving. We were having a party at my friend's house and came up with this great idea. Bruce's neighbor had a small car. I think it was an MG. Well, a bunch of us guys went down to the street and moved the car around the block, literally picking it up so we could

Bruce et al

move it the few feet required. We got the car around the corner. When the neighbor came out to take out his trash, we watched from my friend's window as the guy put down the trash and started back into the house. He stopped, took a double take, and realized his car was missing. He about panicked, and my friend had to rush down there before he called the police. The first time I heard a woman use the "F" bomb was here. I remember James Taylor was coming to do a concert, and the young girl who worked at the cafeteria was going crazy ranting about his visit. I asked her if she was responding to a James Taylor concert like that, what would she do if Elvis was visiting, and she said, "F--- Elvis." I was shocked to say the least.

In the Air Force, we had an annual performance appraisal. It was a 1-9 rating system that was used to evaluate our performance and provide guidelines for promotion. If you received all 9s or if you received a low score (5 or below), the rater had to provide comments to justify his decision. Otherwise, the rating itself was sufficient without comments. The only 8 I ever received was my first one from Staff Sergeant Quinn (who was my supervisor). He gave me three reasons for the rating. One, I would have the opportunity to work up to a nine on my next assignment; two, he didn't want to write any comments; and three, he didn't like "portegees" (referring to my Portuguese heritage). Those were his words. In today's environment, I probably could have filed a lawsuit against him, but back then, who knew?

Airmen Looking at Shrapnel Damage in Revetment

Fortunately, I left that assignment shortly after that. That was the first and last eight rating that I ever received. For the next 25 years, I received nothing but 9s. It taught me a lesson about people. I did receive a promotion to Airman First Class (A1C) while I was there. So, where was my next assignment? Where else? Vietnam. Of course, I had apprehensions about going, as did my family. My younger brother, Arthur, had already had a tour in Vietnam with the Marines, and, Praise God, he returned home safely. Now, it was my turn. I went through the necessary training that was required before leaving: Shots, rifle training, and so on. And then, after a thirty-day leave at home, I returned to McGuire to begin my journey to the Orient, with a stop in Anchorage, Alaska. I arrived at an air base in the southern part of Vietnam called Phan Rang on April Fool's Day, 1971. I was assigned to Detachment 8, 14th Aerial Port Squadron. Guess who met my plane when I landed. Remember that fellow, Wiley, who I used to tease in Tech School when he got his assignment to the RVN? Well, he got his chance for revenge. I was surprised to see him but glad as well. At least I had an old friend to brief me on what to expect. Of course, Wiley took the opportunity to get payback with his stories. But it was all fun. In actuality, my assignment to Phan Rang wasn't too bad. As a matter of fact, in the year that I was there, nothing of major significance happened with the enemy on the base. There were only two incidents that I can recall. Once, there were

One of our barmaids

rumors that the enemy was planning an attack on the base. The Air Force, as a general rule, was not issued any firearms. But since there was the slight possibility of the base being overrun, we were all issued M-16s. However, we were not issued any ammunition. We were told if the base were overrun, the ammunition would be distributed. And what if it were too late to get us the ammo…well, I guess we would just point the gun and say, "bang, bang." Fortunately, it proved to be a false alarm, and nothing happened. The second event was when the enemy lobbed three mortar shells onto the base. One hit a lieutenant's hootch. The lieutenant happened to be on leave at Saigon at the time. Interestingly, he was also dating our unit's secretary, who happened to be one of the local Vietnamese women. Coincidence… I guess we'll never know. Another mortar landed in a vacant field and caused no damage at all. The third hit the revetments where the aircraft were parked. And it landed in one of the few vacant parking spots. The only damage caused was some holes in the steel revetment and in the concrete floor. In this picture, you can see my friends, Roger and Bill, pointing to the holes in the revetment. Most of our problems came from in-house.

We were co-located with the Army's MATCO (Military Air Traffic Coordinating Office) Branch, which took care of the Army personnel who were passing through. We handled Air Force personnel and anyone else that came through our terminal. We worked well with the Army, and MSG Brown, who was in charge of the Army MATCO, became a good friend. He was also a really good scrounger, and because the Army operated a little differently than the Air Force did, he was able to get all kinds of things that we couldn't. He would have clam bakes with lobsters, steaks, and many other things. He was able to get materials for us so that we could build our own club in the back of our hootch, complete with

Airman standing on our six-pack

Our passenger Bus

refrigerators and other accessories to run a bar. Because of my work ethic and integrity, I was put in charge of the bar, hiring the girls who worked for us, and handling the funds. We only had a couple of girls that we actually paid to work, but we had many others who were on our "payroll" so that they could have access to the base and their boyfriends. They would agree to work one night a week for tips only, and the other nights, they could come on base and spend time with their boyfriends. I became like a big brother to the girls. One of our additional duties was being a "bay orderly." What this meant was that when it was our turn, we would

spend a week where we didn't go to work. We would get up, wait for the mama sans that worked at the barracks to come in, and supervise them as they performed their duties. It also meant policing the area and making sure it was kept clean. During the last month or so that I was there, my turn had come up. During the day, I would do what I had to do, and during the evening, I would take care of the bar, making sure everything was taken care of. Our First Sergeant was a big drinker and spent most of his evenings in the bar. As he watched me work, he said he might make me a permanent bay orderly. I surprised him and asked him if he would. And he agreed. So, for the last month, I would get up, police up the area, wait for the mama sans to show up and supervise them as they performed their duties. Never had to return to the terminal to work. Because we were responsible for transporting passengers to and from the aircraft, we had assigned to us a 29-passenger bus and a six-pax pickup. So, I had two more vehicles added to my military license. In the evening, we would use the bus to take the girls who worked for us to the main gate. But before taking them to the gate, we would stop by the club and pick up the other girls who had boyfriends and let them ride out to the gate with us. There was a Vietnamese bus that would take them there, but they preferred riding with us as they could be with their boyfriends. One time, while we were waiting at the club, a couple of guys got on, and they were doing a lot of cursing. Now, I did not like cussing, and I politely told them to please stop as we had ladies

Airmen Relaxing in Our Club

on the bus. They refused, so I told them that they would have to get off the bus. They said if these bitches could ride the bus (referring to our girls), then they could as well. The next thing I know, one of them hit me in the face. I made some stupid comment about us not having been introduced, and he hit me again. Well, our guys grabbed the chocks that we kept under the seats (used for putting under the tires when on the flight line) and were ready to go to battle. I remember telling them to get the girls off the bus first as I didn't want them on the bus if the MPs showed up since what we were doing wasn't exactly legal.

One of the Many Bands

They quickly got off the bus to catch the Vietnamese bus, and the guys who started the trouble took off as well. I guess the MPs were quickly notified of the commotion and arrived at the bus within minutes. When I got off the bus to talk with them, they saw my face was a bloody mess. It really wasn't that bad, but I guess I had a bloody nose and must have rubbed my hand across my face, which made it look a lot worse than it was. Anyway, we told them that a couple of guys had caused the trouble, but they had fled. We couldn't identify them, and we were all OK, so the MPs asked if there was someone else who could drive the bus besides me, and I told him yes. And we went back to our barracks.

Another time, we had picked up a Filipino band and drove them to the Officer's Club, which we often did whenever bands came through. This particular band liked us because of the treatment that we had given them, and asked us to stay as their guests at the club. Generally, the enlisted were not allowed at the Officer's Club as we had our own. But we told them we would stay. Like most bands that came through there, this one had two or three lovely young ladies as part of the group. As the show started, some of the officers started getting really obnoxious, propositioning the girls while they were on stage and carrying on rather rudely and crudely, including throwing ice on the stage. Most of them were drunk. The band leader told them if they continued their behavior, he would end the show right there. They persisted, and he did as he promised. He ended the show and started packing up the equipment. Then, several of the officers started blocking the bus so they could not get on. Fortunately, the MPs showed up and assisted them in getting on the bus, and we drove them back to where they were staying. I found out later that a lot of these officers were fighter pilots under a lot of stress, not knowing if they would make it back each time they went out. So, when they had the chance, they would completely unwind like that. I could somewhat understand that, but I did lose a lot of respect for them. It was years later, when I worked closely with another group of officers at HQ SAC, that I got that respect back.

We did have many foreign nationals who passed through the terminal. One night, we had two large groups that came through at the same time, fully armed. Both had to spend the night to catch out-going flights the following morning. I believe one was a Cambodian group and the other a Laotian group, but I'm not 100% positive now on the nationalities. I only remember that we had to spend the night at the terminal to make sure that they each stayed on opposite ends of the terminal. The fear was that they might get into an altercation with each other with disastrous results. Fortunately, the night passed without incident.

One night, we were playing poker at our barracks club as we always did. My two favorite pastimes are drinking and playing poker. Anyway, we were sitting at the table playing poker, and we heard (and felt) this explosion that sounded awfully close. My friend, Wiley, dove over and under the table so fast it shocked me. I didn't know what was happening. As it turned out, someone had fragged the police barracks next to us. That is, they threw a grenade into the barracks. Evidently, someone had a grudge against the MPs. My understanding is that they found the individual who did it a few days later, and when they were bringing him in, they had an "accident," and the vehicle overturned, and the guy got hurt pretty badly. At least, that's what the story was.

Another incident that we had involved a number of black guys who were returning from the club and were fairly drunk. During those years, when "brothers" would meet, they had a ritual greeting called the "dap." This was an impressive and elaborate form of "greeting," involving a lot of tapping and touching of the hands. It would often last a minute or two. I was sitting in front of our hootch with a friend of mine who happened to be a white guy who could do the dap pretty well (for a white guy), and he was teaching me how to do it. Before we knew what was happening, these five black guys had surrounded us and demanded to know what we were doing. I told them that my friend was teaching me how to do this dap, and the "leader" of the group told me if I wanted to learn to do the dap, I should go to a black guy and not a white guy. The dap was sacred to them, and no white guy should be doing it. While he was talking, someone else ripped the phone off the wall so we couldn't call the MPs. By this time, we thought we were going to get creamed, but fortunately, one of our black buddies heard the commotion and came out and diffused the situation.

As I said earlier, most of our problems came from in-house.

One time, I was returning to the terminal on the perimeter road after running an errand. The procedure was that we had to stop at a designated spot on the perimeter road, check the skies to make sure there were no incoming aircraft and then proceed if the skies were clear. Although the perimeter road did not actually cut across the runway as it was outside the fence, vehicles on the road could obstruct the view of incoming aircraft. I followed the rules, stopping and checking the skies and did not see any aircraft approaching, so I continued on. About halfway across, suddenly, these two F-16s come screaming out of the clouds. I should have stopped as soon as I saw them, but I thought I could make it across before they reached the runway, and so I floored it. They flew right over my head. Fortunately, I was driving the pickup and not the bus at the time. By the time I got back to the terminal, flight ops were on the phone with my boss, wondering who it was that had crossed in front of the runway. That was my first (and only) chewing out, as it were.

Speaking of my boss, I worked for a TSgt Sharpe who loved country music. He played the guitar and was in a group that performed at the club. One day, his supervisor approached me and asked me to keep tabs on him and report back on what he did. It was believed he was rehearsing when he should have been working. Well, I liked TSgt Sharpe and wasn't about to do any spying on him without him knowing, so I told him exactly what I was asked to do. He told me to go ahead and do what I was asked. He didn't care one iota. We had a saying there, "What are they going to do? Send me to Vietnam."

Besides drinking and playing poker, another pastime that we had was throwing knives. There were several of us who liked to throw knives, and we had a little set-up in the back of the hootch beside the bar where we could practice. We had a board nailed to a fence and would throw until we had a big hole in the board, and then we'd nail another one over it. We ended up with a thick layer of boards with a big hole in the center. I remember one night, one of the guys, who was probably the best thrower we had, challenged someone to stand in front of the board. I jokingly said I would but actually had no intention of doing it. However,

One of the Many Aircraft

when I went up to the board to pick up a knife that had fallen on the ground, my friend threw his knife, and it stuck in the board right above my head. When you're drunk, you do crazy things.

While in Vietnam, I would write to Barbara often. I had her picture in my room for all to see, and I did not get involved with any of the girls there. As I said, they all thought of me as a big brother. We talked about getting married when I returned but didn't make any actual plans. When I got back, I had a lot of explaining to do. I would often take pictures of the girls working for us. One day, I snapped a picture of one of the girls just as she spun around on the stool. At the time, she was wearing a very short skirt, but I didn't think anything of it. As I often did, I left my camera under the bar, and a day or two later, I noticed it was missing. I figured she knew I kept the camera there and asked her about it. She denied it at first, but I persisted, and she finally admitted to taking it and said she would return it. I think she took it because she was afraid the picture might have revealed too much. When she returned the camera, the film wasn't in it. She did give me a roll of film, but I told her that it wasn't the same one that was on the camera. She said this one was better. When I had it developed, there were a couple of pictures of one of her friends sitting on her bed in a flimsy outfit. Nothing revealing, but still, I had to explain how these particular pictures came into my possession. Guess I could have just gotten rid of them.

Before I got to the final days here, there was one other incident I recalled. One of the perimeter guards had noticed someone trying to climb over the perimeter fence late at night. Following procedures, he called out three times in English and Vietnamese but received no response. As per protocol, he opened fire. The next morning, when the patrol went out to check it, they found an American soldier shot dead. I'm not sure if he was trying to sneak back onto the base or sneak off the base.

Prior to my leaving, we were told that as the war was winding down, we would be turning the base over to the South Vietnamese. I remember several of the guys said that they were not going to give them "our bar," which we had worked so hard to build. They were going to tear it down before they left. I never knew if they did or not.

The night before I was scheduled to return to the States, we had a going away party. It got a little rowdy, and I got more than a little plastered. I guess I passed out. The next day, one of the girls told me she was mad because I got so drunk. She said they had a surprise for me, but I missed it because I passed out. Never did tell me what that surprise was. She was the same girl who had told me that all the girls regarded me as a big brother. I didn't know if I should have felt flattered or insulted, but at least it kept me faithful to my future wife.

When we were approaching our time for rotation back to the States, we had to fill out what we called "a dream sheet." This is where you indicated where you would like to be stationed when you returned to the States. Having been raised on the East Coast, I had a fondness for the ocean, so I indicated that I would like to be stationed either on the East Coast or the West Coast. They obliged me by sending me to the middle, i.e., Offutt AFB Nebraska. Also, I found out that they no longer needed 605s (Air Passenger Specialists) in the U.S., as most of those positions were filled by civilians. Therefore, any 605s rotating back to the States had to be cross-trained in another career field. For some reason, we were not given the choice but were involuntarily chosen for another career field. One of my best friends was selected to go into the Security Police Career Field and ended up being assigned guard duty around B-52s at K.I Sawyer AFB in Michigan. I, praise God, was selected to come back as a 702 (Administrative Specialist) being assigned to Offutt AFB. And that's where the next leg of my journey begins.

CHAPTER FIVE: RETURN TO THE LAND OF THE BIG BX

(or Awful Air Force Base, Oh My God, Nebraska)

"Therefore shall a man leave his father and mother, and shall cleave unto his wife: and they shall be one flesh."

Genesis 2:24

Offutt AFB was a fairly nice base, even though we used to call it Awful Air Force Base in Oh My God, Nebraska. It is located about seven miles south of Omaha in Sarpy County. The adjoining town is Bellevue. It is also the headquarters of the Strategic Air Command (SAC), which I'll talk about more when I talk about my assignment to HQ SAC.

Offutt's history began in 1890 when the War Department established Fort Crook, named after Major General George Crook, a Civil War veteran and Indian fighter. In 1918, the 61st Balloon Company of the Army Air Corps was assigned to Fort Crook. In 1924, following the creation of an airfield, it was renamed Offutt Field in honor of 1st Lt Jarvis Offutt, a native of Omaha and World War I pilot. Initially, it was used for airmail flights, but as World War II loomed on the horizon, it was chosen as the site for a new bomber plant operated by the Glenn L. Martin Company. Here, they produced the B-29 Superfortress, including the "Enola Gay" and "Bockscar," the two aircraft that delivered the atomic bombs over Japan.

In January 1948, it was renamed Offutt Air Force Base. There is that magic year again, 1948. In September 1948, four days after I was born, the 3902nd Air Base Group became the host unit at Offutt.

Many changes took place over the years, too many to mention here. But I will mention two. On 9 November 1948, it became the host base for the Strategic Air Command. During the Cold War (from February 1961 until July 1990), Operation Looking Glass, a mobile Command Post, was airborne 24/7. A new plane would take off before the one that was currently airborne would land. Twenty-nine years of operation without a single mishap or incident.

Offutt was also depicted in several movies, including Jimmy Stewart's 1955 film, "Strategic Air Command," 1963's "A Gathering of Eagles" with Rock Hudson and Rod Taylor, and 1964's "Fail Safe" with Henry Fonda, just to name a few. It also received mention as "the Omaha Installation" in an episode of "Star Trek."

I was assigned to the 3902nd Operations Squadron. My duty title and job assignments changed over the time that I was there (April 1972-November 1976), but initially, my duty title was Administrative

Specialist, Standardization and Evaluation Section. I was responsible for maintaining all the publications, including technical orders, maintaining office files, and requesting per diem orders for flight crew members who were out for more than ten hours. I was also responsible for requisitioning and maintaining office supplies. The flying operation consisted mainly of proficiency flights on the T-29 and T-39 aircraft. We had to maintain and provide all the tech orders needed by the pilots, and we had to make absolutely certain they were kept up-to-date with all the latest instructions, especially safety cautions. One of the things checked following any mishap was whether or not the pilot was current on the latest instructions. Since I was being retrained in this career field, I had to spend much time studying so that I could pass my proficiency training in this new career field. I completed the training in minimum time, thus making me eligible for promotion to Sgt during the first year I was there. And then to SSgt the next year.

Many things took place while at Offutt, not the least of which was my marriage to Barbara. I'll get to that in a little bit, but for now, let me talk a little bit about some of the things that happened between April and September when the wedding bells rang.

Since I was single when I arrived at Offutt, I lived in the barracks for a while. When I wasn't working or studying, I was out with the guys doing what we learned to do in the Nam. Mainly drinking. There was a club across from the base, and we would often end up there. One of my best friends was Paul, and we spent a lot of time together. We also had another friend who was once a major in the Air Force, but he got RIFed before he had twenty years in. That means Reduction in Force. In order for him to get credit for 20 years, he had to come back in as an enlisted person. Even though his rank was airman, he could retire after his 20 was up as a major. We called him Airman Major. I can't even remember what his real name was. One night, a bunch of us were at the club, and after the club closed, we wanted to go out and eat some food. Denny's was open all night and was about three miles north of the base, so we went there. I had my car, and Airman Major drove his own. When we left Denny's, I told Airman Major I would follow him back to the base. He left Denny's, traveling south in the northbound lanes of Highway 73/75. And stupid me, I followed him. After about a half mile, there was an opening between the two lanes, and he zipped over into the southbound lane, followed by me. When we got back to the base, I asked him what the heck he was doing, and he said, "You said you'd follow me, and I wanted to see if you would." I must have been crazy. That wasn't the only time I risked my life foolishly behind the wheel. More on that later.

I hear the wheels turning in your head, and you're wondering where I got the car I was driving. I arrived at the base without any wheels. I lived on base, the bar was across the street and within reasonable walking distance, and we had friends with cars. But one day, one of my friends, Roger, and I were hitchhiking to Omaha, which was about seven miles from the base. After walking quite a distance without getting a ride, we came upon a used car lot. I asked Roger how much money he had, and he said he had 100 dollars. I also had 100 dollars. So, I walked into the dealership and asked the salesman what he had for 200 dollars (just like my two Studebaker purchases), and he brought me out to look at a 1962

Ford Galaxy. He replaced the battery so it would start. I checked it out and said I'd take it. Remember way back when I talked about the Studebaker with the window that would fall down? When the salesman put the inspection sticker on the windshield and closed the door, the window dropped down. I thought this must be the car for me. I bought the car and paid Roger back eventually, but I gave him rides wherever he needed to go until I paid him back. A win-win deal. More about the car later.

One of the top songs that year was "Brandy" by Looking Glass. Remember, Operation Looking Glass was the name of the 24/7 Airborne Command Post, so the song seemed appropriate for us. I started to like Country Music, partly because that was all they played at the club. Prior to this, I was more focused on rock and roll songs from the 50s and 60s. As a matter of fact, I listened to very few rock songs after 1972. When it comes to song trivia, I am pretty good until you get to songs after 1973. Then, I am pretty much lost. We used to play Trivia songs on the radio (WOW), and I won so many times they told me I was only allowed to win once a month.

So, to get around that, we would use other guys' names in the office to try and win. Prizes weren't that fantastic, maybe free passes to a show or a record album. Nothing too expensive.

Well, let's get back to marriage. When I got home from the Nam, I spent a few weeks on leave. Barbara had moved back to New Bedford, and since I had no car, I had to hitchhike to visit her. Her divorce was now finalized, and we talked a little bit about marriage, but I knew I had to get settled in Omaha first, so we put it off. After a few months, I had saved a little money (despite buying the car and the drinking), and I told Barbara on a phone call if she could get out to Omaha, we could get married. Not much of a romantic wedding proposal, was it? She agreed and started saving her money by selling Avon. We agreed that she would come out in September, and we could get married. We decided on September 15 because the 15th of the month was payday, and we knew we'd always have money to celebrate our anniversary. My friend, Paul, had also planned on getting married in September, but he was getting married to a girl named Gerry in New York. That's where he was from. Queens County, Long Island, to be exact. As it happened, he and Gerry returned to Omaha the same day Barbara and Billy arrived. I had secured an apartment in downtown Omaha, so we were all set there. (I tried to locate the place on Google Maps, but it looks like it's gone to make way for an overpass.) Paul and Gerry agreed to be Best Man and Maid of Honor. Unfortunately, because Barbara was a divorcee, we could not get married in the Catholic Church, so we got a Justice of the Peace in

Bellevue. His name was Judge Orville Entenman. This was my first break with the Church. We stopped going to church after we married and didn't return until 1976. We'll get to that later. A little more about our apartment. Located in the middle of Omaha, just off Dodge Street, it was a fairly good-sized apartment with a big living room that had a fake fireplace and two bedrooms, as well as the usual kitchen and bath. I believe it was on the third floor. We used to think that someday we'd have a real fireplace. One big mistake I made at the time was hanging a poster of Petula Clark in our bedroom. I liked her music and bought an album, and the poster came with it. Barbara did not like that at all. Guess I can't blame her, but in all honesty, it was the music that I liked, not necessarily the woman. To this day, I don't think Barbara likes it when one of her songs plays.

After we got married, Barbara got a job as a waitress at "Big Boys." Big Boys was originally started as Bob's Pantry in 1936 by Bob Wian in Glendale, California, and was known by a variety of names throughout the years. It became famous for being the Home of the Big Boy Hamburger. In 1967, it was bought by Marriott Corporation. They are still in operation today, even though they have undergone a number of ownership and name changes. Barbara enjoyed working there and became known for the phrase "No Tata." This was because of her New England accent, and when people would order fish without tartar sauce, she would say, "no tata," and her coworkers ribbed her about it.

I also decided to get a part-time job to help with our expenses. I got a job working for Gulf-Mart Liquors, a part of the Gulf-Mart Discount Center. Gulf-Mart opened in Omaha in 1967 but unfortunately closed in 1974 due to bankruptcy. Although my stint there was short, I enjoyed it. I worked with a guy named Lenny, and our manager was Ben Finklestein. Ben worked during the day, and Lenny and I worked at night. There was also a security guard who patrolled the area, and he was good friends with Lenny. On New Year's Eve, we were supposed to be open until 10 p.m., but business was virtually non-existent. The security guy (I can't remember his name) came in about 8:30 and told Lenny he should close because no one was out shopping. Lenny hollers out the door, "Anyone there?" Hearing no response, he decided to close the shop, and the three of us broke open a fifth of Wild Turkey. We consumed that and then another pint, I think. How I managed to get home that night, I don't know. One more time, I risked my life doing something stupid. I remember we had guests coming that evening, Dick and Jewell, to celebrate the New Year with us. I came home, sat down to dinner, and passed out, my face in my dish.

Boy, was my wife mad. And who can blame her? That was the start of my end to heavy drinking. As I said, Gulf-Mart was closing its doors in 1974, and they were selling everything at a great discount. Lenny told me one day to help myself to whatever liquor I wanted because they were going to sell the stock at ten cents on the dollar. So, I stocked up my home bar. In the final week, Ben tells Lenny, "Leo's been a very good employee. Make sure he gets something." Lenny says, "Don't worry, it's been taken care of. When we left Omaha in 1976, I gave away a lot of liquor I had left because even though I had a well-stocked bar, I didn't drink much after that New Year's Eve incident.

Let's get back to the job, and then I'll talk about some other activities that occupied our time. As I said earlier, Paul and I were very good workers. We worked in the same organization but in different offices, doing different things.

As mentioned at the beginning of the chapter, my initial duty title was Administrative Specialist, Standardization/Evaluation Section. My immediate supervisor was MSgt Caldwell Anthony. It's easy to make a mistake and reverse the names, and I noticed on my first evaluation report that whoever typed it up did exactly that and listed him as Anthony Caldwell. Evidently, no one ever caught the error, not even him, when he signed the report. I liked working for him. He was a good supervisor and pleasant to work for. One day, however, he gave me the scare of my life. I mentioned earlier that I was usually the first one at work. One day, he and I were the only ones in the office, and all of a sudden, he let us this loud, piercing scream and collapsed on the floor. And he was a pretty big guy. I didn't know what to do. I called for help, and someone in one of the other offices came running in and quickly called for an ambulance. I don't recall what had happened to him, but he turned out fine and was back at work in no time.

I was promoted to Sergeant and then to Staff Sergeant, and with that came added responsibilities. I assumed additional duties as Squadron Ground Safety NCO and Assistant WAPS Monitor. WAPS stood for Weighted Airman Promotion System, and as the monitor, I had to ensure that everyone eligible for promotion had completed what they needed to do, including training in various areas. Later, I also picked up the additional duties of Squadron Customer Account Representative (dealing with publications), Squadron Financial Monitor, and Branch Supply Custodian.

Having the additional duties also meant having to receive additional training. I had the opportunity to go to two schools while assigned here. In September 1973, I went to March AFB, California, to attend the Fifteenth Air Force Noncommissioned Officer Leadership School, Class 73-H, and graduated on October 4. As the Squadron Ground Safety NCO, I was able to attend the Fundamentals of USAF Safety Programs at HQS, Lowry Technical Training Center, Lowry Air Force Base, Colorado. After ten days there, I graduated on 1 July 1975. In addition to these formal training requirements, I also had to complete

a number of other courses, including the Offutt Safety Training Program for Additional Duty Safety Personnel, Supervisor's Safety Course, an 18-hour Defense Race Relations Educational Course, an Air Force Writing Course, Management Training Program for Air Force Supervisors, and a Basic Keypunch Operation and Program Control (my introduction to computers). All part of the job training.

My trip to California for the NCO Leadership School was interesting. But before I talk about that, I have to back up a little and talk about my vehicles. Remember that 1962 Galaxy I bought for $200? Well, Omaha required vehicle inspections every six months. After I had the vehicle for six months, a number of things were going bad on it, including the tires. One day, when I was going home, I was turning left at a light. As soon as I turned, a police car, which was in the lane opposite me, turned in behind me. He had noticed that my inspection sticker had expired and gave me a ticket. I had to appear in court with proof that the vehicle was inspected. I knew the vehicle would not pass inspection, so I traded it in for a Green Opel Manta Rallye with a big black stripe down the

center. When I went to court, the judge asked me if I had the vehicle inspected, and I told her I traded it in. Case dismissed. I really liked that little car. It drove nice, even though it was kind of small. Now, what does this have to do with me going to California? Since Barbara didn't drive (she hadn't got her license yet), one of my friends asked if he could use the car while I was gone. I was flying out, so I wouldn't need the car, and I would be gone for six weeks. I said okay. During this period, something went wrong. He didn't check the oil, and when I returned, the engine had frozen up, and the car wouldn't run. So I had to get rid of it. I traded it in for a 1974 Red Volare Station wagon. More on that later. Back to my trip. I flew out to California on a T-39. This was a small training plane without any luxuries like a bathroom. The pilot told us if we had to relieve ourselves, we would have to use a bucket they had for that purpose and would have to dump it when we landed. I tried so hard not to have to go, but I couldn't make it and ended up using the bucket. When I did return home, there was one other surprise waiting for me. Since I was

gone over our anniversary and my birthday, Barbara had surprised me with a pool table that sat smack dab in the middle of the living room. She knew I loved to play pool and wanted to do something nice for me.

After two years in the apartment, we decided to move closer to the base and found a nice little single-family home in South Omaha, 1909 Missouri Ave, only a few miles from the base. It had a very small front yard. I called it a postage stamp and could cut the grass with a sickle. In the back it had a garage and a short driveway down the alley. It was two stories, had a front

closed-in porch and a full basement. We liked it, and we made friends with some folks down the alley. The only problem was that there was a liquor store down on the corner that attracted unsavory characters. Barbara had always prayed about it, and one day it burned down. I told you I had bought a 1974 Volare Station Wagon. This was the first time I ever bought a brand-new car. And we needed it as our family was going to grow. During the summer of '74, we took a trip to Cape Cod on leave, and I had a bad habit of wanting to get from A to B as quickly as possible, so I drove non-stop, except for gas and rest stops. Barbara ended up not feeling very well. Turned out she was pregnant with Christopher and didn't know it. He was born the following February 27 at the Base Hospital.

The station wagon came in handy those last two years not only because of the growing family but also because of my extra-curricular activities.

As noted above, the job kept me pretty busy. But that was during duty hours. I was no longer a party-goer or drinker, and I was not working part-time, so I had to find other things to occupy my time. It was at this time that one of my senior supervisors, Lt Col. Paul Kennedy, along with Major Charles Emig, decided to form a revolutionary marching outfit to prepare for the upcoming bicentennial 1976. And I jumped at the chance to join. We purchased authentic muskets with bayonets and made our own uniforms. One of the ladies on my street made my jacket, but I made the pants and shirts (I still have them hanging in the closet). We modified our shoes with buckles and bought white wigs to complete the ensemble. The outfit was named the Second Maryland Regiment of Foot, and we received a charter from the Governor of the State of Maryland. This provided us with national coverage, and we were recognized in an article in "Airman" magazine as well as a video spot in an "Air Force Now" film. When American Airlines opened up in Omaha, we were asked to perform and received coverage in their magazine. For two years, we performed

shows throughout Nebraska, participating in parades and performing mock battles. Events such as the Iowa Western Community College Veteran's Day Memorial program, providing the honor guard for the Court of the King and Queen at the Coronation (a local town's celebration), and participating in the parade when Omaha opened the Southside Viaduct Bridge, One such event was at the Annual Rodeo Days at Burwell, Nebraska. A doctor

sponsored us and allowed us to set up camp (Valley Forge West, as we called it) in his backyard. This was truly a big event, and...well, let them speak for themselves. The following is taken right off their website:

"In 1921, citizens of Burwell, Nebraska, decided to put their community on the map with an annual community celebration. They chose to begin a rodeo, which reflected the western heritage of the town. The first rodeo was held in September of 1921, and since that time, nearly every professional rodeo champion who has pulled on a pair of boots has tramped through the historic arena of Burwell. Almost a century later, visitors from all over the world continue to migrate to the small community of Burwell, Nebraska, for a one-of-a-kind experience at Nebraska's Big Rodeo.

From the classic events of rodeo, such as Saddle Broncs, to the wild and woolly action of the Wild Horse Race and Canadian Chuck Wagon Races, Nebraska's Big Rodeo has something for everyone! Family members can visit 4-H animals and exhibits or get a sweet treat on the midway. The Calamus Lake and Fort Hartsuff are nearby, adding to the adventure of Nebraska's Big Rodeo. Don't miss all the action–visit Burwell, Nebraska, in July!"

We were excited to be there and enjoyed performing for the number of days that we were there. One drawback was the extreme heat. Barbara, Billy and Baby Chris accompanied me, and the heat proved too much for her. The good doctor allowed them to stay in his air-conditioned office, and that made her stay a little more comfortable. The rest of us pitched our tents, stacked our muskets, cooked our food over open fires, and just really enjoyed ourselves. When we performed mock battles, I didn't always wear my uniform. Sometimes, I would dress as an Indian, and my son Billy would join me as well, dressed as an Indian. Whenever we visited small towns in Nebraska to participate in a parade or put on a show, the townsfolk treated us like royalty. We were invited to participate in the Bicentennial Celebration in Washington D.C., on Independence Day, 1976. We discussed it and came to the conclusion that if we went to Washington, we would just be one more outfit of the dozens that would be there. We decided we would be appreciated more if we stayed in Nebraska on Independence Day and performed for the locals. On July 4, 1976, we performed in four separate

towns, including two parades (one in the beginning, the other at the end to fit it all in). We started off the first town's parade, jumped into our vehicles and drove to the next town to put on a show, jumped in the vehicles again to get to the next town and put on another show, and then back in the vehicles to get to the final town in time to bring up the rear of their parade. I recall it being a very tiring day but well worth it.

We did enjoy a few other activities while at Offutt. There was lots to do. We enjoyed things like Peony Park, an amusement park that opened in 1919 and closed in 1994. Today, it is a strip mall; the Omaha Henry Doorly Zoo, one of the finest in the country; Ak-sar-ben (Nebraska spelled backward) racetrack and arena (although I don't recall if we ever went there); the College World Series at Rosenblatt Stadium (due to COVID-19, 2020 is the first year the series has been canceled since its inception in 1950). If you didn't like those things, you could go fishing, which we did a few times, usually with Dick and Jewels (remember New Year's Eve). Dick was an outdoorsman and liked doing those things. One show that we attended was the Bill Gaither Trio show. One of their featured performers was a young lady by the name of Sandi Patti, who was making her debut with them. She sang *"We Shall Behold Him"* with such a beautiful voice it brought the house down. If you ever heard her sing it, you know what I mean. If you haven't, well, you're really missing something. Weeks later, the song kept going through my head. At least the melody. I couldn't remember the name, the singer, or the words. The only words I could remember were "face to face." I called a local radio station to see if they could help, and the DJ recommended I call this DJ who worked at a college radio station. He told me if anyone knew the song I was talking about, it would be him. I called the fellow up, and sure enough, he was able to identify the song with the little information I gave him. He told me the lady's  name was Sandi Patti, and I should be able to find her album at the Christian bookstore. I did find the album. I bought it for the one song, but Barbara loved the entire album. So I bought her next one, and the one after that. We ended up with about five or six.

Some things we didn't enjoy, like the May 6, 1975 tornado that ripped through downtown Omaha. It was shortly after 4:00 PM. I believe Billy had just gotten home from school. We heard the warning on the radio and were told to take cover immediately. Fortunately, the basement in our home was designed with tornados in mind, and it had a reinforced SW corner, which provided additional protection. We grabbed some blankets and went down in that corner until we heard the all-clear. Around 5:00 PM, as we heard the all-clear, the phone was ringing, and I ran upstairs to answer it. It was my mother calling from Massachusetts. She had seen the tornado on the news and was calling to see if we were okay. Fortunately, we were as the tornado hit a few miles east of us and went straight up 72nd Street, crossing Dodge, some of the most business-oriented areas of Omaha. Since I had a bus license, I was able to participate in the cleanup by transporting personnel from the base to the damaged areas. It was a mess. I remember one individual commenting that a Catholic Church must have been hit because there were bingo cards all over the place. But so much damage. I believe it was one of the most costly tornados of the time, causing over a Billion of today's dollars in damage. That wasn't the only tornado we lived through. Another time, we were at the base lake for an event. It may have been a Fourth of July event. I had parked the car on the side, at an angle and slightly in a ditch. It started to rain pretty hard, so we all got in the car. A lady with a little child asked if she could sit in the car  until the storm passed, and we said sure. After a while, one of the security personnel was coming along, telling people to get in the ditch as a tornado had been spotted. When he came to us, he saw the mother with the little child and told us we could stay in the car, but if we felt any movement, to get out quickly and get in the ditch. Nothing happened, and we found out later that a small spout had formed over the lake but didn't cause any damage.

 We also had our fair share of winter weather. One snowstorm was so bad it covered the doors, so we couldn't open them, and I had to use the garage overhead to get out so I could shovel the snow. Speaking of cold and snow, there was one embarrassing moment that I recall. It involved a young lady who worked with me by the name of Easter Perkins. Easter happened to be a woman of color or an African-American woman. One spring, it was so cold that the weatherman was predicting possible snow for Easter. Without thinking, I'm going about the office, singing softly, "I'm dreaming of a white Easter…" All of a sudden, Easter looks up and says, "Excuse me!"

I had my first introduction to Amway during this time as one of my later bosses, Major Thelin, and his wife were involved with it. We did sign up under them to buy products but never did anything with it. And didn't renew. We might have pursued it further, but we were destined to leave a few months later. We were reintroduced to it over ten years later, and hopefully, we'll get to that later in the book.

Up until now, all my supervisors were men, but I had a short period where my supervisor was Captain Sharon Gero. She was the executive officer, and I was given the additional duty of taking over the responsibilities of the Chief Clerk in the Orderly Room, as well as maintaining my regular duties.

One time, we did have a serious incident in which a pilot was killed. I can't remember all the details after all these years. I do recall that a pilot was having difficulty with his aircraft and had to eject. Unfortunately, when he ejected, the aircraft was at a turn angle, and instead of going up, the pilot ejected into the side of a hill, being killed. The aircraft itself landed with amazingly little damage. I do remember my commander coming into the office, and I asked him why he wasn't out at the crash site, and he wasn't even aware of what was going on. He immediately rushed out. Later, we were all briefed concerning the fact that he should have been notified and contacted immediately, so some procedures had to be changed.

Another noteworthy event was a visit from President Gerald Ford. Unfortunately, I can't remember all the details. He may even have still been vice president at the time of the visit. I did have one picture, but it was lost over the years, so I have no documentation of his visit.

I was rewarded for my work efforts with two things, as well as promotions. One was receiving recognition as PRIDE NCO of the Quarter, April-June 1973. The other was the receipt of the Meritorious Service Medal.

I finally did get my orders to leave in November 1976. We packed up and headed out to Pease AFB, New Hampshire. I finally got to the East Coast.

See you in the next chapter.

CHAPTER SIX: PEASE AFB NEW HAMPSHIRE

"Jesus answered and said unto him, 'Verily, verily, I say unto thee, Except a man be born again, he cannot see the Kingdom of God.'"

John 3:3

Pease AFB was the closest I had been stationed to home as it was only two hours away. It also has quite a history going back to the 1930s when it was established as Portsmouth Municipal Airport. With the onset of WWII, it was closed to civilian traffic as part of the East Coast defense measures. Subsequently, it was used by the Civil Air Patrol and U.S. Navy until the Air Force took control in 1951 as a Strategic Air Command (SAC) base. After some expansion of facilities, it was renamed Portsmouth AFB, formally opening on 30 June 1956. On 7 September (our son Billy's birthday) 1957, it was renamed Pease AFB in honor of Captain Harl Pease, Jr, a New Hampshire native and a WWII Medal of Honor winner. In 1958, the 509th Bombardment Wing arrived from Walker AFB, NM, with the mission of Strategic Warfare in the event of war. It was to this command that I was assigned. The Wing underwent a number of mission and aircraft changes over the years. In December 1970, the Wing resumed flying training with the FB-111 and assumed FB-111 alert commitments. I was assigned as Wing Administrative Clerk, Maintenance Administration and had duties similar to my previous assignments. These included maintaining publications and forms, handling incoming/outgoing correspondence, preparing reports, maintaining office equipment, ordering and maintaining supplies, inspecting publications and files, maintaining recall rosters (very important since we were an alert base), monitoring suspenses, providing reproduction capabilities, and any other duties a clerk may provide. Over the years that I was there, I also assumed several additional duties, which included Alternate Unit Safety NCO, a member of the Unit Advisory Council and Base Advisory Council, and an inspector and trainer. We enjoyed being at Pease and thought of retiring there, but unfortunately, the base was closed in 1988 as part of the Secretary of Defense's Base Realignment and Closure (BRAC) process. Today, a portion of Pease is home to the Air National Guard, but the majority of it is Pease International Tradeport, which includes Portsmouth International Airport at Pease. Many events happened while we were stationed here, and I will attempt to hit the highlights both on the job on in my personal life.

Let's first get the job out of the way since that was the least "important" of the things that took place. For most of my time there, I worked for MSgt Donald Keever, NCOIC of Maintenance Administration. He was a good supervisor, and I enjoyed working for him. I recall one of the things he taught me was how to "eat" fried chicken. We often ordered lunch and ate in the office, and this particular time, we ordered fried chicken. When he saw how much "meat" I had left on the bones, he showed me what the bone should look like when finished. Nothing but bone. He loved fried chicken. It wasn't until my final year there that he retired, and I assumed his duties as NCOIC, working directly under the Deputy Commander for Maintenance, Col Thomas Wilkinson. Besides our normal activities, inspections were a big pain. We had annual Inspector General (IG) Inspections, Commander's Annual Facilities Inspection (CAFI), and the big Operational Readiness Inspections (ORI). During these inspections, all aspects of our operations were looked at. In my case, it involved making certain all publications, operating instructions, files, and so on were in good shape. Fortunately, we always received great ratings, which resulted in me having to spend much time helping other units get their areas corrected. This led to a few Letters of Appreciation from the Commander.

During this period, the Air Force established what was called the War Skills Program. This involved having wartime "non-essential" personnel receive training in more critical career fields. For example, during wartime, many of the security and maintenance personnel may be deployed, thereby leaving the base without their services. The non-essential personnel who were trained in their areas would step in and fill their shoes while they were deployed. I was selected to be trained in the maintenance field, where I received training on operating heavy equipment such as bulldozers, front-end loaders, dump trucks, etc. This required a two-week initial training and then various training consisting of 3-day periods throughout the year. Those trained in the security police would spend their training days patrolling the base and performing security checks. I got to spend my training days digging holes and filling them again. It would have been much more effective if we had spent our training doing actual work, but that was the fault of those designing the training. At any rate, I enjoyed learning and operating the equipment. Unfortunately, I never used my training to my advantage once I left Pease.

As always, the job wasn't enough to keep me busy, so I got involved in other activities. One such activity was going back to college to get my degree. Since I dropped out after my third year, I never received a diploma, so I took this opportunity to finish by enrolling in the University of New Hampshire by correspondence. Before I was reassigned, I had received my Bachelors Degree in Business Management (Cum Laude) from the University of New Hampshire School of Continuing Studies.

I also spent a couple of years as a Webelos Scout leader for Cub Pack 816 since our son Billy was now old enough to join.

We lived on base housing at 126 White Birch Drive, and we made a lot of good friends while stationed here. The most important thing that happened was our return to the Lord. Remember when we got married, since Barbara had been divorced and we couldn't get married in the Catholic Church, we basically stopped all church affiliation. Well, we met some folks here who were not only involved in the base church but also in the Charismatic Movement. Two couples in particular, the O'Briens and the Thurbers. Barbara got involved with them at first, attending prayer meetings and being introduced to the Charismatic Movement. I was very skeptical and, ashamed to say, I teased Barbara quite a bit, even to the point where I had her in tears. One day, I was challenged by Betsy O'Brien to attend one of the

sessions where she was going to give a talk. I reluctantly agreed, but it turned out to be one of the best decisions I could have made. It didn't happen immediately, but eventually, I accepted Jesus as my Lord and Savior and was baptized in the Holy Spirit. Barbara had already done this. On Dec 25, 1979, I received a Bible signed by the four people who "saved my life." Barbara, Julie & George Thurber, and Betsy O'Brien.

This brought us back into the church and renewed our involvement. I became a Sunday School or, as the Catholics call it, Confraternity of Christian Doctrine (CCD) Teacher for the 7th and 8th graders. My Christian walk was further enhanced by attendance at a Cursillo Weekend held at St. Paul's Retreat House in Augusta, Maine.

I need to spend a few moments explaining the Cursillo.

The Cursillos in Christianity (Spanish: *Cursillos de Cristiandad*, "Short courses of Christianity") is a movement that was started back in the 1940s by Eduardo Bonnin Aguilo (currently under consideration for sainthood by the Catholic Church). It all began when a group of men dedicated themselves to bringing the young men of the island of Majorca, Spain, to know Christ better. Following the Spanish Civil War, a pilgrimage was planned by the Catholic Action Group of Spain to the shrine of St. James at Compostella to provide a time for the young men and women of Spain to dedicate themselves in a renewed way to the working of the apostolate. This pilgrimage had to be postponed several times because of WWII but was finally scheduled in 1948 (that magical year). That pilgrimage set a tone of restlessness and dissatisfaction with spiritual lukewarmness. It also created a "spirit of brotherhood" among those planning the pilgrimage. It was these leaders of the young men's branch of Catholic Action of Majorca who were the developers of the Cursillo method. This group worked together as a team from the very beginning. They prayed together, shared their Christian lives together, studied together, planned together, acted together, and evaluated what they had done together. It remained a localized movement until 1955, when Bishop Hervas (one of the founders) was transferred to Ciudad Real. This was the beginning of the dispersion of the original team, and thus, the movement began to spread, coming to the United States in 1957. Father Gabriel Fernandes, who made his weekend under the original founders, came to Waco, Texas, in 1955, where he met two Spanish airmen, Bernardo Vadel and Agustin Palomino, who were being trained with the United States Air Force. These three put the first weekend on in Waco and formed a school of leaders. As these two airmen traveled, they took Cursillo with them and by 1959, it had spread throughout Texas and Phoenix, Arizona. Also, in 1959, the National Magazine, "*Ultreya,*" was founded, and the first national convention of spiritual directors was held. Following these events, the movement spread quickly throughout the southwest and then to New York, Ohio, San Francisco, Indiana, Michigan, New Mexico and even Florida. Soon, every

Diocese in the country had been introduced to Cursillo. It has undergone several refinements since its inception, but when I attended, it consisted of three days (Friday, Saturday and Sunday) with five talks *(rollos)* per day given by laymen and clergy. The subjects or titles of the talks include piety, study, action, leaders, environment, laity, and Christian community. It focuses on teaching laymen to become effective Christian leaders and to take what they have learned during those three days back into the world in what we called the "Fourth Day." The "Fourth Day" consists of weekly group reunions by Cursillistas (men and women who have attended the weekend), which is to help their spiritual growth following their weekend experience. The three main areas of focus are Piety, Study and Action, and each member of the group has the opportunity to address how these areas were impacted by him or her the previous week. In addition to the weekly group reunions, there is also a monthly gathering of all the groups in the area, which is called an *"Ultreya."* It is difficult to explain the effect the weekend has on someone, but it so impacted me that I helped introduce it to the bases at my next two assignments, Offutt and Germany. I'll talk more about it when I get to those chapters.

While we're on the subject of religion and spiritual development, I must add that Barbara began procedures at this time to have her previous marriage annulled so we could be reinstated fully into the Catholic Church. After discussing the facts of her first marriage with our parish priest, he felt that she really had grounds for an annulment. It took a long time and a few assignments down the road, but finally, on 14 October 1988, the Tribunal of the Archdiocese of Military Services decreed that the marriage was null and void. More on that later.

Another major event was the birth of my son, Adam James, on 9 April 1978. We had a friend who had a baby girl at the same time and had named her with the same initials, AJ.

Not all major events were pleasant. In October 1978, I received a phone call from my brother, Dennis, in the middle of the night. He informed me that our younger brother, Arthur, had died. The news was devastating, and I remember sitting on the edge of the bed and crying. I couldn't believe it. Evidently, he was at a party, and all of a sudden, he keeled over. His friends thought he was joking, but unfortunately, he wasn't. I think the official cause of death was heart failure, but my mother always believed that Agent Orange, from the time he was stationed at Da Nang, Vietnam, was the contributing factor in his death. He was only 27. Arrangements for his funeral and burial were handled by the same firm that took care of my father, and Junior was buried next to him at Mosswood Cemetery. He left behind four sons, Troy, Jamie, William, and Christian. Being only two hours from home was a blessing because it allowed me to return quickly and often.

Let's get back to some more pleasant events. How about eating out? One of our favorite places was Newick's Lobster House (or Seafood) Restaurant) in Dover. The food was always great, and you received lots of it for the price. It wasn't fancy. The food was served on a large paper plate piled high.

Our favorite was the full-stomach clams. I recently looked them up on the web, and unfortunately, most of the reviewers complained that it is not what it used to be. It was once world-famous. As you stood in line to get in, the wall was loaded with business cards of people from all over who had visited there. Now, the reviewers were saying the service was terrible. The food was cold, the fries soggy, prices too high. Well, times do change. One time, our friends George and Julie went there to eat and brought home their "doggy bag." Before returning to the base, they stopped by the shopping mall, which was across the street from the base. While they were in there, their beautiful classic automobile (Mercury Cougar) was stolen. I remember Julie being mad because the Newick's leftovers were still in the car. Don't believe George ever got his car back.

Besides our involvement in spiritual matters with George and Julie, we spent a lot of free time with them, usually playing board games. As Catholic Christians, we had not yet come to the conclusion that drinking was "wrong," so we would often have a beer while playing games. One time, we were playing a game where you would send someone back home if you landed in their space. I landed in Julie's space and sent her back to the beginning. She pretended to be mad and picked up my beer stein, which was empty and pretended to toss the beer into my face. Later, she had gotten up for some reason and left the table, and while she was gone, I refilled my beer stein. Since it was made of metal, you couldn't see inside it. I again landed on one of her spaces and sent her home, and she grabbed the beer stein and, not realizing it was full, tossed it in my face. All four of us were shocked, her probably most of all. She jumped up and started apologizing so much. We were all cracking up. For weeks after that, she was always waiting for me to retaliate. Keeping her waiting was retaliation enough.

While stationed there, Chris and Adam developed some medical problems, mainly ear infections, and had to be treated by the doctors quite a bit. During my fourth year, I received an unaccompanied 1-year assignment to Turkey. That meant that Barbara and the kids would not be able to go with me. We started to make arrangements for Barbara and the kids to remain in base housing while I was gone so the boys could continue to receive the medical care they needed. Meanwhile, we and our church friends were in heavy prayer that I could get out of the assignment. Miraculously, the assignment was canceled. It was immediately followed by another assignment, this time to Germany, but this also got mysteriously canceled. Then I received a call from HQ SAC at Offutt AFB asking me if I would like to return to Offutt and be assigned at the Headquarters. Having just gotten out of two questionable assignments, I jumped at the chance for fear that the next assignment might not be pleasant. And thus, in April 1980, we prepared to leave again. Besides leaving with a college degree, I left with another stripe and was now a Technical Sergeant or E6. And, of course, another son. So now, we were a Party of Five.

I'll see you back in Omaha.

CHAPTER SEVEN: BACK TO OMAHA

"And the Lord, he it is that doth go before thee; he will be with thee, he will not fail thee, neither forsake thee: fear not, neither be dismayed."

Deuteronomy 31:8

We arrived in Omaha in April 1980 and stayed in temporary housing until we could get assigned to Base Housing in Capehart, located about a mile from the actual base, which we eventually did get. The address was 12226 S. 27th Ave, Omaha, but it was far from downtown Omaha.

I was assigned to HQs SAC, specifically, the Missile Tactics Division or SACOS/XOBM. My duty title was NCOIC, Missile Tactics Division, with the responsibilities of managing the administrative support program and additionally providing administrative support to the Joint Strategic Target Planning Staff (JSTPS). This was a unique assignment because the office area was shared by two parallel organizations. The XO was the Air Force HQ SAC portion, and the JSTPS was the equivalent but with multiple agencies represented. This section had its own leadership, which alternated between services. For example, when I was assigned there, the XO was Air Force Major General Christopher Adams. Interesting because my two sons were Christopher and Adam. The JSTPS was commanded by a Navy Admiral. In the area that we shared at the XOBM level, my boss was AF Lt Col McLaughlin, and the opposite side was a Navy Commander (I don't remember his name). Eventually, they did get their own admin support, but for a while, it was all on me. There was a time when the JSTPS/JPTM seat was empty, and the XOBM chief (my boss) had to fill both seats. This was interesting because if my boss came out with a paper that had to be coordinated through both sides of the house, it would have to go up the chain on the XO side, that is, from the XOBM to the XOB to the XO and then across to the JP and then down to JPT and JPTM which was back on my boss' desk. I had to provide support to ten officers, both Air Force and Navy. If you recall, way back in the Vietnam days, I told you I had lost a lot of respect for officers due to the incident at the club. Well, working for these officers helped to build back my respect. They were all hand-selected for this assignment (as was I) and were well-deserving of respect.

I hadn't been there but a few months when one of the officers suggested I apply for Officer Candidate School (OCS). I reluctantly agreed, but over several months, my applications were denied, initially because there were no openings in the area where I was experienced (Administrative). The final rejection was because I was past the age limit. I do believe that was a blessing in disguise because, looking back, I really enjoyed the path that I was on and don't know how well I would have done as an officer.

There really isn't a whole lot to say about the job. I mentioned that I worked with a lot of officers. I also worked with some civilians. Working for both the XO and the JP meant that I was dual-hatted. Probably the worst part of the job was being responsible for so much highly classified material. We had ten safes filled with Top Secret and above documentation, and everything had to be strictly controlled. Any failures here could result in dire consequences, especially for my career. We had one Captain that worried me a lot. He was a very talented individual, and I liked him a lot. He was the one that initially encouraged me to apply for OCS. Because of his abilities, he was appointed to a very special project, which was highly classified and controlled. The problem was because he was such a go-getter and was determined to get things accomplished, he often bypassed some of the security safety measures. I always said that one day, he would either be a General or end up in jail. Don't know whatever became of him.

One of the tasks that I was given was to hire a secretary for the JSTPS/JPTM office. Although our site was assigned an NCO (namely, me), the JSTPS side required a civilian. I interviewed a number of individuals and narrowed the selection down to two for the JPTM to select from. The one selected ended up doing a terrific job and relieving me of a lot of work.

There were a couple of major faux pas that I committed while there. One of my "duties" was to prepare coffee for all the office personnel. We had two coffee urns in the office, and I would make sure that one of them was always filled with coffee. This one time, water had been left in one of the urns, but I hadn't used it for a while because I always made coffee in the same urn. This time, I was using the other urn, and since it was already filled with water, I didn't bother to replace it. The coffee turned out terrible. As it happened, the water had sat in the urn so long mold had formed. I thought everyone would be sick when they found out what I had done. The second big mistake I made had to do with the lock on the door. We had been having a problem easily closing it for some time, and numerous requests to the maintenance department went unheeded. It still worked okay, but it took a little bit of effort to close it. The solution was very simple, so I decided to fix it myself. One day, after everyone had left and I was alone, I took it apart, fixed what was wrong, and reassembled it. It worked fine, at least when operating it from the inside. The next morning, when I got to work, everyone was standing outside the door. Maintenance crews had a step ladder and were attempting to climb through the ceiling to get to the other side. What had happened was when I reassembled it, the "male" portion didn't go directly into the "female" portion but went on the side, so when you tried to turn it with the key, it wouldn't work. The key would turn, but the unlocking mechanism wouldn't. After a while, they got it fixed, but I did get my butt chewed. Maintenance told me, "We don't come in and try to do your work, so don't you try to do ours."

In November/December of 1980, I had the opportunity to attend and complete the Strategic Air Command Noncommissioned Officer Academy, Class 81-B, held at Barksdale AFB, LA. While at the Academy, I decided to overcome the fear of public speaking by entering the Academy's Speech Competition. Individuals would compete and possibly advance at three levels. We were each assigned to a Flight. There were two flights in each Squadron and three Squadrons in the class. I won at the Flight Level and went on to compete at the Squadron Level. I did win at this level also, but I strongly believe that I won because I had a better speech than my competitor. I thought that he was a much better speaker than me. I even enlisted his assistance to help me prepare for the next level. When the competition began, it was decided that a microphone would not be used. We were in a big auditorium, and I'm afraid I did not project well enough to win the competition. At least, that's what I was told. Many towards the rear of the auditorium could not hear my speech.

Additionally, I decided to complete the First Sergeant Career Field Course with the intention of maybe applying for a First Sergeant position at some time. I passed it with a 99% score. Although I never officially became a First Sergeant, I was able to fill in for the First Sergeant both at this assignment and my subsequent one.

As always, I couldn't be satisfied just working on the job, so I got involved in a number of activities. I worked with the Special Olympics and was involved with the Tiger Cubs Branch of the Cub Scouts.

The first time I worked as a chaperone at the Special Olympics, I was assigned to this one kid who was immensely overweight and very slow. I remember one night, he was going to take a bath. He filled the tub to the brim and then jumped in. Water everywhere. As I liked to move fast, it was very tiring with him because of his slowness. But we managed. The following year, I got just the opposite. I was assigned to two teenage boys (a part of a set of triplets, the third being a girl). These two boys were constantly on the go, and I had one heck of a time keeping up with them. I honestly don't know which year was more tiring. But both were enjoyable.

I was also coordinator for the Offutt Chapter of the Nocturnal Adoration Society (NAS). The Nocturnal Adoration Society of the United States is an association for Catholic men and women. It was established in accordance with church Law on November 28, 1928, and is officially affiliated with the Archconfraternity for Nocturnal Adoration established in Rome in 1810. The Nocturnal Adoration Society has a fourfold purpose: To provide a fervent response to Christ's invitation to keep prayerful vigil with Him as he asked His disciples to do in the Garden of Gethsemane (Mathew 26:38-40; Mark 14:37,38; Luke 22:40-46). To deepen the experience of communion with Christ Eucharistic, as He continues His self-offering and saving influence. To live more consciously and actively the full significance of the Eucharist as the sacrament of charity and unity for the Church and the World. To provide an opportunity for the bringing together in prayer men and their families of our communities. (From the Constitution of the Nocturnal Adoration Society)

It involved the exposition and adoration of the Blessed Sacrament throughout the night. We did it only on the first Friday of the month. As coordinator, I was responsible for maintaining the schedule. It would start about 10:00 PM on Thursday and go until 7:00 AM on Friday. We would schedule 1-2 individuals for 1-2 hour shifts. If I could not fill the time slots, I had to be there. If your relief didn't show up, you would have to stay for another shift until relief came. We could not leave the Blessed Sacrament exposed without someone being there. Most of the time, we filled the slots easily, but there were times when I did stay up all night.

Probably the biggest thing that I was involved in was the Cursillo. In order to maintain your spiritual growth after going on a Cursillo weekend, you were supposed to meet weekly with your group and review your piety, study and action of the previous week. When we got to Omaha, we didn't have a group to meet with until one day in the commissary parking lot, I spotted a car with a *"De Colores"* bumper sticker. *"De Colores"* (of the colors) was a phrase that Cursillistas used to greet one another and to show that we had shared a similar experience.  I went over to the car and introduced myself to the driver, and he invited us to join their group, and that was the start of a beautiful friendship. We were warmly welcomed into their group. (Walt and Miriam, Barry and Mary, Linda and Bill)(Linda and Bill are not in the photo) Somewhere along the line, we decided we wanted to put on a Cursillo weekend there at Offutt and started working towards it. It involved a lot of work. We established the Offutt AFB Military Cursillo Center Secretariat, which developed into the Regional Cursillo Center (Michigan, Minnesota, Wisconsin, South Dakota, North Dakota, and Nebraska), and I became the secretary, with Barry being the Director and Father Emil Falcone as Spiritual Director. Our efforts resulted in the receipt of a Certificate of Appreciation from the

 Military Vicar General. With the organization being established, we were able to sponsor a weekend at Offutt. This led to an expansion into the civilian community, with more weekends being put on. Due to some of the changes that folks wanted to make to the weekend to accommodate others who were not Catholic, there was a division. The Cursillo organization had very strict guidelines, and if you did not follow them, you could not call yourself a Cursillo. What happened was that it ended up being called a Christians Encounter Christ (CEC) weekend, utilizing basically the same tools. We still kept our Cursillo affiliation but helped the civilian church establish the CEC.

Our group continued to meet weekly, and we had a monthly meeting when all the groups in the area would get together.

One week, we had a visit from two of my sisters, Anna and Terry. It was such a pleasant surprise to have family visiting. One thing I remember about their visit was taking them to Fr. Flannagan's Boys Town. Fr. Flannagan' Boys Town was established in 1921 by Fr. Edward J. Flannagan as an orphanage for boys in the Omaha area. Two phrases identified with Fr. Flannagan and Boys Town are, "There's no such thing as a bad boy" and "He ain't heavy, he's my brother." Boys Town was highlighted in the 1938 film, *"Boys Town,"* starring Spencer Tracy as  Father Flannagan and featuring Mickey Rooney as one of the boys. Tracy reprised his role in a 1941

sequel, "*Men of Boys Town*". Anna almost burned down the house by putting a bag on top of the stove. Just another little adventure.

Besides receiving another stripe, making me a Master Sergeant, I was selected as XO NCO of the year in 1981 and XOBM Enlisted Professional Performer of the Quarter. Other accolades include letters of appreciation from Major General Harley A. Hughes and Vice Admiral P. F. Carter for my involvement with the Mobile Joint Nuclear Planning Element during GLOBAL SHIELD 83. My going away "trophies" included a certificate making me an Admiral in the Nebraska Navy from JSTPS and signed by the Governor of Nebraska and The Legion of the Mole-Hole. The name Mole-Hole came from the fact that our headquarters were located deep underground in the SAC Building and was commonly referred to as the Mole-Hole. I also received the Air Force Commendation Medal.

A couple of weeks before we were scheduled to leave, we were having our monthly Cursillo Ultreya meeting, and I was the speaker. I remember giving my testimony and talking about how I felt the Lord had been with me throughout my whole life. He had kept me out of the drug and free love scene of the 60s. He protected me during my tour of Vietnam, not only keeping me safe from the enemy but also from engaging with the Vietnamese woman in a manner that I would regret, and basically was guiding me all through my assignments. I also said something to the effect that, in a way, I felt my life was boring and lacked excitement. That turned out to be a big mistake.

On the day that the movers were coming to pack up all our stuff, I got a call from my sister, Mary, from Iowa. She had left her husband and was on her way to Arizona with her children (and four cats, which her children had hidden in the trunk without her knowledge). Her wallet had been stolen with all her money. She asked if she could stop by since she would be passing right through Omaha and if I could help her out. Of course, I told her yes. She arrived at my house while the movers were packing everything. After the movers left, we were getting ready to go to the hotel when my sister could not find her purse. She had laid it down on a table, and the movers packed it. We found it in one of the drawers when we got to Germany. Now she had no money, no keys for her car (they were in the purse), no medication (she was an epileptic) and didn't know what she would do. Our first problem was getting keys for the car since the cats were in the trunk. We finally got the trunk opened, and unfortunately, the cats were in bad shape, and three of them ended up dying. We managed to get a key made for the car, and I told her she was not going to California but would go back to Massachusetts with us, and I would cover her expenses. After we spent a couple of nights in a motel, we headed back to Massachusetts, with me placing everything on my credit card. I mention this only because it came back to bite me later on when I was getting ready to go to Germany.

On the way home, I wanted to stop in New Jersey to visit the family of a friend of mine who had died in a swimming accident at Offutt. I had been trying to convince this individual to attend a Cursillo weekend, and after some time, he finally agreed. A short time after he had attended the weekend and gave his life to the Lord, he was in the pool and drowned. Never figured out what happened because he was a very athletic and proficient swimmer. It was assumed he had some kind of cramp or something. One of the men in our Cursillo group, a LtCol, actually flew with his body back to New Jersey and met his family. I wanted to meet them and tell them what I knew about their son and the type of person he was. It was learned after his death that he had been doing many charitable things for needy folks, which no one even knew about. We did meet the family, and while I was talking with them, somehow, Mary's last cat got out of the car and was attacked by a dog and killed.

Well, we finally reached home. Mary was able to fix things with her husband, and we spent a few weeks on leave enjoying ourselves with our families.

After our vacation was over and it was time to leave for Germany, things really started to get "exciting," if that's the word I want to use. My plan was to load up the station wagon and drive to Boston, where my sister Anna lived. I was going to sell her the station wagon and rent a car to drive to McGuire AFB since we were flying out of there to go to Germany. Unfortunately, I found out that my only credit card was maxed out from the trip back from Omaha, and I was unable to rent a car. We ended up having to take a train from Boston to New York, where we would catch a bus to McGuire. "We" included me, Barbara, Billy, Chris and Adam, with each of us having three bags apiece. That's a lot of luggage. Due to certain circumstances, we arrived at New York's Grand Central Station late, and the last bus to McGuire had already left. I sat there pondering what to do. We could either spend the night at the station or see if we could find a hotel to stay at. Barbara did not want to spend the night at the station, and I couldn't blame her. Finally, a cab driver became aware of our dilemma and came over and told us for 100 dollars (1984 dollars), he would get us to McGuire. I was doubtful, but he assured me he could. Somehow, he got all our luggage and the five of us in his cab. It was very crowded, and I think he damaged his trunk when he tried to close it. But true to his word, he got us to McGuire. We checked in at the terminal, had our baggage loaded on the plane and waited for departure. After some time, we finally boarded the plane and waited, and waited, and waited. They eventually had us get off the plane and go back into the terminal. It turned out the aircraft needed a part that maintenance did not have available, and they had to have it flown in. We waited for hours before the part arrived and was installed. At last, we were ready to go, and we reboarded the plane. I don't remember how many hours we ended up waiting before we were allowed to board. While waiting, I realized that I had no hat with my uniform because it was in my luggage. I had to be in uniform to fly on the military flight, so I had kept my uniform out but forgot the hat. There was a store at the terminal, but they had no enlisted hats, only officer flight caps, which were different from the enlisted because they had a silver braid on them. I ended up buying the officer's cap and then sitting in the terminal with a razor blade, cutting the braid off. Well, we finally were ready for takeoff and boarded the plane, totally exhausted with a long flight ahead of us. Let me get some sleep on the plane, and I'll pick up the story in the next chapter.

CHAPTER EIGHT: OFF TO GERMANY AND HAHN AB

"For here have we no continuing city, but we seek one to come."

Hebrews 13:14

When we finally arrived in Germany, we were a ragtag group. We truly looked like a mess. Not only did I have a hat with the braid torn off, but I had forgotten to put the brass back on my uniform after I had gotten it back from the cleaners. None of us had gotten much sleep in the last 48 hours, and it showed. The young lieutenant who was there to pick us up told me later he had no idea what the Air Force had sent him.

His name was Lieutenant Keo Zaiger. A young lieutenant straight out of school was sent to Hahn to make preparations for a new organization that was being formed. He was told that they were sending him an administrator to help him get things set up. He had been having a difficult time with all the red tape. He couldn't get the things he needed because he didn't have the proper paperwork, and he couldn't get the proper paperwork because he had no administrator to order the forms he needed. Kind of a Catch 22. He needed a vehicle and couldn't get one, so he finally contacted a general at Ramstein, who told the motor pool to give him a vehicle. He believes they gave him the worst one they had, a beat-up VW bus. And that's the vehicle we had for the first few weeks. More on that later.

Well, we all piled into the van and headed for Hahn Air Base to begin our tour. Hahn AB was built in 1952 in the Hunsruck of Germany and remained active until 1994. Today, it is a civilian airport. In case you are wondering what the Hunsruck is, it is an area located in the Southeastern part of Germany surrounded by the Moselle-Saar, Nahe, and Rhine river valleys and the Taunus mountains. Initially, we stayed in temporary lodging until we could locate a place to stay. Although my orders identified my duty assignment as the 7451st Tactical Intelligence Sq (USAFE), Hahn Air Base, my actual work location was approximately 12 miles north of the base at a place in the middle of the woods called Wueschheim Com or as it was known, Metro Tango. The area was already involved with intelligence gathering, but our unit, which would eventually be known as the Tactical Reconnaissance Exploration Demonstration System (TREDS), dealt with images from the TR-1/U-2.

Working with Lt Zaiger, I had the responsibility to prepare the way for a major new initiative in tactical intelligence "from the ground up." Our unit would eventually grow to over 600, including command support for over 100 civilian employees for two U.S. contractors. I had to create all administrative functions and all support items. This included developing a welcome package for the newcomers, developing an orientation program, maintaining a $150,000 office equipment account, setting up programs to assist the newcomers in finding off-base housing and providing all individuals with identification cards, vehicle registration, and ration cards (which were strictly controlled because of their sensitivity). After a couple of years, I had to also assume the responsibilities of the First Sergeant. Responsibilities also included establishing and monitoring a Weight Management Program. Other regular programs that I had to monitor, especially later on, were the Performance Report Monitoring Program, the Awards and Decorations Program, the Leave Processing Program, and any other administrative program you can think of. Eventually, my administrative branch grew to five people, so I don't want you to think that I had to do all the work myself. I ended up with a very capable staff to do the actual work. My job was to supervise.

Initially, we shared a desk in an army building that was already established, but a new building was being constructed for our use. As the unit grew, some old metal trailers were brought in to give the employees a place to work until the building was finished. I believe we had about five or six of these big trailers, with the admin staff occupying one of them. The trailer that I was using almost killed me. When I opened the trailer following a rainstorm, I got a slight shock, and I reported this to the Safety division. They came out to check the trailer and found out the grounding was wrong, and the electrical current was flowing through the trailer. When I opened the door, because my feet were in water, I completed the circuit. He told me it was a wonder I wasn't electrocuted. God was and is always with me. Eventually, the new building was completed, and we moved in. It was a nice building and very comfortable to work in. The Commander was very proud of it. And then came the problem with the smokers. Because rooms were shared and not everyone was a smoker, the rule was that there would be no smoking in the rooms unless you were the only one that occupied it. The First Sergeant happened to be one who didn't share an office, and he was a smoker. So, the smokers would always be visiting the First Sergeant. This got to be a problem, so the rule was changed to no smoking in any of the workspaces, but you could smoke in the hall by the front door until the Commander came in one day and found a cigarette burn on his new carpet. OK, no smoking in the building, period. You could smoke outside in front of the building. Until a general came to visit and had to walk through a "cloud of smoke." All smokers would have to move to the break area at the back of the building. We were afraid that eventually, smokers would be moved ½ mile down the road to the old Boy Scout camp, which was used for overflow parking. Personally, I had quit smoking at this time. Actually, I never smoked in front of my children but would occasionally have a smoke when I was alone. But by this time, I had quit. It turned out that if you wanted to find out what was going on around the squadron, you hung out with the smokers because that's where all the scuttlebutt was obtained, and so I started smoking again. Eventually, I quit when we returned to the States, and I haven't smoked since.

Let's come back to the work situation later. Right now, let's talk about the family situation and getting settled. As I mentioned, we were initially in temporary quarters called Hotel Gass in the town of Buchenbueren, just outside the base, and had to find some off-base housing because it would be some time before we could get base housing. An enjoyable part of this was eating out, and there were a lot of German restaurants around (after all, this was Germany). I was able to buy a rather cheap car, an Opel

Kadett. This enabled us to look around for a home off-base. I remember one time we were looking in the town of Sohren. As we were walking around, we got hungry, so we started to look for a place to eat. I had bought a German translation book and learned enough to ask for directions, so when a German man approached us, I mustered up the best German I could and asked him for directions for a place to eat. He proceeded to tell me (in German) a place to eat, and I couldn't understand a word he said. Fortunately, he used a lot of hand gestures, so after I thanked him, we moved on and found the restaurant. We found a really nice home about ten miles from the base and about three miles from where I worked. It was a large, single-family, two-story home with a full basement, a garage, and a big backyard with a couple of fruit trees. The address was Hasericherstrasse #2, 5581 Blankenrath. I don't recall the Landlady's name, but she was a pleasant older woman. We enjoyed the home, especially the boys because they had a big backyard with fruit trees. They also enjoyed exploring the basement. This resulted in a near tragedy. One day, Chris and Adam were playing down there, and they found an old meat slicer, the kind you turn by hand while sliding the meat, similar to the one in this picture. They decided to use their ingenuity and use it as a "log mill" and try to cut some of their Lincoln logs. In the process, the tip of Adam's little finger was cut virtually off. We had to rush him the ten miles to the base hospital with Barbara holding his finger in place until we got there.

Let's take a minute or two and go back to the beginning. As the unit was starting to grow, it was one of my responsibilities to drive to Ramstein to pick up the newcomers. We still had that wonderful VW bus. One day, I was going to pick up Mark and his family (wife and two kids). When I arrived there, I needed to refuel, so I pulled up to the base gas pumps. An individual was in front of me, so when he finished, he handed me the pump. I proceeded to fill the tank when, 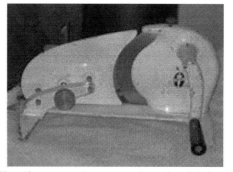 after a few seconds, I realized that the pump he handed me was a diesel pump. I stopped and told the attendant, and he said it should be all right and to just finish with the regular gas, which I did. After we loaded the folks and their baggage, we headed back to Hahn. After about 20 miles, the bus started acting up, and I pulled over at the first place that was safe to do so, a restaurant or rest area. The van would not restart. I called back to the base, and they sent someone to pick us up and return to Ramstein. As it was late in the evening, we managed to put the family up in the base hotel, while I had to stay with the vehicle, using a hand crank to empty out the tank. It proved to be fruitless, and we had to get another vehicle to return us to Hahn. An investigation was conducted to see if I was at fault because I had not done a full vehicle check before leaving Hahn, but the findings were that the vehicle was already defective, and I should not have been using it, to begin with. We eventually were able to get a new vehicle.

One of the things we saw that we thought was weird was a man urinating on the side of the autobahn. We found that wasn't that uncommon. At one of the fasching celebrations, we saw men urinating against the walls of buildings. They had few rest areas and public places where you could stop. One time in our travels, we did stop at a rest area with a bathroom. While I was in there tending to my business, a woman attendant came in and asked if I needed help. What happened was one of my sons had knocked on the door of the attendant's room, and she thought it was me.

I mentioned the Fasching (aka Karneval, Fastnacht, Fasnacht, and Fastelabend, depending on where you are in German-speaking countries). That was the big celebration time in Germany prior to Lent, similar to the Mardi Gras in New Orleans. Towns all come alive, celebrating with parades, music, and all kinds of celebrations around every corner.

Let's go back to the town of Blankenrath. We could sit in our window as the parade would go by, and they would toss candy out, trying to get it inside the window. Everyone would wave and yell out "Halloo" or something similar. It was a really fun time. Additionally, a lot of the restaurants would have sidewalk stands, and you could walk around getting sample drinks of wine and other goodies. It was truly a fun time. We liked the town of Blankenrath. Like many of the little towns, the people were really friendly. Many of them spoke English, but they would wait for you to at least attempt to speak to them in their language. Once you made that attempt, they would address you in English. One of the things that Barbara liked was that you could walk to the store every day and pick up what you wanted for that day. You didn't have to stock the fridge. Our little store was just on the corner from where we lived, a couple minute's walk. On Sunday, the church bells would ring, and the town became like a zombie movie. All the people would suddenly come out of their homes and begin the walk up the hill to the church. We attended a few times. The services were in German, but since it was a Catholic Mass, we knew what was going on and what to expect. Just couldn't understand the sermons. Most of the time, we drove to the base for church and became involved in the base parish.

Blankenrath was located about 14 kilometers from the Mozelle River and the city of Zell, and we enjoyed taking the ride down to the river. Actually, we enjoyed driving all over the area. By the way, I got rid of the little Opel and bought a used Mercedes. More about that later. One year, we drove to the Black Forest, famous for its cuckoo clocks, about a three-and-a-half hour drive. By this time, I had a VW Passat. We made it a weekend camping trip and really enjoyed it. We had one tent that the boys would stay in, and by opening the hatchback of the VW, we created a "Camper" by hanging a tarp over the back, and Barbara and I were able to sleep in the car. Unfortunately, we never bought a clock while we were there. Guess we just didn't have the money at the time. Since I already mentioned three of the cars I had while here, let me take the time to give you their history. The Opel was my first car because I needed something cheap and quick, didn't know enough about the area to shop around and didn't have the time. I saw it on sale at the base and bought it. We wanted something a little nicer to travel in, so I eventually traded it in for a nice, used, baby-blue Mercedes. I had it for one year, and it came up for inspection. Cars had to be inspected every year. The inspector found a lot of rust on it, and that was one thing that could cause you to fail inspection. So, I got it patched up and took it back for reinspection. This time, the inspector went even deeper and found more rust in the floor of the trunk, which was covered by a floor mat. Because he had failed to find it during the first inspection, he said he would go ahead and pass me, but he guaranteed me it would not pass the next year's inspection. But I did have a whole year to replace it. One day, I received a call from a friend of mine from church who was getting ready to rotate back to the States and he asked me to meet him on base. I drove to the base during my lunch hour and met him. He said he knew that I was looking for another car and said I could have his VW Passat if I wanted it. He said I could take it, get it inspected, drive it for a while and then send him whatever I thought it was worth. It turned out to be a really good deal and a really good car. We did a lot of traveling in it, including the trip to the Black Forest. One day, I was on my way to the base to attend a bowling game with the team. It was a wet day, and for some reason, the German work crews decided to mow the sides of the road. The main road between the base and our work site was a two-way highway, one lane going in each direction. The type of equipment the Germans used to mow the grass was a truck with a long, extended arm with a mower attached to the end. They would drive slowly down the side of the highway with the mower extended. Naturally, this caused the traffic to get backed up. You had to stay behind the truck unless you had a clear opportunity to pass. Along the side of the highway was a row of trees spaced about thirty feet apart. Here, once again, the Lord was watching over and protecting me. Because the traffic was backed up, I was sitting in a long line, and I happened to glance at my rear-view mirror and see this car coming fairly fast. I quickly assessed that he was not going to stop in time and turned my wheel to the right to move out of his way and give him a little more stopping distance. He rammed the rear of my car, sending it flying into the field between two of the trees. The rear of the car received extensive damage, although there was no damage to the front. Had I not turned the wheel, I would have been pushed into the vehicle ahead of me. If the angle hadn't been just right, I would have plowed into one of the trees. The insurance company totaled the car, so now I had to get another one. My son Chris tells me the first tool he and his brother Adam ever bought was a hammer, and they lost it since it was left in the back of the car. Since we would be going back to the States within the year, I decided to buy a new American car, and I ordered a Dodge Caravan and picked it up in Bremerhaven. We kept that until we rotated back to the States and had it shipped home. That was the second time I bought a brand new vehicle, the first being the Red Volare I sold to my sister.

Because of the amount of work during the first year trying to get everything established within the unit, getting new people set up, and moving into the new facilities, I didn't have time to get involved in too much outside of work. But once everything was up and running smoothly, we had a good administrative team on board, and we were well-established in the new building, so I could start doing other things. I'll get to that in a bit.

One of the really memorable events was a trip to West Berlin for a conference. A group from the unit went together by train. We rode through the night, both coming and going, so we didn't get to see too much of the countryside, but we enjoyed the train ride nonetheless. I did take some video of us on the

train. Although we were there on official business for the conference, we still had time to enjoy ourselves by getting to see a little bit of West Berlin. We didn't get to go over to East Berlin partly because of the classified nature of our job and our unit, but we could clearly see the contrast between the two sides. I remember going to an Irish Pub, and it was a blast, singing all these Irish songs. They had a huge mirror on the ceiling, so it gave it a weird feeling. I have some video of that also. Berlin is an interesting city. The year 1948 (my birth year) had some significance here also. In June of 1948, the Soviets blockaded all rail, road and water access into West Berlin. This was the onset of the Cold War. Two days later, the United States, along with its allies, began the greatest peacetime air supply in history, known as the Berlin Airlift. Aircraft flew in and out of West Berlin's three airports (Tempelhof, Tegel, and Gatow) almost non-stop, bringing in food, coal, and other necessities. At one time, a plane was landing at Tempelhof every 45 seconds. By May of the next year, realizing the blockade wasn't working, the Soviets ended it. The allies, however, continued the airlift until September of 1949 to ensure the city was well-stocked. Over 227 thousand flights had delivered 2.3 million tons of supplies. At the Pentagon, there is a monument dedicated to the Berlin airlift. Similar monuments also stand at Tempelhof and Rhein-main Air Base. The monument consists of three concrete prongs that soar upward, representing the three air corridors the airlift used to reach Berlin. The base is adorned with the names of the Americans who were killed in the airlift. The monument at Rhein-main is flanked by two U.S. Air Force airplanes, representative of the ones that flew in the airlift, a Douglas C-47 Skytrain (or Goonie Bird) and a Douglas C-54 Skymaster. The British also used Yorks and Dakotas.

I wasn't the only one who got to travel. Barbara got to go to Lourdes with ladies from the church. There is so much I could talk about during our tour, but I won't be able to cover everything. Some of it was good, some not so good.

One of the regrets had to do with our son Billy. Let me take some time here to give you a little background on him. He was born William Carlos Rocheteau, III on September 7, 1967, to William and Barbara Rocheteau, 8 lbs, no hair, in New Bedford, MA. He slept well and was walking at one year old. He and his Mom loved one another as they lived alone with no father around. He was a fast learner, and at four he learned to tie his shoes and ride his bike. He didn't want his Mom to get married again because he wanted to marry her. When he was almost 5, he and his Mom flew to Nebraska to get married to Leo (that's me). He started kindergarten in Omaha. He was shy and didn't want to go to school, but he did. He loved his family. He was very athletic and loved to ride his bike, go swimming and ice skating, and play baseball and football. He also loved to sketch. Some

of his drawings can be seen in the Appendix. At the age of 9, he played an Indian with me to celebrate the bicentennial in reenactments. He was a member of Webelos, Cub Scouts. He loved to go camping and fishing. When he was 7 ½, his brother Christopher was born.

The family moved to New Hampshire when he was nine, and when he was 10 his brother Adam was born. He was always ice skating in New Hampshire. The family moved back to Omaha in 1980, where he took up dirt biking and BMX racing. When he was about 13, we bought him a bike for Christmas, and he loved it so much he was always playing with it. One day, he got his finger stuck in the frame and tried as he could but could not remove it. We had to cut the frame to get his finger out. He became very adept at riding in the BMX races and won many trophies. At the age of 17, we were transferred to Germany, which proved to be the turning point in his life. And that's where we are in the story. But I will continue with the rest of his story, and you'll understand why. He found it difficult to adapt to the new settings and ended up hanging out with the wrong people and getting in trouble with the German police. and spent about a week in a German jail before we could get him out. Eventually, he had to return to the States or risk going to jail in Germany for an extended period. I was called in by the First Sergeant one day, and he told me that Billy may end up going to prison in Germany because of some of the things they believed he was involved with unless we got him out of the country. The Commander gave me the option of cutting my tour short and requesting an assignment back to the States. After talking things over with the family, I decided to stay, and Billy was going to go back to America. Looking back, that may not have been the best decision for the family. He returned to the States in 1986 and stayed first with his grandmother and then an aunt, and eventually ended up in California when he got his life together and got married. In 1994, he was a passenger in a car that struck a tree and was thrown from the car and fatally injured. Germany was the last time we saw him alive. I'll come back to this point later in the story when I get to 1994.

After our first year in Blankenrath, our Landlady raised our rent because she thought she wasn't getting enough. We gladly agreed because I felt it was still a good deal. The Landlady eventually realized that she could probably get triple the rent if she fixed the place up, so in the second year, she said we would have to leave because she was remodeling the building. We applied for base housing and were accepted. We were actually going to move into base housing, which was located about 15 miles from the base (about 5 miles from where I worked). This was the time period when Billy moved back to the States. Because we now had one less child with us, we no longer qualified for the house that we were going to get, and other arrangements had to be made quickly. We received quarters in the actual housing apartments at Hahn, but because of the change, our moving date was also changed to about a week later. It now coincided with the day that the Landlady had scheduled for the remodeling crews to come in and start "demolishing" the house since she expected us to be gone by then. We managed to get everything packed and out of the house, even while the remodelers were there. By the time we left the home, it looked like a bomb had gone off. They had torn out all the windows, bathroom fixtures and other items and tossed them in the backyard. We found out later that she fixed the place up really nice after a few months and doubled or tripled the rent on it. But by this time, we had settled into our apartment on the base. A third-floor unit, which was a fairly good size with a nice balcony. Got to meet the neighbors and enjoyed some fun, neighborly activities, along with a few embarrassing moments. More on that to come. Oh, what the heck? Let me get through some of them now.

A bunch of Kids had a little plastic swimming pool on the side of the building on the grass. They were having fun and enjoying themselves in the water. Mighty Superman decides to pretend he's going to jump into the pool with them. He takes a running start, jumps up and pretends to land like Superman in front of the pool. However, landing on wet grass isn't that easy, and after landing, I slid right into the pool, collapsing it and getting soaked while all the water flowed out. How embarrassing. As mentioned earlier, we lived on the third floor and in the basement, each apartment had a cage (more about the cage later) and what was called a maid's room, mainly used for storage. One day, I came home from work and went down into the maid's room to get something. When I came out, I automatically walked up the three flights and into the apartment…but since I was in the maid's room, my apartment required me to go up four flights. Oh well, I forget what my neighbors were having for dinner that night, but they were sure shocked when I came barging in. How embarrassing. Going down into the maid's room wasn't that unusual for me. I did it fairly often. One time, I came home, left my briefcase on the stairs and ran down to the room to get something. I was only going to be a second. However, it took much longer for me to find what I was looking for. When I came back upstairs, I found my briefcase in the middle of the parking lot, surrounded by security personnel, and my wife nodded her head and said, "Yes, I think that belongs to my husband." Somebody, being security conscious, saw the briefcase, notified the police, and they responded instantly. Unattended packages were a big no-no in the environment in which we were in. I was lectured severely for violating a security measure that was taken seriously. How embarrassing. Already mentioned the men's room incident. Not so embarrassing were some of the things we did as a community. On Halloween, the neighbors went all out for decorations, so we naturally joined in. One of the things we did was construct a haunted house. Before any kids could collect their "treats," they had to get their "tricks" by going through the haunted house. You would enter at one end of the apartment building, which was decorated with a huge face. One year, it was Dracula, and the next year, I believe it was a ghost. The doorway was the mouth. Once you entered, you would go down into the basement, walk the full length of the building and come out the other end. The regular lights were replaced with dim orange bulbs. We would hang fake cobwebs from the ceiling and put camouflage netting along the one wall that was opposite the cages. Each family would design their own haunted cage. One year, we had someone dressed as a gorilla in our cage, and I would hide behind the camouflage netting just opposite the cage. When people would stop to look at the "gorilla," he would charge at them. In their shock, they would back up right into my waiting arms. We were terrible. Everybody loved it, though. The neighbors were nice, and we would often have picnics or barbecues together. Our closest friends were the Krevejkos and the Arritas, both wives being named Michelle.

OK, let's get back to work. I have already talked about the new building. The work was very interesting. As I mentioned, we were testing a new intelligence-gathering program called TREDS. I wasn't involved in any of the tactical work. My job was strictly administrative. We had a very good group that consisted of officers, enlisted, and government contractors who were responsible for collecting the data and analyzing it. They took their work seriously and did a great job. But it wasn't all work and no play. We had a baseball team and a bowling team, which I was a part of. For once, I got involved in some sports. We had occasional parties or picnics, morale days as we called them. I had the responsibility of setting them up, which was a fun job. While I was acting as First Sergeant, I initiated a weekly letter that went out to all sections. I gathered information from the weekly base First Sergeant meeting, the base paper and bulletin, the Base Personnel Office, and various other sources. This helped to keep the unit apprised of what was going on even though we didn't get to the base very often. Most of the personnel had secured housing in the German community or in the housing that was located 15 miles from the base. Speaking of parties, one of the parties that we had was a costume party. It was a really enjoyable party. One of the captains had created an awesome costume. Using a couple of phone books, he created "shoes," which gave him additional height. His entire body was covered, including his head. He came in, never said a word, and stood in a corner. Everyone was trying to guess who he was. Eventually, before the night was up, his identity was discovered, mainly through the process of elimination.

One of the things that I would do while working was take a lunch break and use it to read or take walks. One time, I decided to walk in the woods in what I thought would be a circular pattern that would bring me back to the site. I remember I was reading the bible and walking along, and every time I tried to go a certain direction, I encountered a thick underbrush and had to go a different direction. Eventually, I did come out of the woods about a mile from where the site was. Speaking of walking, one of the things we enjoyed was volksmarching. Well, at least me and the boys. Not so much Barbara, although she did go along with us sometimes. We got to see a lot of the German countryside and even some castles and catacombs at some of the places we went. I got involved with the church, taught Sunday school, became a scout leader with the Webelos, was Captain of the Squadron Bowling Team, and organized Squadron Morale Days. Even managed to develop a Cursillo team and put on a Cursillo weekend. This is a picture of the men who went on that weekend. I'm the one on the left with the tie, the glasses, the little facial hair. That was a real challenge but a very rewarding one.

Speaking of Church, we did get heavily involved, and we had a terrific Chaplain, Father William Dendinger. He helped us quite a bit. Remember, we started Barbara's annulment way back in New Hampshire. Well, after we left, things fell through the cracks, and nothing was completed. After counseling with Father Bill, he got things rolling again. Unfortunately, his assignment back to the States came through before things were completed again. He was stationed at Bolling AFB, Washington D.C. More on this later.

One day, I received a call from the Office of Special Investigations (OSI) at Hahn. They wanted to know why I hadn't shown up for an interview. I was a bit confused and asked them what they were talking about. They told me I was being recruited to work for the OSI, and I was supposed to come in for an interview. I told them I never got the message and scheduled a time for the appointment. We talked for a while, and I told them I would be glad to work for the OSI, but I didn't want to come to Washington, D.C. I never liked cities but preferred the country. I was assured that that would not be a problem. A short time later, I received  an assignment to Little Rock, Arkansas. I thought it would be a good assignment, but my wife had her misgivings. All she knew about Little Rock was the race riots of the 60s and all the violence that took place there. I did as much research as I could and finally convinced her that that was in the past. That Little Rock was a nice place, inexpensive, with lots of fun things to do. She finally felt comfortable with the move, and we prepared to leave. We had the van shipped to Philadelphia, where we would pick it up after landing in the States. At the last minute, I received a notification that my assignment was changed. I would no longer be going to Arkansas but rather to the OSI detachment at…you guessed it…Bolling AFB, Washington D.C. We had to make arrangements to have our household goods rerouted. Fortunately, I planned on taking a 30-day leave before reporting for duty, so there was plenty of time for the shipment to be rerouted. I wrote to Father Bill to let him know that we also were being assigned to Bolling AFB. He wrote back and told us that his was a good assignment. The only thing he didn't like was the traffic. Another reason I didn't want to go to Washington. Well, I left Germany with another AF Commendation medal and a certificate for completing the Senior NCO Academy Course by Correspondence. The time had finally come for us to leave. And we did.

CHAPTER NINE: RETURN TO THE STATES (BOLLING AND ANDREWS)

"Yea doubtless, and I count all things but loss for the excellency of the knowledge of Christ Jesus my Lord: for whom I have suffered the loss of all things, and do count them but dung, that I may win Christ." Philippians 3:8

We returned to the states in April of 1988. It was an uneventful trip, considering the type of trip we had going to Germany. We arrived at the airport, picked up our van and headed up to Massachusetts. We spent the 30 days of leave doing all kinds of things, many of them with my mother. We took her around to see a lot of her old friends whom she hadn't seen in a while. We went to Provincetown on a whale watchers cruise. The trip to P-Town was the first time Chris and Adam had ever seen two guys holding hands while walking. I think it was a culture shock for them. Mom was at the time volunteering at a Senior Citizens Nutritional Center in Hyannis, and we would go visit, talk and entertain the folks who were there. They all liked Mom, and we enjoyed our visits. But the thirty days went by fast, and it was time for me to head to my new assignment. I took Barbara to New Bedford, where she and the boys would stay with her mother, Mildred, until I could get us settled with housing in Washington.

When I got to Washington, I got a hotel in Alexandria for a week's stay. I got the paperwork started on base for Base Housing and was getting settled into my job. I was assigned to the Air Force Office of Special Investigations (AFOSI) as the Assistant Chief, Information Management Services Directorate. Did I mention that the USAFOSI was established in 1948? That's right. General Order No. 1 of 2 January 1948 officially established the Office of Special Investigations and appointed Special Agent Joseph Francis Carroll (a senior FBI official) as the first Commander. Its purpose was to consolidate all investigative activities of the Air Force under one jurisdiction, and thus, it was patterned after the FBI. August 1, 1948, is considered the operational date following a number of directives prior to that date.

My duties were to oversee the productivity of and support provided by personnel in four subordinate branches. This included the Administration Section, The Supply Section, the Movie Studio, and the Graphic Arts Department. I'll come back to the job in a little bit.

About three or four days after arriving, I decided to put my van in the shop for an oil change and some minor work. I left it there and went to the hotel, which was within walking distance, with the intention of picking the vehicle up the next day. While at the hotel, I received a call from home saying that my mom had passed away. She had not shown up for work that day at the Center, and folks were concerned, so they called my sister,

Leonna, who lived in the house behind my mother's. Leonna went down to mom's house and found her lying in bed with a book in her hand. She had died in her sleep. I immediately took off to go pick up the van before they closed, and early next morning, reported to work to get an emergency leave pass, and headed back to the Cape. I remember being stopped for speeding just before going through the Baltimore Tunnel. The officer was a female, and I told her that my mom had just died, and I was rushing home. She let me go with the admonition to watch my speed, but she did not give me a ticket. That was a very trying time for all of us. But we got through it as a family.

Eventually, we got back to Bolling. Life had to go on. In a short time, we received housing on Base, 314 Martin Street. It was a nice little home, nothing fancy but comfortable. I became the Base Housing Senior Area Representative or "mayor" of our housing area. All that meant was that I had to attend the Base Meetings with the commander and report to the folks in our area anything that was going on. I was also responsible for ensuring that people in our area complied with all base regulations regarding housing, kind of like a home-owners association (HOA). One time, one of the residents approached me and asked if I could intercede for her because she was being asked to vacate base housing (basically being evicted). I don't recall the actual problem, but I remember going to see the commander. Unfortunately, the situation, which I was not fully aware of, was such that she could not remain on base and had to leave. One of the memorable things was that our unit was one of the units selected to participate in the inaugural parade of President George H. W. Bush on Jan 20, 1989. We spent weeks rehearsing, marching on top of one of the parking garages on base. Unfortunately, we were close to the end of the parade, and by the time we got to the reviewing stand, a lot of people had left. It was cold that day. We were also on the tarmac the day he left office. Our neighbor was one of the presidential chefs, and I was able to get a bottle of the presidential champagne (which I still have unopened). When he left, we were able to visit on the tarmac with the dog, not the president, just his dog, Millie. There are a lot of things to cover over the next 20 years. I'll try to get through as much as I can. I had involvement in Special Olympics, Toastmasters, Church, Gideons, acting on stage and screen as well as on the job and at church, Amway, building our new home, retirement and much more. I won't get through all of it in this chapter, so some of it will show up in the next following retirement.

Let's start with church, beginning with the base church, St. Michael's Parish. One of the positive events was that since Father Bill was stationed here, he could continue the work he started on Barbara's annulment, and it was finally approved. After we received the approval, we decided to get remarried in the Catholic Church, and on Valentine's Day, 1990, we exchanged vows with our sons present and one of my coworkers as best man and Joanne McCoy, who worked for the church, as Maid of Honor. Father

Bill did the honors. Now we get to celebrate two wedding anniversaries. Since I'm talking about marriage at the moment, let me talk a little about the steps we took to make our marriage work. We attended a number of different marriage enrichment programs. One such program was a Marriage Encounter. Another was a program called "A Weekend to Remember," sponsored by Family Life Today. We actually attended three of them. Both the Marriage Encounter Weekend and the "Weekend to Remember" offered something special, and both were Christian-oriented.

We both became heavily involved in the Parish, both with teaching Sunday School (or, as they put it, being a Faith Formation Instructor) and being president of the Parish Council as well as being on the Parish Funds Council. I was also a Lay Eucharistic Minister. Barbara got a part-time job as Sister Virgine's assistant. On Martin Street, we lived close enough for her to walk to the Chapel, but we knew she would have to get her license soon. More on that later. One of the fun things about working with the Parish

Council was being on the entertainment committee. We had several Filipinos in the Parish, and they had quite a knack for putting on entertaining shows. We celebrated Parish Appreciation Days, picnics, special church feast days, and whatever else we could. Food was always plentiful and delicious. Some of the programs we put on involved some of the men on the council and in the parish doing some crazy things. On one Parish Appreciation Day, we staged a Hawaiian Hula Dance with five of the men (including yours truly) dressed as hula dancers, complete with wigs, "grass" skirts, and balloon bras. All rehearsals were kept hush hush, and the secret wasn't revealed until the actual show. Fr Bill and Sister Virgine were dubbed the King and Queen, and the five men were

introduced one at a time as a Princesses. Yours truly was Princess Leoni. Then, to the tune of "Tiny Bubbles," with Barbara walking around the room spreading bubbles, we did the hula dance. Another time, I dressed as a barnyard rooster and performed some crazy antics while the people sang about the maladjusted rooster. When Father Bill was transferred to the Command Chaplain staff, we (the crazy men) celebrated his farewell by "singing" (lip-syncing) a couple of songs from Sister Act, "*I Will Follow Him*" and

"*Hail Holy Queen,*" while dressed as Nuns. We were billed as the "*Singing Nones of the Lost Habit.*" Present at the ceremony were some of the highest-ranking individuals in the command.

We spent two years residing at 314 Martin Street when the Base decided to renovate the homes in that part of the base.

So, we were reassigned to the opposite end of the base at 5573-G Patrick Circle. Two years later, the base decided they would renovate these homes, and we were forced to move again. This time, we decided to purchase a home, so we set out looking and found a lot in Accokeek at a development known as Clover Park at Whitehall. Homes were being built by Ryan Homes. On the 13th Day of August 1993, we purchased our lot described as Lot 44, In Block Lettered "C" as shown on a plat entitled "Whitehall, Section 3," which said plat is recorded among the land records of Prince George's County Maryland, in Plat Book 21, at Plat No. 3, being the same property described in a deed recorded among the aforesaid land records on May 20, 1993. Parcel I.D. #5-57005-15-002. Just thought I'd include all this legalese from the deed since I thought it was kind of funny. We'll come back to the house later. I must say, the job the base did on renovating the homes was really something. In addition to renovating the homes, when the new base commander came in and looked at the riverbank of the Potomac River along the north side of the base, he was disgusted. You could tell where the Naval Yard ended and the Air Force began because it was terrible. There was a lot of underbrush, overgrown and fallen trees, trash, etc. He exclaimed here we had a million-dollar property that looked like the slums. And he proceeded to clean it up to the point where it was beautiful. He added a levee along the riverbank and created a beautiful park where people could enjoy walking, picnicking, playing, and just having a good time. We sometimes wished we could move back there. While living on Martin Street, I compiled my collection of poems and got it copyrighted under the title of "Leo's Lines – A Collection of Poetry, 1967-1989," copyright # TX80 003. I also entered some of my poems in poetry contests. Never won any prizes but did get Honorable Mention for a few of them, namely "*To Gain From Loss,*" "*When I Complain,*" and "*Into the Future.*" "*To Gain From Loss*" also won the "Golden Poet Award for 1989" and was included in "Great Poems of the Western World, Vol. II, along with about 13,000 other poets. Actually, it was just a gimmick to get you to buy the book, which, of course, I did. You can find me on page 1150.

As long as I'm speaking about the poetry, let me add that I did submit a number of them to some songwriting companies, one in Boston (Hallmark) and two in Nashville, Tennessee (Top Records and Music City Music). I was quite pleased with the results from the one in Boston but disappointed in the ones from Tennessee. The songs recorded in Boston include "*When I Complain,*" "*My Mother, My Brother, My Dad,*" "*Rock Me Off to Sleep,*" "*Only He,*" "*Trained in Jesus,*" and "*I Needed a Friend.*"

"*Only He*" was actually a contest entry by the owner of the company. He wrote the main lyrics, and the contestants wrote the last verse. Unfortunately, I didn't win the contest, but I did get a recording of my version. Never did get to hear the winning version. Music City Music did "*Deep In the Heart,*" "*I Cannot Lie,*" and "*Barbara.*" Top Records did "*Our Last Goodbye,*" "*A Lonely Face in a Sea of Life,*" and "*Homelessness is No Way to Treat a Lady.*" I actually got the inspiration for that last one from a bumper sticker on the back of a "House of Ruth" truck. The "House of Ruth" is an organization located at various locations in and around Washington D.C. Their website states, "Founded in 1976, House of Ruth empowers women, children and families to rebuild their lives and heal from trauma, abuse and homelessness. House of Ruth offers comprehensive support for women, children and families."

I was disappointed in the songs done in Nashville, not only because I didn't like the way they were sung, but because they changed some of the words, which actually changed the meaning of the song. Although the songs were recorded, they were never published. Who knows, maybe someday. I did copyright them as an album. I do have to tell you about the terrible April Fool's Trick I played on Barbara. As the name implies, "*Barbara*" was written for her. I wrote it to the tune of "*Venus*" by Frankie Avalon. I had sent the song off to be recorded, and while we were waiting, I typed up an official-looking letter addressed to me saying the song was accepted for publishing. I enclosed a bogus check for $1,000 as an advancement along with the letter, sealed it in an envelope, and addressed it to myself. Our mailbox was a slot in the door. The mailman would slip the mail in the door, and it would land on the floor. As we were going out somewhere on April 1st, I dropped the letter on the floor so it would be there with the rest of the mail when we came home. Barbara was so excited when we came home and found the letter…but then when she found out it was a hoax, she got so mad. Well, can you blame her? Never pulled another one like that. Well, enough about the poetry and songs.

Maybe I should talk a little more about the job. As I said earlier, I was assigned to Headquarters, Air Force Office of Special Investigations, as Assistant Chief, Information Management Services Directorate, and later as Director. We provided support for not only the headquarters but all 19 districts and 200 worldwide detachments and operating locations. The job consisted of a host of administrative functions, which I will not list, but I will talk about a few of the ones we received kudos for. When I arrived there, they had been short-handed, and a lot of things were way behind. We had a backlog of publications awaiting editing, and within two months, we decreased that by about 70%, getting 35 AFOSI publications edited, published, and distributed. During the first year, I was also able to complete the Senior Noncommissioned Officers Academy in Residence (I had already done it by correspondence). This time, I went to Maxwell-Gunter AFB, Alabama, graduating on Dec 14, 1988, after five weeks of training. It was actually returning from this trip that I spotted the bumper sticker that resulted in writing "*Homelessness Is No Way to Treat a Lady.*"

I also helped to organize an effective writing training course and time-management course using the Franklin Planner. If you are not familiar with it, it was a time management system developed by Hyrum W. Smith in 1984 and put into paper form, namely a comprehensive 3-ring binder with all types of inserts designed to help you with organizing your time. Smith said he named it after Benjamin Franklin. Initially, we had trainers come to us, but eventually, we were able to send some of our folks to be trained to be instructors, saving us over $4,000 per year.

During Desert Shield, many of our agents were deployed. Administrative support was essential, and we were able to provide 24-hour administrative support to the Crisis Action Team (CAT), coordinate official and personal mailing and message addressing for all deployed personnel, provide 24-hour computer graphics support, and identify replacement personnel during the extended deployments. One noteworthy achievement was the "Adopt-a-Det" program. Through this program, over 12 large boxes of miscellaneous items were sent to AFOSI personnel deployed in support of Operation Desert Shield/Storm. As a result of my participation in the Desert Storm Welcome Home Ceremony, I received a letter of appreciation from the Air Force District of Washington (AFDW) Commander.

Some other kudos and letters of appreciation (LOA) include AFDW Information Manager of the Quarter (1 Apr – 30 Jul 90), USAFSIA's Nominee for Outstanding Field Support Manager of the Year 1993, numerous LOAs for such things as organizing AFOSI picnics, National Prayer Day participation, being Emcee for the AFOSI Annual Prayer Breakfast, Change of Command Ceremony, participating in the Air Force Day service at the Washington National Cathedral, helping to organize the AFOSI Gator Ball, LOAs for being in the Mentorship Program and Special Olympics. A little bit about those last two items. The Mentorship Program was established to help children in some of the schools have a positive role model. Those of us who volunteered were assigned a school in the local area, and once a week, we would go there and spend time with one or more of the students. The goal was to give them positive feedback and let them know that they were something special.

As I had participated in Special Olympics at Offutt, I was happy to participate here. In Washington, the Special Olympics was held at the Gallaudet School for the Deaf. I was assigned as part of the security team, and our responsibility was to patrol the campus at night and ensure that everyone was safe and no one was doing anything they shouldn't have been doing. I don't recall having any difficulties during my time there.

Some of my additional duties included POC for Academy Goals Development, Combined Federal Campaign, Newcomers Orientation Tours, Alternate Voting Officer, and Internal Management Control Officer.

One of our biggest projects was moving the Academy over to Andrews AFB. It required a lot of coordination. The move went flawlessly, and we were established in a nice new building. And the work continued. About the same time that the Academy was moving to Andrews, we were moving into our new home. See the speech that I gave at Toastmasters for a summary of the move in the appendix. We literally watched the house being built as we would drive by there at least once a week to check on the progress. We came by one day close to the finish, and while checking out the back of the house, we realized that it sloped precariously dangerously down into the gully. I brought this to the attention of the site manager, and he had them shore up the embankment. Now, we at least had a little backyard, although not much for little kids to play on. We chose this lot specifically so we could have a walkout basement. Barbara had envisioned having a daycare in the basement with the walkout to the backyard. This would not be feasible because the backyard was not suitable for little kids to play in. My boys loved it, though, as did their friends because the backyard was basically wooded with a stream running through it. They built a campsite out there. They tied ropes to the trees so they could swing out. I never did complete building steps to go down into the gully, but that didn't bother them. They would tie a rope up and shimmy down into the gully and use the rope to climb back up. I eventually built a deck in the back, but I'll get to that in the next chapter. Before we even moved into the house, the site manager sponsored a block party so all the neighbors could get together and meet one another. It was quite enjoyable, and we did get to meet a lot of the neighbors before moving in. For a while, it became an annual affair, but somewhere along the line, it tapered off and ended.

I'll come back to the house in a little bit, but now let me say a little bit about Toastmasters. I think I stumbled upon the Toastmasters Club accidentally one day. They met at the Base Chapel, and someone invited me to sit in. I enjoyed it and decided to join. I had given a couple of speeches at the Academy and had even competed and won in the speech competitions. So, I thought I'd give it a try. If you are not familiar with Toastmasters, it is very structured. There are a number of manuals that you have to work through by giving speeches on a variety of subjects as well as outside presentations. You work up to different levels: Competent Toastmaster (CTM), Able Toastmaster (ATM), ATM Bronze, ATM Silver, and Distinguished Toastmaster (DTM) (the highest level). Toastmasters International is set up in Districts, Divisions (Optional), Areas, and Clubs. I belonged to District 27, Division E, Area 52, and Club 3308, Bolling AFB Toastmasters. Other clubs in Area 52 were 3173, NSWC Energetics (Naval Warfare Center at Indian Head), 3614, NRL Forum and 3617, NRL Thomas Edison (both at the Naval Research Lab next to Bolling), and eventually 1149, Dialogues (DIA) and OSI Articulators. You also have different leadership positions that you have to fulfill in order to advance. These include your basic club officers: President, Vice President-Education, Vice President-Membership, Vice President-Public Relations, Secretary, Treasure, and Sergeant-at-Arms. There are, of course, other leadership positions at the Area, Division and District levels, but instead of presidents, you have Division, District and Area Governors. During my time in Toastmasters, I served in almost all club positions and eventually Area Governor. I achieved up to ATM Silver, but I never succeeded to DTM. The initial Communication and Leadership Program topics include The Icebreaker, Be In Earnest, Organize Your Speech, Show What you Mean, Vocal Variety, Work With Words, Apply Your Skills, Make It Persuasive, Speak With Knowledge, and Inspire Your Audience. There are a number of Advanced manuals that include a variety of topics such as Communicating on Television, The Discussion Leader, Entertaining Speaker, Storytelling, Technical Presentations and more. I especially enjoyed Storytelling and the Entertaining Speaker. I helped establish two Clubs, one at DIA and one at AFOSI. We conducted Speechcraft Programs where you would go into a school or organization and put on an abbreviated training program.

I helped put one on at a local school. I was able to conduct and participate in speech competitions, regular and humorous. Overall, Toastmasters was a lot of fun, but it was also very educational and helped me grow considerably. It taught me how to give criticism and how to accept criticism since part of the program involved critiquing one another's presentations. In order to advance in TM, you had to do a number of presentations outside of the club environment. My job with OSI and my involvement with the church gave me many opportunities to do this. One such event was delivering a ten-minute speech at the Dr. Martin Luther King JR Service of Remembrance. My subject was the legacy of Martin Luther King Jr as it related to the Catholic Church. I also had the opportunity to speak at Career Day at McGogney Elementary School and to be the guest speaker at a Christian Men's Fellowship Luncheon. Well, enough about my speaking career. Let's talk about my "acting career."

You might say my "acting career" started back at Offutt when I was with the Second Maryland Regiment of Foot, but it really took off here. While at the OSI Academy, I had the opportunity to perform many roles. The administrative staff were often used in roles to help the students train. One time, I got to play an abusive father. Another time, I got to play a father who was irate over what someone had done to his daughter, and I was going after the guy who did it who was protected by the agents. My two favorite roles were a sheik and a spy. The spy role was a two-day affair. On the first day, I was to meet my contact (one of the young ladies who worked with me) at the bar in a local hotel, and we made arrangements for a drop-off. The next day, we were to meet in a church parking lot to make the exchange (supposedly some classified information for cash). When the time came, I parked my car a distance from the church and started jogging (I wore my jogging outfit). As I ran past the church, I spotted the OSI agents in various locations. They were set up to block the parking lot as soon as I drove up. My contact came and parked in the parking lot. Meanwhile, I had made a loop around once, and I stopped to talk to a couple of guys who were working on their yard. After my contact parked in the lot, I jogged by, stopped by her car, exchanged packages, and kept running. As soon as the agents realized I wasn't in a car, they jumped out of their cars and started chasing me. I was trying to get to my car, but they finally caught me not too far from where I was talking to the two guys. As they tackled me to the ground, the two guys came over and were getting ready to interfere when the agents told them to back off. They identified themselves as federal agents and said this was official business. The two guys backed off. After the "arrest" was completed, the agents let me go. I went over to talk to the two guys to let them know it was a training exercise, and they told me I should have given them a heads-up because they were getting ready to go into their house and get their guns. Another time, I got to dress up as an Arabian Sheik, complete with a turban. The agents assigned to me were supposed to give me a tour of DC, and I was supposed to try to convince them to find a woman or drugs for me. We didn't have a limo, but we had a big town car. We drove up to Arlington Cemetery for the changing of the guard, and all these people were looking at me and taking pictures, thinking I was someone important. We often had to play "the rabbit." This meant the agents were supposed to tail us. We would be given an itinerary, but the agents weren't. One time, one of the young ladies who worked for me was the rabbit. She was supposed to go to the Springfield

Mall to buy something, then come out and go to her next stop. The agents followed her into the mall, but when she came out, she used a different exit. As the agents were unfamiliar with the mall, they were disoriented and couldn't remember where they had parked the car. The mall parking lot was full, and as they were driving a rental, they were just too confused. At that time, we didn't have alarms where you could press the button on your key chain, and the alarm would sound to help you find your vehicle. They ended up calling back to headquarters, and someone went to pick them up. They went back later that night when the parking lot was empty to find the car. Another time, this same lady made an unscheduled stop at the school where her daughter was to drop something off for her daughter. As the agents sat in their car waiting for her, someone got suspicious of them and called the police. Another call back to the headquarters.

Since we're talking about my acting, let's talk about some of my "professional" roles. My first one was as a grunt soldier in that blockbuster movie, "Mars Attacks." I was given a free haircut, an old 50s uniform, and a rubber gun. We were to stand in front of the Capitol, in front of a line of tanks, and pretend to be shooting. I was standing right in front of the tank upon which Rod Steiger climbed to give the orders to shoot. They had to bring a step ladder out for him to climb onto the tank. They told us the sound and the fire would be added in through special effects. Other than the fact that it was cold at the time of the shooting, and we had to stay in a big tent trying to keep warm until it was our time, it was an enjoyable experience. I think we were paid $50.00 for the day. The last two that I was in actually took place after I retired, but I'll talk about them now. One was in the movie "Contact" with Jodie Foster. At the auditions, I was told to show up on the day of shooting in a blue suit. Unfortunately, I didn't have a blue suit, so I showed up in a brown suit. It turned out the roles were color-coded. Had I worn a blue suit as instructed, I would have been a Senator and might have been situated in front of the camera while James Woods was questioning Jodie Foster. Because I wore the brown suit, I was cast as a news reporter at the far back of the room with a very slim chance of getting camera time. I did sit down on Angela Basset's chair until someone told me to move. Though I didn't get any air time and didn't get to meet any of the real stars, I did get to see how Jodie Foster prepared for her scenes. She was very intense. The final movie that I was in was G.I Jane. I played a 2-star Army General during the ball room scene. We filmed at a fancy hotel in downtown D.C., 1701 Kalorama. I always say I had to get out of the Air Force to get promoted to General. But once again, my camera time was non-existent. I had two scenes. One was walking up the stairs, and the other was milling around in the ballroom with a glass of wine. On the stair scene, someone rushes past me carrying the newspaper article about "G.I. Jane." You can spot me for about half a second. In the milling around scene,

I don't think the camera caught me at all. The fellow in the photo with me looking at the map kept changing his position each time we redid the scene in the ballroom, hoping the camera would catch him. Don't know if it ever did. Never did get to see Demi Moore. I believe she was in Florida at the time, filming another scene.

That was the extent of my big screen experience.

My other acting was the result of my son, Adam. Adam had started performing with the Hard Bargain Players (HBP)in an outdoor theater in the woods called Hard Bargain Theater in the Woods in Accokeek, MD. In 2003, he played Francis Nurse in *"The Crucible"*. When I took him to audition for John Steinbeck's play *"Of Mice and Men,"* they asked me to audition, and I got the part of Candy, the aging ranch handyman who lost one of his hands in an accident. Adam got the part of Crooks, the black stable-hand. We got to do one scene with just the two of us and Lennie. It was a very enjoyable experience, although it was time-consuming. The second time I got to act with Adam was in "The Night of the Living Dead" (2008). I played the sheriff, and during one performance, my gun wouldn't fire, so I hollered, "bang." The "theater" itself is a natural amphitheater built in the early 1930s by Alice and Henry Ferguson who owned the farm. Initially, it served for their own entertainment and that of their friends. The Fergusons donated the land and founded the Ferguson Foundation in 1954. It serves as an educational center that focuses on land stewardship and historical farming practices in the region. Besides the Theater in the Woods, the property includes a Tobacco barn originally built before the Civil War. The property was listed on the National Register of Historic Places in 2014. Besides performing here, Adam also did a few plays with the Fort Tobacco Players in La Plata, one of them being *"The Trip to Bountiful."* In one show, *"Lysistrata,"* an ancient Greek comedy by Aristophanes, *Barbara* and I were sitting in the seats waiting for the show to start. The producer came over to where we were sitting and asked if any of the patrons in our row knew CPR. When asked why, he said because I would need it during the second act. I wasn't sure what he meant until my son came out wearing a flimsy ladies' nightie.

Wow, I've wandered way off. Let's get back to the house and family. Haven't told you anything about the boys other than the fact that they liked to play in the back yard. When we first arrived in D.C., we were concerned about their schooling, so we enrolled them in a Catholic elementary school, St. Ritas, in Alexandria, Virginia. After graduating from elementary school, they went back to public school. School without Walls and Francis Junior High School. After we moved into our house, they attended Gwynn Park High School in Brandywine, from which they both graduated. They both have their own stories to tell, which are numerous, many of them, I'm sure, of which I was not even aware. I'll talk about some of them in a bit.

In order to afford to send them to St. Rita's, Barbara and I both got part-time jobs stocking at the Bolling Commissary. That was an interesting experience. One time, we felt something wasn't right because they were making us do things that didn't make any sense, such as bringing all the stock onto the floor, whether it was going to be put up or not. We believed that management was getting paid by the number of pallets that were moved or some such thing. It got to the point where I brought my camera in and started taking pictures so I would have some evidence of what they were making us do. Somehow, the manager got wind of what I was doing and told me that it was illegal to be taking pictures, and if I didn't turn the camera over to her immediately, she was going to call the commander and have me arrested. It just so happened that she and the commander were good friends. I couldn't afford the risk because of my job so I relented and turned the camera over to her. I quit the job shortly thereafter.

Remember I said earlier that Barbara needed to get her license. Well, I bought her a car and decided to give her driving lessons. Not a very good idea. One day, while we were in the parking lot practicing, we got into an argument, and she got out of the car right there. Husbands cannot teach their wives to drive. She eventually did get her license, and before long, she was driving around the base. It was still some time before she had the confidence to drive off base. She had been going to see a doctor about 12 miles from the base, and you had to take US 95 to get there. I had been taking her there for quite some time, and finally, I told her she had to drive herself. I refused to take her. So, she got Chris to go with her, and without her knowledge, I followed her up there, waited until she was finished, and followed her home without her knowing it. She did fine even though she was mad at me for making her do it.

So, let's talk about the boys and some of their antics. Chronologically not sure where the stories will fit in. Some while at Bolling, most after we were in our new home. One time, Chris and friends almost got held up on Livingston Road. He, Jamie, Wendy, and Stephanie were walking home from the 7-11 a couple of miles from the house when a car stopped beside them. One of the guys got out of the car and asked them if they needed a ride. When they said no, he pulled a gun and told them to get on the ground. At about that same time, a car came driving by, and the guys in the car decided to take off. The other three were too afraid to walk any further, so they hid while Chris ran the rest of the way home and got Nevin, who was sleeping at our house. They went back into Nevin's car and picked up the other three. Chris says that he always felt his guardian angel was watching over him because this wasn't the only time something like this had happened. One time, when he and some friends were at the Oxon Hill Movie theater waiting to see "The Crow," a bunch of guys approached, stole one of the friend's tickets, and threatened them with a supposed gun, which was never revealed. (You know, hand-in-the-pocket type of thing.) While at Bolling, we had a curfew on base, and there were many nights when the boys would sneak out without us being aware. One time, they were with a bunch of friends and were spotted by the MPs. They all high-tailed it. Adam was one of the few that made it home. Chris got caught. We received a call from the main gate saying they had Chris. Adam, by this time, was safe in bed, and we never knew he had been with them. Later, a neighbor told me she had spotted Adam sneaking back in the house, so one day, while we were talking, I casually hinted at the fact that we knew he had been with Chris. Don't know if he ever found out how we knew. Anyways, we went to the gate to get Chris, and while we were there, the MPs became involved with something far more serious, a highly belligerent person on drugs, so they just let us take Chris home. Remember the incident back in Germany where Christopher almost caught off Adam's finger? Well, Adam got his revenge when they were fooling around, and Adam had a knife. Without thinking too smartly, Chris grabbed the knife with his hand by the blade. Now, both have slight scars on their hands as mementos. When Adam was about 12 or 13, one of his friends was a young girl named Melissa Shields. I have a video of them dancing together at one of our barbecues. I mention this only because, after many years of separation, they finally reconnected, and in 2022, they ended up getting married some 30 years later.

Living in the D.C. area provided us with lots of things to do. One of these activities was the free concerts with star performers at the DAR Constitution Hall, located at 1776 D Street NW. The DAR, or Daughters of the American Revolution, is a non-profit organization open to any woman who can prove her lineal connection with the American Revolution. They sponsored these free concerts. One of my favorite ones was when B. J. Thomas was performing. He was already one of my favorite singers, plus one of the first movies Barbara and I saw together was *"Butch Cassidy and the Sundance Kid,"* and B.J. did the theme song, *"Raindrops are Falling on my Head."* When he became a Christian, he sang a song called *"Home Where I Belong,"* and I really liked that song. It basically talks about how this earth is not our home. It is only temporary, and we are just passing through. When his biography came out with the same title, I purchased it, and this concert gave me the opportunity to get it autographed. We also saw the Air Force Band perform, Bruce Springsteen, and some others.

With the boys in school, many of the activities centered around field trips with them, like going to the Zoo or to some of the many museums in D.C. There were also amusement parks, such as Six Flags in Upper Marlboro, and if you didn't mind driving a little bit, Kings Dominion, about an hours' ride south of D.C.

As both boys grew into manhood, they encountered many adventures. It is not my intention to tell their stories. That is something that they will have to do in their own time. I have included some as memory served me or as they were related to me by them, but the rest is on their shoulders.

Back to work. One of my bosses was the Deputy Chief of Staff for information Management, Lt Col Hudson. Even though he gave me rave reviews on my performance report, he and I often bumped heads over certain things that we did not agree on. One time, when I was in his office, we got into it over something. I can't remember what, but it was loud enough for the people in the outer office to hear. I was sticking up for the folks who worked for me. That's all I remember. But we were able to work through it, and eventually, he retired. Not long after he retired, I received a call from Mark DeMatteo. My name had been given to him by Col Hudson, and he wanted to talk to me about a business proposition. I agreed and attended the meeting. It turned out to be an Amway meeting. To make a long story short, we signed up and although we never built it to any large size, it proved to be an important turning point in my life. We began going to meetings and sponsoring a few people. Every Thursday, we would go to Mark's house for product pickup. Following the weekly plan, where we would bring prospects for the business, we would have some follow-on training about the business. Occasionally, he

would have further training either at the hotel or at a local late-night restaurant. These late-night training sessions weren't about the business, but rather, they were about your spiritual life. Mark was an expert on many topics, but his passions revolve around Jesus Christ, creationism, and the history of our nation. I could sit for hours listening to him teach. Sometimes, on Thursday night, following product pick-up, he would teach all night for those who were willing to stay. It reminded me of the bible story where Paul was preaching for so long that one of the listeners, a man named Eutychus, fell asleep and fell out the window and died. Paul brought him back to life. (Acts 20:7-11) When we went to the major functions and heard the speakers' testimonies, it was more of the same, and we realized that Amway was more than just a business. We came to really respect the leaders, especially Mark. We built a small team and went to a lot of functions, sometimes four major ones a year, with a few minor ones. Heard a lot of great speakers, both in and out of the business. People like Clebe and Deanna McClary (U.S. Marine), Rudy Rutiger (portrayed  by Sean Astin in "*Rudy*"), Kenneth Copeland, Chris Gardner (*The Pursuit of Happyness* guy, portrayed by Will Smith), Oliver North (USMC LtCol, Ret), C. Mason Weaver (author of "*It's OK to Leave the Plantation*"), Ben Carson (Neurosurgeon and US Sec of HUD), and many more. Some of these resulted in autographed books.

Unfortunately, there came a time when there was a rift in the business. Some of the leaders proved to be not what they were pretending to be. Our upline leadership could not in good conscience stay under their leadership and broke away, and we followed them. I won't go into all the details because I don't have all the facts. But the business continued for a while under the new leadership. We were a part of it as it transitioned from Amway to Quixtar and then back to Amway. We got a chance to go to Ada, Michigan, and tour some of the facilities. Some of the functions took us to North Carolina, South Carolina, Tennessee and some places I can't remember. I remember one time the function was in Tennessee. Doris,

one of the individuals on our team, had an RV, and she offered to drive us all down there. "We" included Barbara and I, Doris, my two sons, Wendy, and Rob Stucky and his wife. Rob and Doris are still part of the team as of this writing. We had a great time driving down, but on the return trip, something went wrong with the RV as we were coming across the panhandle of Maryland. We couldn't get it to go over 40 miles an hour. We stopped at an RV place to have them look

at it, but they couldn't fix it. We eventually got home, but it took us awhile. We still enjoyed ourselves, singing and having a good time. Most of us, anyway. Some just slept. It was during this trip that I wrote a song to the tune of "*I'm a Believer*" by the Monkees, talking about building the business to Diamond. Unfortunately, we just couldn't seem to build a big enough team to make a profit and had to quit going to everything. We still remained part of it, but mostly for just buying products, even though we still have a very small team and do get an occasional check.

With all the training that I was getting going to the meetings, something was gnawing at me. But I'll get back to that later because it takes place after my retirement from the Air Force, and I still have some ground to cover on this side of the retirement.

Shortly after we had signed up in Amway, tragedy struck again. We were notified that our son Billy was involved in a serious car accident in California and was in critical condition. I stayed with Chris and Adam, and Barbara flew out to California to be with him. When she arrived there, he was on life support, and Barbara was told that he would not make it. She had to make the decision to remove him from life support. One of my regrets in life was that I did not go there with her. Thank God her father and uncle were there, but it was still a very difficult time for her. A few years later, Adam conducted a memorial service for him at his church in Bryans Road, The Worship Center, in order to provide closure.

Although I was hoping to make Chief Master Sergeant before I retired, it didn't seem like that was going to happen, so I decided to put my papers in.

Father Bill agreed to do the retirement for me. One of the young ladies who worked for me handled all the details and emceed the program. It was rather nice. A couple of my sisters showed up, which was a pleasant surprise. It was a very nice program. Unfortunately, my Certificate of Appreciation for my service was signed by President Clinton, not one of my favorite Commanders-in-Chief. But it is what it is.

And life goes on.

CHAPTER TEN: RETIREMENT BECKONS, A NEW CAREER BEGINS

"And whatsoever ye do, do it heartily, as to the Lord, and not unto men; knowing that of the Lord ye shall receive the reward of the inheritance: for ye serve the Lord Jesus."

Colossians 3:23-24

Once I retired from the Air Force, I had to make a decision to do something else. I was a bit tired of working behind a desk, pushing paper and pencils, and so I decided to try something completely different. I got a job working for Orkin Pest Control. The job was as an inspector, not as a technician. It would involve me making appointments to visit people and give them a free inspection. If I sold them on receiving treatment, I would receive a commission. The job required me to go to Atlanta, Georgia, for two weeks of training on how to identify possible damage from termites and also to identify different types of pests that might be in and around the home. Upon returning, I would receive a small salary for a month but was expected to get paid on commissions once I started making sales. I enjoyed what I was doing. I got to visit a lot of different homes, from some really beautiful places to some really rundown places. Once, I was called to a trailer park by the manager. One of the tenants had left without taking her pet cat with her. The cat had been in the trailer and was infested with fleas. It was so bad we had to call in a team to totally fumigate the place. The poor cat did not survive.

Another time, in November, I visited this beautiful home that was all decorated for Christmas. As I was briefing the owner, I told her I had never seen a more festive home. She thought I said I had never seen a more infested home. She about panicked. The only part I didn't like about inspecting was when I had a home that had no basement but only a crawl space underneath. You never know what you're going to find in those places. Well, to make a long story short, I was not making any money on this job, and I was using up all my savings and driving up my credit cards. The people who could afford our services didn't need it, and the people who needed it couldn't afford it. Even the one month when I was a top salesman, I couldn't make any money. So, as it was nearing Christmas, I knew I couldn't continue. I had to find something better. The boss kept saying it would get better after the holidays, but I couldn't wait to find out. One of the ladies in my Amway upline, Anne Harrell, worked for Sterling Software in Tysons Corner in Virginia. She told me she'd see if she could get me an interview for a job. She did, and I was hired. I liked the job, even though it was sitting back behind a desk as a technical editor. But I hated the commute. It would take me an hour to get to work and an hour to get home. Sometimes even longer. One day, my car broke down on the Wilson Bridge. This was the old Wilson Drawbridge across the Potomac. I was right in the middle of the bridge, causing a traffic backup. I think the backup even caused an accident to occur. Finally, a tow truck came and pushed me off the bridge. Well, not off the bridge, like into the water, but over to the Virginia side of the bridge where I could pull safely over to the side. I was able to get the car towed to a nearby dealer and called someone to come and get me. I eventually made it to work, and when I explained what had happened, someone said, "Was that you?" They were one of the people affected by the backup. One day, my boss called me into his office and told me there was an opening at Bolling AFB, in DIA (Defense Intelligence Agency), where they were implementing a new program. He asked me if I wanted it. It took me about 10 ½ seconds to decide. What a relief. Back at Bolling. Working at the Defense Intelligence Agency. The new program that we were implementing was called "Athena." It was a website on the government's classified server where intelligence analysts could go to get information on NBC Warfare. That is, Nuclear, Biological and Chemical Warfare. Eventually, Cyber Warfare would be added. The team that I was on built the website. My primary responsibility was to search all other websites, both classified and unclassified, to find any information in these areas that I could then link to on our website. So, every day, I would search NSA, CIA, ONI, FBI, and all the alphabet government agencies (even those that didn't exist), as well as the local news outlets and other unclassified websites. Anything that I could find that dealt with NBC was linked to the website under a variety of subject headings. My job was to determine what was the most appropriate heading to link them to. When our analysts were working on a project, they could come to the Athena website and check out all the things that came out recently on that one website. Later, it grew to include what was known as Artemis. I worked on this job for 15 years and got to the point where I could practically do it in my sleep. One day, I forgot my access badge, and when I went to the security desk to get a temporary badge, I found out I didn't exist. Somebody had dropped the ball on my security clearance renewal, and it didn't get updated, so my card was canceled. I could not do my work. I could not even come to work without having an escort. They recognized the mistake that was made but said it would take a while to fix it. By a while, I don't mean a few hours or even a few days, but rather a few weeks. Here, I've had top-secret and above-security clearance for over 35 years, and now, because someone made a mistake, I can't go to work. The solution was to have me work at home doing a partial job, that is, just research unclassified sources and save the articles to a disk. Then, once a week, I would bring the disk into DIA, and they would upload the information to the website. I could live with that. So, for about a month, that's what I did until finally, they had the security situation straightened out, and I could come back to work.

I was working here on September 11, 2001. We all know what happened that day. I was sitting at my desk when someone cried out that a plane had hit the World Trade Center. At first, I thought they were talking about a small plane, but as we all gathered around the boss' office (he was the only one with a TV), we saw what was unfolding in New York as the second plane hit. You could see the Pentagon from our windows, and soon, someone said there was smoke coming from the Pentagon. It was at that point we realized we were under attack. The base was immediately placed on lockdown: nobody in, nobody out. Barbara was visiting the base that morning and was on her way home when the base went into lockdown. She was stuck in traffic with no place to go. Well, we finally got through that, but things weren't the same. There were constant patrols along the Potomac in front of our building. I used to walk at lunchtime on the beautiful Potomac (remember when I said the Base Commander had fixed it up really nice). Well, we could no longer do that. The whole area was placed off-limits. Somewhere along the line, things got back to normal. And then, one day, we got word that Athena was going to move to Charlottesville, Virginia. We could choose to relocate and go with Athena to Virginia, or we could look for a new job. I didn't want to relocate because I didn't want to sell the house, but the commute would be about three hours one way. God came through for me again. Northrop Grumman had an opening at Ft. Belvoir at the Army Cyber Security Command. Oh, I guess I forgot to mention that I now work for Northrop Grumman. No, I didn't change companies, but Sterling got bought out by Computer Associates in 2000, who then sold Sterling's Federal Systems Group to Northrop Grumman. And that's how I ended up working for Northrop Grumman. This time, my job consisted of doing contracts for purchasing and renewing computer software programs that were used by the Cyber Security Command. I was amazed at how much money was spent on these programs. I was working here when the earthquake hit. We were in a meeting on the ground floor, and when the place started shaking, one of the people in the room, who was from California, said, "It's an earthquake." We all immediately vacated the building, some a whole lot faster than others. Because one of the individuals in the meeting was in a wheelchair, and nobody thought to make sure he got out, we had to implement some new emergency evacuation procedures to ensure all persons who were physically handicapped had someone assigned to make sure they made it out safe. We also implemented a procedure for ensuring that the area was empty following an evacuation order. During my time here, we underwent a building remodeling project of major proportions to include the building of a parking garage. Prior to this, parking was at a premium, and if you didn't get to work early enough, you may have had to park at the commissary or BX parking lot and walk to work. I always got to work early. Well, the problem with working under a contract is that that contract has to be renewed every few years. And it's a bidding war. After five years at the Command, the portion of Northrop Grumman that handled this contract was outbid, and a new company got the contract. Fortunately, they were going to keep most of the people that were under the current contract. Not only were they going to keep me, but I was going to get a raise, plus I would be getting a severance package from Northrop Grumman. At least that's what I was told until they found out that under the new contract, my position was changed. Based on the wording of the job description, the position that I was in now required certain computer certifications that I did not have. I had a choice. Go back to school to get the certifications needed or find a new job. Well, I decided since it had been about 20 years since I retired from the Air Force, maybe it was time to retire again. And so, in 2015, that's what I did.

Wow, I went from retirement to retirement. I must have missed a lot of stuff. Let's go back and catch up.

Sometime during this period, I was driving an Oldsmobile Cutlass. I had this while I was working for Orkin. I put the Orkin magnetic sign on the side of the car, which was perfect because the car was white, and Orkin vehicles were white. Somewhere along the line, two things happened to the car. The rearview mirror broke off, and I lost the reverse in the transmission. It was like the car was telling me don't look at where you've been. Look at where you're going, and don't go back. Keep moving forward. That's an OK message, but it meant every time I parked the car, I had to make sure I was in a position to drive forward or on a slope where I could roll backward. I had one car that was a real lemon. Nothing but problems. One day, Barbara was driving it, and it stopped about a mile from the house. I called a tow truck to go and get it, and by the time they got to where it was, someone had sideswiped it. At least that's what they told me. When I went to the place where they had towed it, I saw that the driver's side had been hit. When I asked them about it, they said it was like that when they found it. Well, I stopped paying for it, and they repossessed it, but eventually, it went to court, and I ended up paying for it plus the towing charge, minus what they got for selling it, which was about $100 in salvage. As long as I'm talking about car trouble, let me tell you about the Volvo my brother Johnny gave me for nothing. I picked it up from Massachusetts and had to fix a few things on it. But there was a lot more I had to do to get it to pass inspection. We drove it to North Carolina to attend a function, and on the way back, smoke started coming out from the rear wheel. It was me, Barbara, Chris, Adam and Wendy. I was so fed up with the car I was just going to leave it. Wendy wanted me to leave her with the car, and she would drive it home. I believe she didn't even have a license at the time. Anyway, I told her no. I found a guy who was willing to give me enough money for bus fare and sold the car to him for it. I canceled the insurance on the car, but I failed to turn the plates into the MVA. The MVA has a stiff penalty for driving a car without insurance. Because I didn't have the name of the guy I sold the car to, I could not verify the date I got rid of the car, so I ended up paying a hefty fine on a vehicle that cost me nothing. As long as we're talking about insurance, one time, my insurance wasn't renewed, and I wasn't aware of it. I was with Allstate at the time, and I thought it was renewed automatically. I wondered why I hadn't received a bill for them in a while, so I called them, and they told me that my insurance had been cancelled. They said they sent me a renewal notice, and I never responded. When I tried to renew it, they said they could not because it had been over a certain period of time that I hadn't paid. While I was talking to them, I was on the computer contacting Progressive Insurance and by the time Allstate was finished telling me why they could not insure me, I had already signed up with Progressive. Still had to pay a hefty fine to the state. But during that period without insurance, I accidentally ran a red light at a busy intersection and just barely missed getting T-boned. If that car had hit me after I ran the red light and I had no insurance…well, I dread to think what the consequences would have been. One more thing to thank Almighty God for.

Since we're on a roll with these automobiles, we might as well continue. Not necessarily in chronological order, but we've had a number of auto-related happenstances. Once, while parked at work at Bolling, I came out ready to go home and found my right side window shattered (sliding door on the van). A construction worker had swung his front-end loader too far and hit the window. Fortunately, he was good enough to leave a note so I could contact their insurance company and the problem was taken care of. One morning, I woke up and discovered an attempt was made to break into my van. Fortunately, they did not succeed but did manage to cause damage to the passenger side door. Another incident was my fault. I left my vehicle parked in the road in front of my house, accidentally left the hatchback open, and left my briefcase for church (with the Sunday's collection in it. The next morning, I received a call from someone at the church just down the street from where we live. They found my briefcase in the parking lot with the contents strewn about. The cash was missing (about $50.00), but all the checks and everything else were there. I replaced the cash out of my pocket and made certain that it never happened again. One Saturday morning, my son knocked on our bedroom door quite early. He asked if we were both there, and I said, "Yes, why do you want to know?" He replied, "Because the van is missing." Sure enough, someone had stolen the van sometime during the night. I called the police, and they came and filled out a report. The following Monday, I rented a car from the rental agency about three miles from home. On my way to work, I noticed my van parked in front of an apartment complex just off of 210. I called the police and waited until they came. The only damage done to the van was the ignition keyhole had been removed, and the vehicle evidently started with a screwdriver. We filled out the police report and had the vehicle taken to my mechanic, who replaced the ignition. About a year or so later, when it was time to renew my registration, I received a notice saying they could not renew the registration because the vehicle had been reported stolen. The police never cleared the report, and I had to go through all kinds of hassle to get it straightened out before I could renew the registration. Well, enough about vehicles.

Let's talk about a much more important issue. Remember in the last chapter when I said something was gnawing at me? Well, there have always been some things within the Catholic Church that I could not understand. I loved the church, as I said in the past. I enjoyed the services. I enjoyed the pageantry of the special services such as the Lenten and Easter services, midnight Mass at Christmas, and so on. However, I still had questions about some of their doctrines. As I got more involved with the people in Amway, listening to many of the speakers, I was encouraged to read the Bible on my own. Not only to read it but to study it. The more I read and the more I studied, the more questions I had. Questions that were not being addressed within the church. I got to the point where I felt I was no longer being fed within the church, and I couldn't reconcile some of the things I read in the Bible with what the church was saying. We started to shop around for another church, first by going to other Catholic churches to see if the messages were different. When my son got married to Susan, and we wanted to know a little bit about her religious background, we attended some services at her church in Brandywine. This was a cute small Church painted white on Cherry Tree Crossing that Susan's family attended. It was under the Church of God denomination. We had attended a couple of services when the pastor announced that he was leaving due to health concerns of his wife and the fact that he lived an hour away. A new pastor was sent in, Dr. Ronald Washington. The first time we heard him speak, I felt this was someone I could follow. His message was right along the lines of what I had been hearing and studying about. We continued to attend, eventually becoming members and even getting on the board. One day, I accompanied Pastor Washington to a meeting he had with the Church of God hierarchy. It appears the small church had borrowed some money from the denomination for some much-needed repairs and was unable to pay it back. Not only that, but they needed to make some more repairs. The Bishop refused to extend the payment period or to provide any more money. Pastor Washington asked if they could take some time to pray about it, and he was told that this wasn't about prayer. It was about business. We left. Pastor Washington moved the church down the street to the Brandywine Elementary School, where he rented space. He no longer felt he could continue with the Church of God with the attitude they were showing, where business was more important than prayer and faith. Some of the people followed him. Some did not. Others joined the church later. Many of them were relatives of Pastor Washington. Two ministers were ordained, William and Wakefield. I was ordained as a Deacon. Pastor's wife, Sister Velma, was also a minister.

Pastor Washington had an interesting story. He was a homicide investigator with the Metropolitan Police Department in Washington D.C. and one day, he was attending a wedding reception off-duty. A man came in with a gun, attempting to kill the bride, and Pastor Washington intervened. He ended up killing the man, but not before he was fatally shot. I say fatally because the doctors said he was dead, but they revived him and brought him back. He eventually left the police force and became a minister. You can read his story in his book, *Forgiveness and Reconciliation.* Copyright 1993. One day, he took sick, and as he lay on his death bed, he called some of us to his side and told us that we needed to seek out a new Pastor. He cautioned us about one minister who would try to take over our church and told us not to let him. He recommended we contact John Edwards, an Evangelist who was a friend of his and who had spoken at our church before, to see if he would be willing to Pastor us. We contacted Rev Edwards with the proposal, and he told us that he was not a Pastor. He was an Evangelist. He said he liked to blow in, blow up, blow out and let the Pastor pick up the pieces. But he agreed to give us a trial run of about six months. That was over twenty years ago, as of this writing, and he is still our Pastor. He is a man who preaches the Gospel truth…nothing less and nothing more. His own testimony is an inspiration to us all. A former DJ (the Turk) with WDJY in DC, he turned away from drugs, booze and women to follow the Lord. There is nothing really special about our little church. Initially, we met at the Brandywine Volunteer Fire House Activity Hall. We have between 15-20 faithful members, a choir of 3-4 members. It was my responsibility, as Deacon, along with Barbara, to set up every Sunday Morning. We'd go in about 9 AM, set up the chairs, the banners, the sound equipment and Communion if it happened to be Communion Sunday. At 10:15, we'd have Sunday School. We have three teachers, and I am blessed to teach every third Sunday. At 11:15, the church began and lasted until about 12:30. Since COVID-19 struck, we have been meeting via Zoom. This had both its good points and bad points. The bad is we miss the gathering in person. The good I no longer had to set up, but much more importantly, people who would not be able to participate in person are able to attend and thereby hear the unadulterated Gospel message. No compromise, no political correctness. Just the truth as God intended.

Let's go back to our reason for attending this church. Christopher was seeing a girl named Susan Townshend. She got pregnant, they got married, and we got involved. Susan's parents were Adonah and David Townshend, who were members of the little church. Needless to say, Adonah was very upset over the secret marriage and her daughter getting pregnant. She had always hoped to have a beautiful wedding for Susan (whose actual name was Adonah Susan). Nonetheless, we managed to get along. On February 1, 1999, a beautiful daughter was born, and we had our first grandchild, Caitlyn Helen Brandao. We were all present at the hospital when she was born. Her birth resulted in a bond between the Brandaos and the Townshends that would last for 21 years. We did many things together. Unfortunately, Christopher and Susan's marriage did not last, and they divorced within two years. Both of them remarried shortly thereafter, Susan to David Grubaugh and Christopher to an old friend, Wendy Ramsey. Oddly enough, both couples gave birth to sons only three months apart. Susan and David named their son Sean David. Christopher and Wendy named their son our first grandson, Trevor Demetrius. Trevor was a birthday present for Caitlyn, as he was born on February 2, 2002, the day after her birthday. Unfortunately, this

marriage, too, was doomed to failure, and Christopher and Wendy went their separate ways. In January 2009, we went to Medieval Times with Trevor and Caitlyn and all three sets of grandparents, the Townshends, the Ramseys, and the Brandaos. Had a great time. Eventually, Trevor ended up leaving with Wendy, and we only got to see him a couple of times a year as they moved to Kentucky. Caitlyn, on the other hand, became an intimate part of our lives, living with us in her early years and then later on when she turned 15. In between times, she lived with her family (mom, stepdad, and brother Sean) in Florida. I'll come back to Caitlyn,

Trevor and Sean a little later. We became very close friends with the Townshends, eating out together a couple of times a week, playing dominoes or cards (blitz), having poolside barbecues at the Townshends, and spending just about every holiday together. Adonah was a graceful hostess, always going all out, especially on the holidays. She put together a very beautiful dinner table. She had a knack for decorating for every holiday, the Fourth of July and Christmas being her

favorites. David was relatively quiet. Loved his westerns and loved to play dominoes or blitz. His goal was to win. We did a lot of traveling together but only by car. Adonah would not fly anywhere. Some of the places she encouraged us to go with her include Radio City Music Hall in NYC (Barbara went there), Sight and Sound Theater in Pennsylvania, Florida to visit David and Susan, Virginia  to visit her brother and lots more through just driving around. She attended Rolling Thunder one year and met a young man who was visiting here from India. She invited him to come to her home. And that's how we met Parajat Jamdar. Pari, as we called him, became a very good friend. He was here for his job for a few days but visited a couple of times over the years. He became like a son to Adonah. Everywhere we went with him, he had his camera out taking pictures. One year, we went together along with Caitlyn to distribute Christmas Wreaths at Arlington Cemetery as part of the Wreaths Across America Program and got to meet the owner of Worcester Wreath Company, Mr. Morrill Worcester of Harrington, Maine, who was responsible for the wreaths. We spent time talking with him, and he told us his story. If you are not familiar with this program, it began as a fulfillment of a promise made by Mr. Worcester. As a young boy, Morrill won a trip to Washington D.C and the trip, especially the visit to Arlington Cemetery, had such an impact on him that he promised that someday he would do something to honor

Adonah, Mildred & Barbara

the veterans who gave their lives for this country. In 1992, the opportunity came when he found himself with a lot of excess wreaths at the end of the Christmas Season, and he made arrangements to have them delivered to Arlington. This was the start of a program that has grown every year. In the beginning, he stayed under the radar, and he would take no donations because he wanted this to be his gift to the veterans. In 2005, a picture of the gravestones at Arlington with the wreaths lying in front of them and covered with snow went viral on the internet, and thousands of requests began pouring in from all over the country, from people wanting to either help, place wreaths at their veterans' cemetery, or just share their story. He was unable to fulfill all the requests that came in, so he began taking donations and sending wreaths to as many veteran cemeteries as he could. Every year, a caravan of

Harry, Parijat & Barbara

trucks departs Harrington, Maine and makes the trip to D.C., stopping at various veteran cemeteries along the way. You can read the entire story on their website. We got Adonah to travel with us to Cape Cod for one of our family reunions, and she really enjoyed herself, although she later remarked to her cousin that it was like the United Nations and had scared her a little bit. It was at one of these reunions, in July 2002, that she had the opportunity to meet Barbara's mother, Mildred.

Another thing we did together was to visit a nursing home in Waldorf where Rene, Adonah's cousin, spent some time after having a stroke. Adonah would decorate the place real nice, and we would sing, talk and maybe play bingo. I would sometimes make balloon animals. The residents loved it.

Harry at the Piano

David eventually developed some health problems and slowly went downhill. The night before he went to be with the Lord, Barbara spent the night with Adonah. Barbara was the one who found David had passed in the night. Fortunately, before David died, we spent time talking with him about the Lord and were assured that he gave his life to Jesus before he died. A few days before he died, we sat with him, and he asked us to sing some Christian hymns with him.

The next two years were very rough for Adonah, and we tried to be there for her as much as we could, with Barbara often spending the night with her. She had her occasional good days, but she really missed David. Less than two years later, while visiting her brother Glen in Virginia, she went home to be with the Lord.

Susan and David had bought a nice house in Pennsylvania a few years earlier and made it a home. We visited them a few times.

Let's back up and talk about the grandkids: Caitlyn, Trevor and Sean. Yes, we include Sean even though he is not blood-related. We spent more time with him growing up than with Trevor, and since he is Caitlyn's brother, we include him as one of our grandkids. We did many things with them while they were growing up, and if I tried to cover everything, it would take a whole book. And like any proud grandparent, I took plenty of pictures. I'll start with Caitlyn and bring Trevor and Sean in as we go along. As I already mentioned, she was born February 1, 1999. She came in at 9 pounds, 8 ounces. In the beginning, Susan was having a very difficult time, so Caitlyn stayed with us

for a while. We have a small office in our bedroom, so we put a crib in there, and that's where she slept. One night, we found her on the floor. She had climbed out of the crib. That was the beginning of her adventurous spirit. Because she lived with us, we got to see many of the baby firsts. Things like walking, talking, and exploring. We were there when she got on the bus for her first day at school and was there when she came home. As she grew, she loved to go exploring, and she and I would often take hikes in the woods or at one of the many parks in the area. Sometimes, Sean was with us. Sometimes Trevor. Sometimes, all three. Besides walking along the creek behind our house, one of our favorite places was Piscataway Park along the Potomac River. They have a nice boardwalk where you can walk, but you can also play along the riverbank. Another favorite was walking around the pond at Costco Park and visiting the Nature Center. Once, we rented the paddle boats, but that was too much work for me. But it was fun. She loved dinosaurs and had just about all the dinosaur movies and many books on the subject. At one time, she even went by the name "26," which was the name of one of the dinosaurs in the movie *Dinotopia*. If someone asked her her name, she would respond, "26." I accompanied her on an overnight field trip to Ferguson Farms, where we enjoyed looking at all the different animals, including snake exhibits, having a "scary" bonfire at night, and doing a number of different activities. Caitlyn even got to milk a cow. We got to go to Medieval Times with the Townshends and the Ramseys. Had a great time. Because Caitlyn lived with us for many years during two different periods (her early years and then her teen years), we  did most of the activities with her. Before Trevor moved to Kentucky, we were able to do a few things with him, but after the move, we saw him maybe once a year. During those times, we did such things as go to the Go Kart Races in Bowie or the Paint Ball place in Waldorf. Sean was able to accompany us on these outings as well. When Caitlyn graduated from High School (Gwynn Park, same as her mother and father), she wanted to go to Missouri to visit one of her friends who had moved there. So, as a graduation present, we took a ride to St. Louis, where she was able to spend a few days with her friend. Got to see the Gateway Arch and visit the Missouri Botanical Gardens, which were really quite beautiful. Seventy-nine acres of 20 gardens with various themes, including a Chinese garden, a Japanese meditation garden,  and a fragrance garden for the visually impaired. You could either walk the entire grounds or ride the shuttle train, which stopped at the various gardens. When we left St. Louis, we made a side trip to visit our old friends from the Amway days, Jim and Becky Sager. They had moved to Branson, Missouri, where almost the whole family was involved with the Sight and Sound Theater there. We got to see "*Moses*" for the second time, but this time it was free as we went as their guests. We also received

the backstage tour and were shown a number of different sets and how they operated. Very impressive. I might mention here that one of their daughters, Nicole, is a great Christian author who has written a number of novels concerning a fictional place called Arcrea. Highly recommend her books. While in Branson, we went to the Branson Dinosaur Museum with lots of life-size dinosaurs. Unfortunately, we didn't get to visit Dolly Parton's Stampede Dinner Attraction or any of the other many attractions that are there. Somewhere along the line, I picked up the art of making balloon animals, swords, and other items. This, along with my ability to do a few magic tricks, led me to purchase a clown outfit and entertain at parties. Every time I visited the Cape, I would stop at the Joke Shop on Main Street in Hyannis and pick up a few more magic tricks. Although most parties were relatively small, I did get one gig in Alexandria, VA, for a family that owned a restaurant. I believe it was a family from India. They had closed the restaurant to have a birthday party for one of their children. There were a lot of people there, and I received $300.00 for my performance. I was performing at a party one time, and when I bent over, my clown outfit ripped. It was then I realized I was putting on too much weight to continue as a clown. I continued to do balloon creations at family reunions and at the homeless outreach. The latter started when the Gideons were contacted by The Homeless Outreach organization to hand out Bibles at one of their annual activities. I went there as a Gideon to pass out testaments, but I happened to have a bunch of balloons in my pocket, so I started to make a few swords (or crosses, as I called them) to pass out as well. Later, I apologized to the lady who ran the program, Carol, and she told me I was an answer to a prayer because she was trying to find someone who did balloon animals for the kids. So, from then on, at each function, Easter, Back to School, and Christmas, I would come early and make creations with and for the children before handing out the testaments. I eventually had to quit because I had hurt my shoulder from a fall, and this prevented me from working the balloons as quickly as I had to. Then came the pandemic and no more social gatherings.

I need to back up a little and talk about Barbara and her daycare. If you recall, we chose the particular lot for our house because we wanted a walk-out basement, and that was the only lot left that was suitable for a walk-out basement. Because of the slope of the backyard and the gully behind the house, it turned out to be not suitable for young children, and so the plan of turning the basement into a daycare fell through. However, when Caitlyn was little, Barbara started taking care of her. She had a young cousin named Geordan (son of Susan's sister, Dawn) whom Barbara also cared for. Then, one of our neighbors across the street had a son named Micah, about the same age, and she started caring for him as well. As word spread, Barbara got more and more kids to take care of. So, even though we didn't use the basement, she did get her daycare. Over a period of time, she took care of about 12 children, although not at the same time. After she stopped doing daycare, she started "bussing" kids to a private school, Beddow High School, a couple of miles from the house in Accokeek. This started when Micah was enrolled in it, and Barbara started driving him there. Again, word of mouth brought her a number of other students going to that school who needed transportation. She really enjoyed it until most of those she was transporting graduated, and she stopped doing it.

Much of what I've been talking about happened after my second retirement, so let's jump to the next chapter and look at that.

CAITYLN

With her Stuffed Animals

With Her Angel

With her Balloons

With Mamaw Barbara

With Daddy

With Papaw Leo

With Mamaw Doni

With Mommy

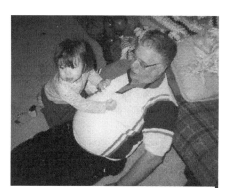
With Grandaddy David

I'll hide it here. No one will find it.

Tinkerbell is back!

We are not amused.

Ooh, this isn't chocolate milk.

Oh, Mr. President, what happened to your party?

And now, on page two, I want...

Looks nice but taste yucky

No, I'm not bigfoot

Anybody seen the rest of this creature?

Oops, you caught me.   *I hope I'm getting paid for this.*   *Now where did I park my car?*

TREVOR

This piece has to go somewhere.

Do you mind moving your feet?

Do it now, nobody's looking.

I've got my laser eyes on you.

I really do need to see the dentist.

She'd better not touch my drink

See, my lips don't even move.

Aw, isn't she adorable.

I got this

SEAN

Go ahead, make my day.

Straw, twigs or brick...huh

Get ready to fetch

It got struck.

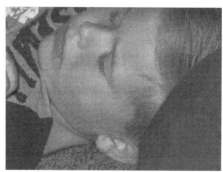
Wake me when it's time to go to bed.

How adorable

CAITLYN, TREVOR, AND SEAN TOGETHER

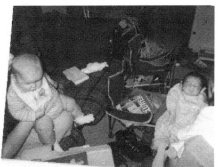

Are they talking about me?

Boy, you're short, Trevor

Who's short now?

The family on the Cape

Trevor & Caityln

Wendy & Trevor – Susan & Sean

Picnic with the Townsends

At Chuck E Cheese

Climbing the hill in back of the house

Mildred, Barbara & Jane

Pari & Adonah

Barbara's brother Mark

CHAPTER ELEVEN: RETIRED AGAIN – WHAT DO I DO NOW

"Let not your heart be troubled: ye believe in God, believe also in me. In my Father's house are many mansions: if it were not so, I would have told you. I go to prepare a place for you. And if I go and prepare a place for you, I will come again, and receive you unto myself; that where I am, there ye may be also." John 14:1-3

Let's return to retirement. Since I was no longer with Northrop, what do I do? We tallied all our money and expenses, and it looked like we would do okay even if I didn't get another job. But Barbara got tired of me hanging around the house and being underfoot, so I had to do something. So, I signed up to be an Uber Driver and then added Lyft. I would usually wait until after morning rush hour to get on the road and then quit by three before the afternoon rush. Sometimes, I'd work later, but not often. I was doing ok. I tried Uber Delivery as well, but I hated making deliveries in downtown DC. Sometimes, I'd get a call to go to a restaurant in Alexandria and bring the food to an office in DC. It was terrible trying to find a place to park, and often, I'd have to call the person to have them meet me at the car. I enjoyed the long trips like out to Dulles or BWI Airports. I dreaded the short trips in DC. I had bought a 2009 Jeep Commander, which I was using to do Uber/Lyft, but it wasn't very economical. Still, it was comfortable, people liked it, and I kept it clean. I always had goodies in the Jeep for people to snack on. Most of my reviews were very good, but I did get one or two bad reviews. Unjustified, in my opinion, but C'est la vie. One day, while coming home, I blew a piston or something in the engine. I was told it would cost about $5,000 to replace it, so I bought another van, this time a Chrysler Town and Country. Frankly, I

don't know why I let myself get talked into getting the Jeep instead of another van in the first place. My wife drives a Ford Focus, which I also had registered to drive Uber, but I found it too small and uncomfortable, so I never used it. When I blew the engine, I stopped driving for a while until I got the Town & Country van, but I only made one trip for Uber with it. For some reason, I just stopped going out.

I did start to do a lot of remodeling around the house after I retired. My first project was to build a small deck in the back, about 8' by 12". Then, I decided to add another 8 feet to it and extended it to the edge of the drop-off. After I finished the back deck, I decided to build a front porch. Someone once told me that front porches were so you could intermingle with your neighbors by sitting on the front porch and talking with them as they walked by. Decks were built so folks could isolate themselves from their neighbors. I decided I wanted both.

Then, I built an office in the basement for myself. Chris had already claimed half the basement for his own private bedroom/apartment. Later, I decided to close in part of the porch so Barbara could have a little greenhouse. Initially, it was just screened in, but then I built some plastic inserts that could be inserted into the screen windows to block out any snow, wind, or rain when needed.

One day, I received a call from an old friend, Lenny Brown. I knew Lenny while I was in the Air Force. He and I were in the same Toastmasters Club on Bolling. He asked me if I could meet him for coffee, and I said sure. We met at a local McDonalds. He said that he had heard that I was no longer a practicing Catholic and was wondering if I was interested in joining the Gideons. You know the Gideons

International as the people who place Bibles in hotels and motels. I've seen many of their Bibles in hotels on my Amway excursions. After we talked for a while, I said sure, and I filled out an application. I found out that Gideons International (TGI) is much more. It was founded in July 1899 when three men, John H. Nicholson, Samuel E. Hill, and William J. Knights, met at a YMCA in Janesville, Wisconsin, for the first meeting of a group of Christian traveling salesmen. Their purpose was to provide fellow Christian salesmen a means to maintain accountability with other Christians while on their travels. They began placing Bibles in hotels in 1908 but have since branched out to schools, colleges, universities, prisons, hospitals, nursing homes, police stations, firehouses, the military, and any other venue available, including what we call Personal Witness Testaments (PWTs). We carry PWTs wherever we go with the intention of handing them out to someone along with our personal testimony, hopefully being led by the Holy Spirit and not our own wiles. The sole purpose is to reach men and women, boys and girls, with the Gospel of Jesus Christ. Similar to Toastmasters, it is organized in levels beginning with Gideons International, headquartered in Nashville, Tennessee. You have Zones, States, Regions, Areas, and, instead of clubs, the local group is known as a Camp, based on Judges 7:21, "And they stood every man in his place round about the camp." I belong to Delmardic State (Delaware, Maryland, D.C), East Region, Area 4, Camp U07107. Each Camp has elected positions of President, Vice President, Secretary, Treasurer, and Chaplain. Additionally, you have the appointed positions for each of the

programs within the Camp: Church Ministry Chairman, Membership Chairman, Gideon Card Program Chairman, and Bible Distribution Chairman. We have a weekly early morning prayer meeting and a monthly meeting, as well as State and International Conventions. Wives of Gideons join as Gideon Auxiliary and play a vital part in prayer,

Bible distributions, and money raising. They have their own leadership throughout the organization. A book recently came out by Jeff Pack, titled, "*Witness to History: The Story of the Gideons International.*" It is a very detailed history of the Gideons. I've served in various officer positions as well as Area Director for Area 4, which is responsible for the District of Columbia and four counties in Maryland (Charles, Prince George, Calvert, and St. Mary). Joining Gideons was the next step in my Christian walk, as it gives me ample opportunity to spread the Gospel message.

In June, my van, which I had purchased a year earlier, was sitting in the driveway when a driver hit it around 3:00 a.m., messing up the front end. It also damaged the rear of the Jeep Commander. Naturally, his insurance company, which happened to be the same as mine, would take care of all the repairs. While being fixed, I also had the two front tires replaced, which I had planned to do anyway. The insurance paid for a portion of the one tire as a result of the accident. I start out with this story as it plays a role later on. Later in July, we drove to Cape Cod for our annual family reunion.

In August, a member of the PG North Camp offered us the use of their Condo in Myrtle Beach since they were not able to use it that year. My wife and I were delighted as we had been wanting to get away by ourselves for some time.

The day came for us to leave, and we departed early on Saturday morning. In South Carolina, about 20 miles south of Goldsboro, our van broke down. Fortunately, I had just gotten off the highway and due to construction at that particular intersection, we were slowed to a crawl as each car had to stop at the stop sign. (First "miracle") It was there that the van broke down, and I was able to pull over just past the stop sign, not too far from a Country Golf Club. I called my auto club, and they dispatched a tow. While waiting, a couple of police officers stopped to check on us. I explained the situation and asked if there were any hotels in the area, as I knew we would be spending the night. He told us there were a couple that he recommended we NOT go to, but there was one about a mile ahead that was decent. (second "miracle")

The tow truck showed up, and the driver told us that the place the auto club had destined for him to tow the vehicle was not a good choice, as there was only one old man who worked there, and there was no telling when he would be able to work on the vehicle (third miracle, as we shall see later). He recommended another place, and we said OK, even though it was the weekend there would be no one there until Monday. We figured we'd just stay at the hotel. He took us to the hotel so we could unload our baggage, and then he took our vehicle to the destination, leaving a note for the management.

At the hotel, we found they had no rooms available due to a golf tournament that was in town. We decided to get a cab or Uber to Goldsboro, but we were told there was no Taxi service, Uber or Lyft, in the area. While trying to decide what to do, one of the gentlemen who was there for the tournament recognized our dilemma and offered to drive us to Goldsboro. We accepted, and he would not accept any money for taking us there. (fourth miracle). The tow truck driver called us later to make sure that we arrived at Goldsboro. Had we not, he was going to send his girlfriend to pick us up and take us to Goldsboro. He had previously called his boss to see if he could take us, but his boss had told him he had other assignments, so he couldn't.

We spent the weekend at a nice hotel in Goldsboro and, on Monday morning, called the shop where the van had been taken. After a few hours they called us back with the diagnosis on the van. The transmission was shot. I had only had the van for a year. It was 2015. The gentleman told us he had checked with the Chrysler dealer and found out the van was still under warranty, and Chrysler would take care of towing it to the Chrysler dealer in Goldsboro and would take care of the repairs (another miracle, I lost count).

We got a rental and went on to Myrtle Beach for the week, had a great time, and returned the following weekend to pick up the van with a brand-new transmission. Drove the van quite a bit in August and September, working at two county fairs. On the last day of the Charles County Fair, I had started out to go to the fair (about 15 miles) when the van started making terrible grinding noises around the right front tire. I turned around, went home and parked the van for the weekend, using Barbara's Focus for the rest of the weekend.

The following Monday, I started to take the van to the mechanic but could barely budge it. I stopped to check it and found metal pieces in the driveway. Called a tow, and the driver told me it was a miracle the wheel hadn't fallen off. I had the vehicle towed to the folks who had initially worked on the repairs in June and found out that the axle had been cracked at the time of the accident. It was so minor it wasn't noticed. All the jostling from the driving over rough terrain (the Fair parking areas), the trips to Cape Cod and South Carolina, and the replacement of the transmission had caused the minor crack to expand and eventually give way. The repairs were made with a new axle, which was covered by the insurance because it was related to the previous accident.

In short, all these things could have cost us a bundle, could have happened while traveling on the highway, could have resulted in injuries, could have taken it to the wrong mechanic, etc. Because of some very good people (God sent), the whole series of events cost us little monetarily and only some small inconveniences along the way, which we managed to enjoy, nonetheless. God does work wonders if we only trust Him.

Let's back up a little and see where we are. 1997, retired from the Air Force; 2015, retired from Northrop Grumman. Started attending what is now Christ's Mission Ministries, serving as a deacon, financial committee chairman and Sunday School Teacher. I am nearing the end of my story up to this moment. As I write this, it is the summer of 2023. Many things have happened over the past few years. Adam got married for the second time, this time to Melissa Kelly, whom he had known since they were about 11 or 12. They currently live in Fredericksburg. Over the past few years, family and friends have gone on to be with the Lord, among them my two brothers, a sister, a brother-in-law, a nephew, a niece, my granddaughter's other grandparents, a number of my Gideon brothers and sisters, some church members, and neighbors. A reminder to me that life is very short. As I mentioned in the beginning, Psalm 90:10 tells us, "The days of our years are threescore years and ten; and if by reason of strength they be fourscore years, yet is their strength labour and sorrow; for it is soon cut off, and we fly away." And again, James 4:14 reminds us, "Whereas ye know not what shall be on the morrow, for what is your life? It is even a vapor that appears for a little time and then vanishes away." In March 2020, the terrible pandemic known as COVID-19 hit our country and changed, possibly forever, the way we live. People spend most of their

time in their homes. When they do go out, they are masked, and many are afraid to make contact, which hinders communication with others. Crime seems to be skyrocketing all over the place, adding to the fear of people going out. We are more and more becoming a community of strangers. This is not what life was meant to be like. The country shut down, and three years later, it is still not back where it used to be. Probably never will be. As I saw in a meme recently, "Normalcy will not return; Jesus will." When sister Terry was diagnosed with cancer, the family began a weekly prayer time via Zoom. This has been a blessing and gives us some community time together. God said it is not good for man to be alone. We need one another. I don't know what lies in store over the next few years. I am not getting any younger, and one day, I, too, will go home to be with the Lord. Perhaps Jesus will return before my time is up. Perhaps not. However, reading 2 Timothy 3:1-7 makes me wonder. It says, *"This know also, that in the last days perilous times shall come. For men shall be lovers of their own selves, covetous, boasters, proud, blasphemers, disobedient to parents, unthankful, unholy, without natural affection, trucebreakers, false accusers, incontinent, fierce, despisers of those that are good, traitors, heady, highminded, lovers of pleasures more than lovers of God; having a form of godliness, but denying the power thereof: from such turn away. For of this sort are they which creep into houses, and lead captive silly women laden with sins, led away with divers lusts, ever learning, and never able to come to the knowledge of the truth."* Sounds like the world today.

But my assignment is not to worry about the last days. My assignment is to continue to spread the Gospel until He does return. As Bobby Richardson, one-time second baseman for the New York Yankees, once said at a meeting of the Fellowship of Christian Athletes, "Dear God, Your will, nothing more, nothing less, nothing else."

The recent election did not go the way I had hoped it would. Many of the things that made America what it was are disappearing. But God is still on the throne. He is still in charge. He is still sovereign. And I have to trust Him no matter what is happening around me. This may be the end of this book, but it is not the end of my story. I have no idea how long my "dash" will be. Perhaps someday I'll add another chapter but until then, God's Blessing upon everyone who chances upon this story. I pray you enjoyed reading it.

I've added some things in the appendices that may or may not be of interest. Many of them are the kudos that I received in this lifetime, certificates that have been collecting dust over the years. I do want to make one thing clear. Any kudos I may have received over the years, I owe all to God. The Bible tells us in Colossians 3:23, "And whatsoever ye do, do it heartily, as to the Lord, and not unto men." Living by those words and what my Father taught me about hard work paid off. As I close, let me end with the words of Solomon from the Book of Ecclesiastes:

1 The words of the Preacher, the son of David, king in Jerusalem.

2 Vanity of vanities, saith the Preacher, vanity of vanities; all is vanity.

3 What profit hath a man of all his labour which he taketh under the sun?

4 One generation passeth away, and another generation cometh: but the earth abideth for ever.

5 The sun also ariseth, and the sun goeth down, and hasteth to his place where he arose.

6 The wind goeth toward the south, and turneth about unto the north; it whirleth about continually, and the wind returneth again according to his circuits.

7 All the rivers run into the sea; yet the sea is not full; unto the place from whence the rivers come, thither they return again.

8 All things are full of labour; man cannot utter it: the eye is not satisfied with seeing, nor the ear filled with hearing.

9 The thing that hath been, it is that which shall be; and that which is done is that which shall be done: and there is no new thing under the sun.

10 Is there any thing whereof it may be said, See, this is new? it hath been already of old time, which was before us.

11 There is no remembrance of former things; neither shall there be any remembrance of things that are to come with those that shall come after.

12 I the Preacher was king over Israel in Jerusalem.

13 And I gave my heart to seek and search out by wisdom concerning all things that are done under heaven: this sore travail hath God given to the sons of man to be exercised therewith.

¹⁴ I have seen all the works that are done under the sun; and, behold, all is vanity and vexation of spirit.

¹⁵ That which is crooked cannot be made straight: and that which is wanting cannot be numbered.

¹⁶ I communed with mine own heart, saying, Lo, I am come to great estate, and have gotten more wisdom than all they that have been before me in Jerusalem: yea, my heart had great experience of wisdom and knowledge.

¹⁷ And I gave my heart to know wisdom, and to know madness and folly: I perceived that this also is vexation of spirit.

¹⁸ For in much wisdom is much grief: and he that increaseth knowledge increaseth sorrow.

The only accomplishments that will follow me into the next life are the souls of those who, by my words and examples, chose to accept and follow Jesus.

"Let us hear the conclusion of the whole matter: Fear God, and keep his commandments: for this is the whole duty of man. For God shall bring every work into judgment, with every secret thing, whether it be good, or whether it be evil." Ecclesiastes 12:13-14

So, in conclusion, as you travel on this road that we call life, please be certain that you take the time to travel the Roman Road. What is the Roman Road?

ROMANS 3:10. *As it is written, there is none righteous, no, not one.*

ROMANS 3:23. *For all have sinned and come short of the glory of God.*

ROMANS 5:8. *But God commendeth his love toward us, in that, while we were yet sinners, Christ died for us.*

ROMANS 6:23. *For the wages of sin is death; but the gift of God is eternal life through Jesus Christ our Lord.*

ROMANS 10:29. *That if thou shalt confess with thy mouth the Lord Jesus, and shalt believe in thine heart that God hath raised him from the dead, thou shalt be saved.*

See you in eternity!

APPENDICES

APPENDIX 1	BHS-66
APPENDIX 2	A CAR – A SUMMER – A BROTHER
APPENDIX 3	BARBARA
APPENDIX 4	MY MOTHER, MY BROTHER, MY DAD
APPENDIX 5	HIGH SCHOOL AND COLLEGE DIPLOMAS
APPENDIX 6	NON-COMMISSIONED OFFICER LEADERSHIP SCHOOL
APPENDIX 7	SENIOR NON-COMMISSIONED OFFICER ACADEMY
APPENDIX 8	SPEECH COMPETITION CERTIFICATES
APPENDIX 9	MERITORIOUS SERVICE MEDAL
APPENDIX 10	AF COMMENDATION MEDAL
APPENDIX 11	AF COMMENDATION MEDAL, 1ST OAK LEAF CLUSTER
APPENDIX 12	GREAT NAVY OF THE STATE OF NEBRASKA
APPENDIX 13	ORDER OF THE MOLE-HOLERS
APPENDIX 14	DAD & I AT WORK SPEECH (Speech Given 26 Jan 94, Category: The Monodrama)
APPENDIX 15	HOME SWEET HOME SPEECH (Speech Given 21 Oct 1993, Category: Make Them Laugh)
APPENDIX 16	POETRY CERTIFICATES
APPENDIX 17	TOASTMASTER CERTIFICATES
APPENDIX 18	SERVING WITH PRIDE
APPENDIX 19	BILLY'S SKETCHES
APPENDIX 20	JAMES' ARTWORK
APPENDIX 21	GALLERY OF FAMILY AND FRIENDS

BHS/66

Blessed is the leader so the author said
And how true/each all they were and more still
Our four leaders were they then and now their own as always will
Jeff and Doug, the two on top, remember from Osterville they came
And one Pearl was the jewel which kept the story
And Linda blushed and was priceless
The class was large yet larger still the talents of them all/big or small
They each in their own way had a contribution to make the years at BHS the best
Shari, Sandy, Lynn and Gale
Jimmy, Bobby, Moe and Dale
Just a few who made the ranks
Who to their school did give their thanks
And Franny, too, can't be forgot
Our very own Junior Miss
Cape Cod and our state / a beauty great
Deserving well her crown
"Atlantis" paved the way and she the queen became
But then at "Winter Wonderland" Wendy drew her court
And she the crown maintained
The activities were many / variety was there
And each chose his own and mastered it
The Raider Reader was our voice as still it is
And the band played on proudly representing our school
Sports was there of every type for every one that could
And those that could not did else
Our cry was shouted loud and echoed and feared
And still is heard today
B-A-R-N-S-T-A-B-L-E the way it should be heard
BHS I am proud
I grew up in your halls
I gazed with hate upon your walls
And complained
Yet loved it all

APPENDIX 1

A CAR - - A SUMMER - - A BROTHER

Remember 66 - - I do - - that was the summer that was
The summer of the Studie
What fun and what times
You know we always seemed so far apart, so different; you had your world and I had mine
But it seems that one summer, one car brought us together for a while
It wasn't much of a bond but still it was
Remember the fight - - what was that for - - oh yes the tires but that was over as soon as it was begun
That night at the carnie was great
Remember the broken windshield - - John was a crazy friend
Maybe it was because he was crazy that made him a friend
because we all were
And then again - - They're Coming to Take Me Away - -
And they almost did but we had no screwdriver
What memories, what pleasures
Remember 66 - - what a year
The two-wheeler we pulled across from the Melody Tent - - Did we?
Anyhow that was funny
And funnier still was the flying record and the visit to the hospital
For some reason it didn't hurt - - had someone else thrown it, it might have
And that was the shoe polish, the songs, the words
Remember the highway rides, the rocking, the singing
Oh yea, Red Rubber Ball was big
And then there was Barbara, or was it Brenda that year
I guess to you that's unimportant
I met Mar that year - - she's a wonderful girl
And the ball games started - - and the parties at Joshua's late at night
Then too, the night - - or the morning - - on Main when a sneeze broke the silence and the cops were there
So many things to remember and these are but a few
Remember 66 - - I do - - that was the year I graduated
- - and met my brother - -

APPENDIX 2

BARBARA

Barbara, when you're near
I feel the pains of love life disappear
I sense the glow of love I've felt before
And hope that once more love's here

Barbara, when you smile
The heavens seem to stop but for a while
They seem to keep a watchful look of love
With all the stars above on you

Oh, Barbara, Oh, Barbara,
        Make my wish come true

Barbara, take my hand
And walk with me upon this lonely land
Don't let me face the dangers all alone
But give me your own sweet love

Barbara, say once more
The words I know you said a time before
But make them mean a whole lot more for me
And I too will be for you

Oh, Barbara, Oh, Barbara,
        Make my wish come true

Written to the tune of "Venus"

APPENDIX 3

MY MOTHER, MY BROTHER, MY DAD

While I was growing up I turned to daddy for advice
He taught me about women, about working, about life
My character was largely built on what he had to say
The example that he gave me almost each and every day
Don't get me wrong, he wasn't perfect but as far as daddies go
He was loving, kind and gentle and he taught me all I know
By the time he passed away, I was fifteen and a man
And I'll carry on his name as best I can

I will always remember; never forget all the fun that we had
I love you; I miss you, my mother, my brother, my dad

My brother was my friend, a few years younger than I
He wore the green of the U.S. Marine and lived a life of Semper Fi
We lived, we worked, we played together and shared a life of fun
With cruising, dating as a pair, we often seemed as one.
He loved to live his heart was big his children he adored
But at the age of 27, he passed through heaven's door
The hole he left within our hearts can never be refilled
Except with love of Jesus as we know the good Lord's will
I will always remember; never forget all the fun that we had
I love you; I miss you, my mother, my brother, my dad

When father died my mom was there to carry on the task
Of raising nine of us to be a family true and fast
She held us all together with faith in God above
All our hearts and our hurts were bandaged by her deep, devoted love
I thank the Lord I had the chance to spend some time with her
Before he called her home to join my dad and dear brother

I will always remember; never forget all the fun that we had

I love you; I miss you, my mother, my brother, my dad

(Recorded by Hallmark Records)

APPENDIX 4

APPENDIX 5

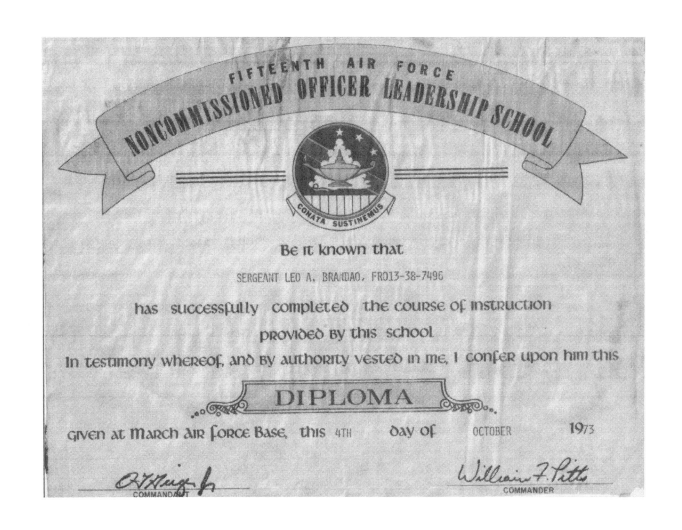

APPENDIX 6

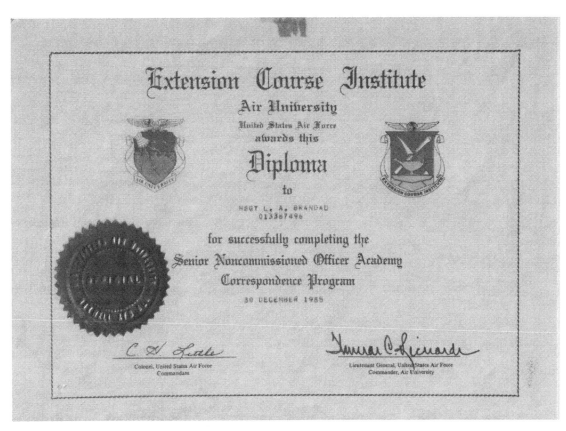

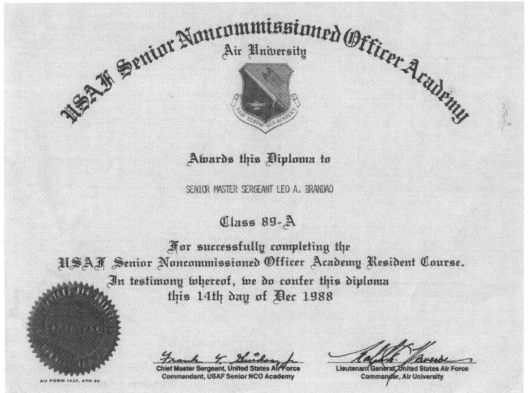

APPENDIX 7

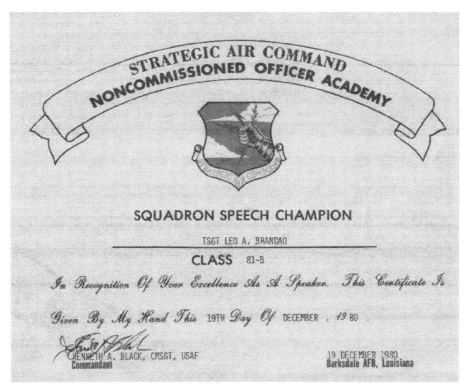

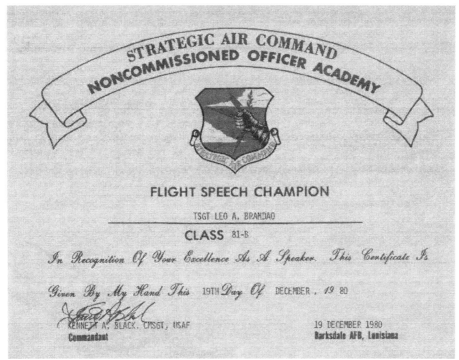

APPENDIX 8

THE UNITED STATES OF AMERICA

TO ALL WHO SHALL SEE THESE PRESENTS, GREETING:

THIS IS TO CERTIFY THAT
THE PRESIDENT OF THE UNITED STATES OF AMERICA
AUTHORIZED BY EXECUTIVE ORDER, 16 JANUARY 1969
HAS AWARDED

THE MERITORIOUS SERVICE MEDAL

TO

STAFF SERGEANT LEO A. BRANDAO

FOR

OUTSTANDING SERVICE

12 APRIL 1972 TO 10 NOVEMBER 1976

GIVEN UNDER MY HAND IN THE CITY OF WASHINGTON
THIS 13TH DAY OF DECEMBER 19 76

Commander in Chief
STRATEGIC AIR COMMAND

SECRETARY OF THE AIR FORCE

CITATION TO ACCOMPANY THE AWARD OF

THE MERITORIOUS SERVICE MEDAL

TO

LEO A. BRANDAO

Staff Sergeant Leo A. Brandao distinguished himself in the performance of outstanding service to the United States as Administrative Supervisor, Flight Management Branch and as Squadron Chief Clerk, 3902 Operations Squadron, 3902 Air Base Wing, Offutt Air Force Base, Nebraska, from 12 April 1972 to 10 November 1976. During this period, Sergeant Brandao's outstanding professional knowledge, initiative and devotion to duty were responsible for timely and efficient administrative support during the transition from conventional aircraft to a modern jet airlift fleet for the support of the Strategic Air Command and during the subsequent transfer of the support airlift function to Military Airlift Command. He served with distinction, enthusiastically performed duties normally accomplished only by senior ranking personnel, and consistently achieved outstanding results. The singularly distinctive accomplishments of Sergeant Brandao reflect great credit upon himself and the United States Air Force.

APPENDIX 9

DEPARTMENT OF THE AIR FORCE

THIS IS TO CERTIFY THAT

THE AIR FORCE COMMENDATION MEDAL

HAS BEEN AWARDED TO

MASTER SERGEANT LEO A. BRANDAO

FOR

MERITORIOUS SERVICE
31 MAY 1980 – 1 JUNE 1984

GIVEN UNDER MY HAND
THIS 19TH DAY OF NOVEMBER 19 84

B.L. DAVIS
GENERAL, USAF
COMMANDER IN CHIEF
STRATEGIC AIR COMMAND

AF FORM 2204, JAN 61

CITATION TO ACCOMPANY THE AWARD OF

THE AIR FORCE COMMENDATION MEDAL

TO

LEO A. BRANDAO

Master Sergeant Leo A. Brandao distinguished himself by meritorious service as Noncommissioned Officer in Charge, Missile Tactics Division, Tactics Directorate, Strategic Air Combat Operations Staff, Headquarters Strategic Air Command, and Noncommissioned Officer in Charge, Missile Tactics Branch, Tactics Divison, Single Integrated Operational Plan Directorate, Joint Strategic Target Planning Staff, Offutt Air Force Base, Nebraska, from 31 May 1980 to 1 June 1984. The exemplary leadership, professional competence, and devotion to duty displayed by Sergeant Brandao directly enhanced the deterrent capabilities of this nation's strategic forces. His efforts resulted in improved management of critical weapon system planning factors, effective administrative procedures for the Mobile Joint Nuclear Planning Element, and development of a new storage, documentation and retrieval program for over 400 extremely sensitive documents. The distinctive accomplishments of Sergeant Brandao reflect credit upon himself and the United States Air Force.

APPENDIX 10

DEPARTMENT OF THE AIR FORCE

THIS IS TO CERTIFY THAT

THE AIR FORCE COMMENDATION MEDAL
(FIRST OAK LEAF CLUSTER)

HAS BEEN AWARDED TO

SENIOR MASTER SERGEANT LEO A. BRANDAO

FOR

MERITORIOUS SERVICE
12 JULY 1984 TO 18 JUNE 1988

GIVEN UNDER MY HAND

THIS 21ST DAY OF DECEMBER 19 88

William L. Kirk
WILLIAM L. KIRK
General, USAF
Commander in Chief
United States Air Forces in Europe

AF FORM 2224, APR 85

CITATION TO ACCOMPANY THE AWARD OF

THE AIR FORCE COMMENDATION MEDAL
(FIRST OAK LEAF CLUSTER)

TO

LEO A. BRANDAO

Senior Master Sergeant Leo A. Brandao distinguished himself by meritorious service as Noncommissioned Officer in Charge of the Administrative Branch, 7451st Tactical Intelligence Squadron, Deputy Chief of Staff Intelligence, Headquarters United States Air Forces in Europe, Hahn Air Base, Germany, from 12 July 1984 to 18 June 1988. During this period, Sergeant Brandao's selfless dedication and administrative expertise aided immeasurably in the fielding and activation of the imagery portion of the Tactical Reconnaissance Exploitation Demonstration System. Sergeant Brandao established orderly room procedures and initialized military support programs for squadron personnel and assigned contractors. As First Sergeant for the squadron, he ensured that morale remained high throughout his tenure. Sergeant Brandao's personal integrity served as an example not only to military personnel, but to those he aided in off-duty community support programs as well. The distinctive accomplishments of Sergeant Brandao reflect credit upon himself and the United States Air Force.

APPENDIX 11

THE GREAT NAVY OF THE STATE OF NEBRASKA

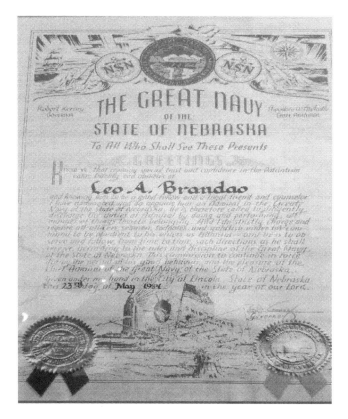

The citation reads:

To all who shall see these presents, Greetings. Know ye that reposing special trust and confidence in the Patriotism, valor, fidelity and abilities of Leo A Brandao and knowing him to be a good fellow and a loyal friend and counselor, I have nominated and do appoint him an Admiral in the Great Navy of the State of Nebraska. He is, therefore, called to diligently discharge the duties of Admiral by doing and performing all manner of things thereto belonging. And I do strictly charge and require all officers, seamen, tadpoles and goldfish under his command to be obedient to his orders as Admiral – and he is to observe and follow, from time to time, such directions as he shall receive, according to the rules and discipline of the Great Navy of the State of Nebraska. This commission to continue during the period of his good behavior, and the pleasure of the Chief Admiral of the Great Navy of the State of Nebraska. Given under my hand in the city of Lincoln, State of Nebraska, this 23rd Day of May 1984 in the year of Our Lord.

Signed: Bob Kerry, Governor

APPENDIX 12

LOYAL ORDER OF THE MOLE-HOLERS

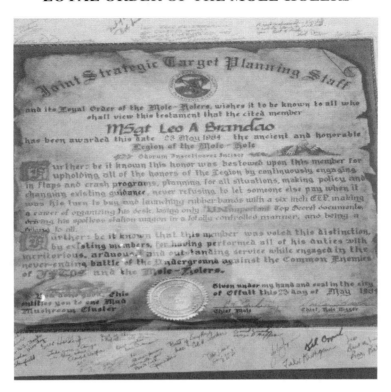

The Citation reads:

Joint Strategic Target Planning Staff and its Loyal Order of the Mole-Holers wish it to be known to all who shall view this testament that the cited member, MSgt Leo A Brandao, has been awarded this date, 23 May 1984, the ancient and honorable Legion of the Mole-Hole (*Odorum Insectivores Incisor*). Further, be it known this honor was bestowed upon this member for upholding all of the honors of the Legion by continuously engaging in flaps and crash programs, planning for all situations, making policy and changing existing guidance, and never refusing to let someone else pay when it was his turn to buy and launching rubber bands with a six-inch CEP, making a career of organizing his desk, losing only "UN" Important Top Secret Documents, driving his spotless station wagon in a totally controlled manner, and being a friend to all. Further, be it known that this member was voted this distinction by existing members for having performed all of his duties with meritorious, arduous and outstanding service while engaged in the never-ending battle of the Underground against the Common Enemies of JSTPS and the Mole-Holers. Given under my hand and seal in the city of Offutt, this 23 day of May 1984.

Signed: P. F. CARTER, JR, Vice Admiral, USN and HARLEY A. HUGHES, Major General, USAF

APPENDIX 13

DAD & I AT WORK

Speech Given 26 Jan 94, Topic: The Monodrama

'Twas the Spring of 1955. I was a mere lad of but 7 years old when first invited to accompany my dad on one of his many jobs, the first of what would be many trips. My father was a landscape gardener – this I did not know at the time. All I knew was that he took care of this beautiful estate which lay near the water in the village of Wianno on Cape Cod, Mass. A beautiful estate it was with the bay on one side, beautiful sandy beaches, a lovely boathouse, and on the other side of the house, the front side you might call it if you consider the roadside as being the front, there was the most beautiful of rose gardens that you could imagine, with hedges so high, I could not see over them. Like playing in a maze, it was, with such gorgeous flowers as you would ever want to see. Roses of all sorts and colors and so many other lovely flowers. Now, at the age of seven, I didn't really appreciate the splendor of these, but as the years went on and I began not only to accompany my father but also to share the work with him, I began to appreciate the splendor of these creations and the work that went into them.

My father was not an educated man. He came to this country when he was about 17 and used what talents he had brought with him from his native Cape Verde Islands – working the land.

Tending to this estate was his primary job, given to him by virtue of his employment with the Daniel Brothers, a local landscape gardening contracting business. The estate was owned by two spinster sisters, the Parletts – their first names escape me. Whether either of the two had ever been married, I do not know, for I knew them only in their later years as old but gentle women who welcomed my presence on the estate. The Winters they spent in warmer climates, and the estate was basically closed, but come to Spring, they would return to enjoy the splendor of this estate. Why anyone would want to leave such a beautiful place, even in the cold of winter, I could not understand, but I suspect their advanced years may have made it difficult to withstand the sometimes harsh Winters of the Cape. But I enjoyed it when I could, during school vacations, looking forward to accompanying my father. As I grew and my younger brother began to accompany us on these trips, we began to make them adventures. While father would tend to his duties, we could roam the grounds and let our imaginations take over. One day, we might be explorers in the deepest jungles of Africa, winding our way through the tall hedges. Another time, we might be cowboys and Indians riding across the prairies, finding ourselves rolling down the lush green grass of the lawn. Or we might be fishermen on the shore or clammers, having learned the art of finding the clam or quahog beds from our father. We could swim in the water when Father was in eyeshot to ensure we did not endanger ourselves, but we did occasionally slip away on our own. I recall one winter when the bay was partially frozen over, not unlike these past few weeks... It wasn't the normal course of things – only in extremely cold winters. My brother and I thought we'd be brave and attempted to cross the bay. We got maybe halfway across

when we realized our mistake and headed back, only to find the ice breaking up around us. My father did come to our rescue – and following our much-deserved punishment – we never ventured out across that frozen tundra again. This estate was only one of which my father tended. This was his 7-4 job, but the income was not sufficient to raise a large family (there were nine of us eventually) and so he had others he tended to each day of the week, some small, others somewhat larger. I remember the names – Greico, Adams, Goodspeed, Aylmer, Frazier, Crockett - each name evokes memories. I remember my first love- finding her soon after I started making these trips with my father. Her name was Karen Aylmer, the daughter of one of the owners. I was seven. She was perhaps six. I remember playing in the leaves with her during the fall while my father worked. I wonder what ever became of her.

When my brother and I were old enough, my father would leave us to tend to one job while he went to take care of another. One of the more luxurious estates was that of the Greico family, again located on the ocean with lovely beaches and luscious landscapes. My father left us here one day to mow the grass while he went to take care of business at another location. He would return and pick us up later that day. My brother and I worked hard and finished long before expected, so we had time to kill. The curiosity of young boys often leads them to places they shouldn't go, and our curiosity led us to explore the wine cellars of the estate. Like the Parletts, the owners were here only during the summer, and as this was the fall, they were not present. I'm not certain what the potent potable was that we decided to experiment with - possibly a bottle of rum – but it proved to be a bit overwhelming for a couple of young boys. I don't know how much of it we consumed, but when my father came to get us – well – suffice it to say that that was one act which we never again repeated – and the punishment my father imposed upon us was only a small part of the reasoning for our decision.

Much of what I learned about life came from these jobs. As I grew and became more responsible, I took over many of these jobs, so when my father died, I had established myself as a responsible landscape gardener in my own right. I kept such jobs as the Adams, the Goodspeeds, and the Fraziers and picked up a few others such as the Cassidy's. Like my father, I eventually had a regular job, working 8-5 as a produce clerk at the A&P Company, and I would tend to these other jobs in the late afternoon or on weekends. It was hard work, and the money I made from them was quickly spent. But the lessons I learned, and the reputation I established as a responsible, hardworking individual remained with me for many years, even until today. My only regret about being in the military these past 20 years is not having been able to share that same joy with my young sons as they were growing.

APPENDIX 14

HOME SWEET HOME

Speech Givem 21 Oct 1993, Category: Make Them Laugh

Today (Oct 21) is the birthday of John Howard Payne, born in 1791. Who is John Howard Payne, you might ask? The author of dozens of plays and an actor of some repute, today he is remembered practically entirely for the song "Home Sweet Home," a song that I'm sure all of you are somewhat familiar with.

After more than a quarter of a century of being on my own, it finally happened. I became what most of you probably have been for a long time. A (in a whisper while looking around) "Homeowner."

The past six months have been a very exciting time for my wife and me as we searched high and low to find the home of our dreams. A mansion with enough space so we can each have our own private areas, our kids can have room to grow with separate areas for studying, sleeping, and playing. A kitchen big enough so we can both work in it at the same time without crawling over each other. Enough bathrooms so we don't have to stand in line waiting, and a sauna for resting after a long hard day at work. A living room and formal dining room where we can entertain and a family room and dinette where we can live. Rooms that we can each use to pursue our hobbies. A beautiful deck and yard area big enough so we can invite all our friends over for big holiday barbecues and other backyard activities. A swimming pool for those hot summer months and two fireplaces for those cold winter months. The home of our dreams. Unfortunately, we never found it in our price range, so we settled for what we could afford.

But nonetheless, we love it. In preparing for this major change in our lives, I wanted everything to go as smoothly as possible, so I approached it logically. We selected the house we wanted, the lot we wanted, and the date we wished to move. That done, I let the realtor and mortgage company handle the paperwork and I set out to develop my plan of action.

I looked at the pre-move, the move, and the post-move. In order to make a few dollars, I decided to do a DITY move. In the military, that is a do-it-yourself move. After doing it, I can think of a few other names to call it, but I won't.

I decided to start packing well in advance as much stuff as possible and converted one room in the house into a storage room for the packed boxes. I obtained boxes and tape from whatever sources I could and began to pack, pack, and pack. The room eventually became so full of boxes that I decided to start moving them out to the carport about a week before the scheduled closing. I stacked them nice and neatly and covered them with plastic in case it rained, but there was no rain in the forecast for a while. As the due date approached, I began to get nervous because something was not happening. The VA was not coming through with the appraisal. All else was done and ready to go, but no appraisal. Calls to the VA proved fruitless. They were still within the allotted time frame. We had overlooked one small detail. You see, progress on the house was moving so fast that we moved the closing date up a month but didn't notify VA. They were still operating with the old dates they were given.

Needless to say, Murphy's Law was at work, and in the interim, it rained and rained and rained. The plastic wrap I had put over the boxes worked great. The boxes on top were dry. But I neglected to take into consideration what would happen if water accumulated on the carport. You guessed it. The bottom boxes became, well, soggy, to say the least. Unpack repack. And life goes on.

Finally, victory. The appraisal was done the closing was scheduled. I should have been forewarned when notified of the closing date, but I'm not superstitious. August 13th, Friday. Oh well. We arrived at the location in plenty of time and completed and signed all the paperwork without a hitch. Did I say without a hitch? Wrong! There was a small mistake in the amounts. Only about 200 dollars, not much, but some of the paperwork had to be re-accomplished. Not a problem. We are in a computerized age. These were all on the computer. The mortgage lady would be back in a couple of minutes. Well, five minutes. She did come back within ten minutes…to tell us the computer was down and they were trying to fix it. About 15 minutes later, she returned and said they couldn't get it fixed. Not a problem. We can still do it by hand. She finally did. We signed we left, we visited our home, and we made the final arrangements to move in the following Monday. The truck was rented, and the weekend was spent packing the last few items. We were ready.

The move itself went fairly smoothly. My two teenage sons pitched in and really helped out a lot. Some of my friends helped carry the big items in, and we survived. With one small incident. The color TV. Now, this isn't a small portable, but it's not a great big one either. A macho-type guy like me can handle it easily. Right? Wrong! Carrying it in, I slipped and lost my balance. Being a toastmaster has trained me to think quickly and make decisions instantly. Save me or the TV? No question. The TV! Trying to keep it from crashing into the cement, I softened the blow with my body. Ouch! My legs were bruised from the knees to the ankles. But we survived the move and life goes on.

That week, I was on leave, and we spent the time getting as much stuff put away as we could, but I came back to work the following week. Had to! Needed to test for Chief. While I was hard at work putting my answers down on paper, my wife called the office. Since I was "out of pocket" while taking

the test, Mrs. Rudy handled the situation. My wife was hysterical. It seems a small problem developed with the upstairs toilet. It was overflowing. She had no idea how to shut it off. (I failed to show her the little knob under the toilet. I thought everyone knew about that.) Not to worry. I have a teenage son. They know what to do. There's a rubber ball inside the tank. Pull that up, and the water will shut off. Teenagers sometimes don't know their own strengths. He not only pulled it up, but out as well. Under the circumstances, I can understand. Picture everyone running around hysterically as the water overflows the bathroom, down the stairs, through the floor, into the basement. I'm talking almost an inch of water in the basement. Brand new white carpet being soaked through like a sponge. Well, finally, a stroke of genius. She called one of the maintenance folks working on the houses next door. One of them finally came in, shut the water off, and had the plumber come in and fix the ballcock at a cost of $64.00. It took about another week to dry up using water vacs and fans. But we survived, and life goes on.

We were at last settled in the home and ready to welcome visitors. We got lots of visitors. Someone offering to do our landscaping, someone offering to sell us firewood, someone offering to seal our driveway, someone selling decks and patios, someone selling Kirby Vacuum Cleaners (well, at least they gave us a fruit basket), someone from Jehovah's Witness.

You get lots of mail, too. One of the first things I found in my mailbox was a, you guessed it, a bill. Remember I said our original date was back in July. Well, I had the phone and utilities hooked up at that time. And the bills were there when we moved in for the first month. I hadn't realized I could spend so much in absentia.

But despite the visits, the junk mail and the phone calls, we enjoy our home. I enjoy working in the yard. The spacious backyard…if you consider the woods in the gully. You see, the backyard drops off after about 12 feet straight down. My first project is to build steps down the gully because it's awful hard carrying firewood up the steep hill.

CONCLUSION: Be it ever so humble, there's no place like home.

APPENDIX 15

POETRY CERTIFICATES

APPENDIX 16

APPENDIX 17

APPENDIX 18

BILLY'S DRAWINGS

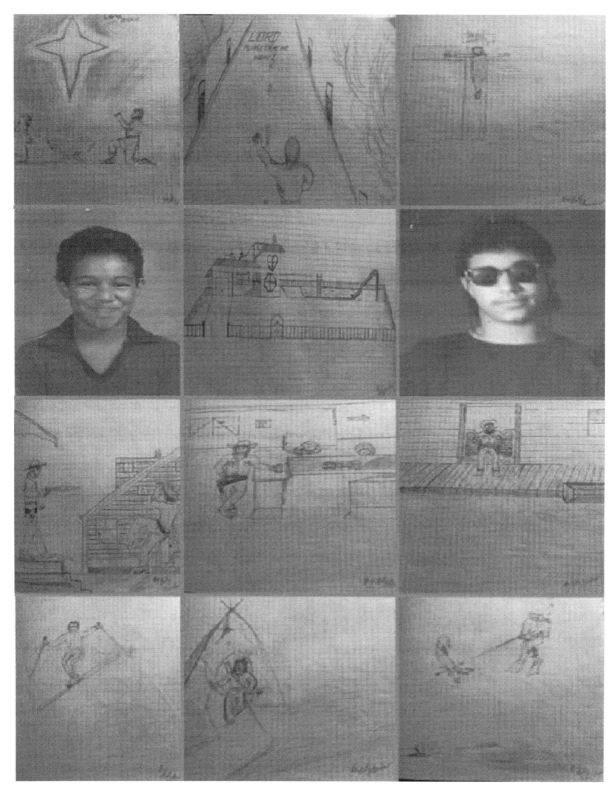

APPENDIX 19

JAMES FORTES' ARTWORK

APPENDIX 20

GALLERY OF FAMILY & FRIENDS

APPENDIX 21

Made in the USA
Columbia, SC
05 September 2024

9db1375d-e2bb-4f28-87cf-ed2876f1e314R01